Tomorrow&Always

ALSO BY BARBARA BRETTON

SOMEWHERE IN TIME
THE BRIDE CAME C.O.D.
RENEGADE LOVER
DADDY'S LITTLE GIRL
BUNDLE OF JOY
STRANGER IN PARADISE
SENTIMENTAL JOURNEY
ALL WE KNOW OF HEAVEN
MRS. SCROOGE
MOTHER KNOWS BEST
A FINE MADNESS
HONEYMOON HOTEL
NOBODY'S BABY
SECOND HARMONY
PLAYING FOR TIME
SHOOTING STAR
PROMISES IN THE NIGHT
THE EDGE OF FOREVER
NO SAFE PLACE
THE SWEETEST OF DEBTS
LOVE CHANGES
STARFIRE
THE RELUCTANT BRIDE

BARBARA BRETTON
Tomorrow & Always

Harlequin Books

TORONTO • NEW YORK • LONDON
AMSTERDAM • PARIS • SYDNEY • HAMBURG
STOCKHOLM • ATHENS • TOKYO • MILAN
MADRID • WARSAW • BUDAPEST • AUCKLAND

For my husband, Roy, with love and gratitude, for
twenty-five years of showing me what the word *hero*
really means. I love you more than I can say,
Bretton. Thanks for giving me your summer.
This one's for you!

With special thanks to Karin Stoecker, whose
enthusiasm and daring made this book possible.
Your kindness in Chicago meant more to me than
I can ever say.

 HARLEQUIN BOOKS

TOMORROW & ALWAYS

ISBN 0-373-15236-1

Copyright © 1993 by Barbara Bretton

This edition published by arrangement with Harlequin Enterprises B. V.

® and TM are trademarks of the publisher. Trademarks indicated with
® are registered in the United States Patent and Trademark Office, the
Canadian Trade Marks Office and in other countries.

Printed in U.S.A.

I am almost ashamed to be living in such peace while all the rest struggle and suffer. But, after all, it is still best to concern oneself with eternals, for from them alone flows that spirit that can restore peace and serenity to the world of humans.

—Albert Einstein
Princeton, NJ

PROLOGUE

Late August, 1776

ANDREW MCVIE SAT on the slope behind the lighthouse and waited. He wasn't certain what it was he waited for, but the need in him was so great it could not be denied.

He had awakened near Milltown before dawn that morning, as sharp of eye and clear of head as if he had slept a full night and more. The innkeeper, a good woman named Annie Willis with two sons serving under General Washington, had offered him fresh coffee and bread still warm from the ovens but he found himself unwilling to spend the time.

"A body cannot subsist on patriotism alone." She wrapped a loaf of bread in a clean white cloth then handed it to him. "Think of mistress Willis when you sup, and pray her boys come home to her again."

Patriotism. The very word that had filled his soul with fire not so many years ago held no meaning for him now. Indeed, there were times when he felt as if he'd never known what it truly meant to sacrifice everything on the altar of revolution.

They called him a hero. They said he risked his life to go where others feared to tread because he understood that the need of the colonies far outweighed his own pitiful need for comfort. But they were wrong. All of them. Since he'd lost Elspeth and David he had been moving through the days both blind and deaf to anything but the pain inside his heart. It was easy to risk everything when you had nothing of value left to lose.

But now even his effectiveness as a spy had been taken from him.

He shifted position on the rock and rested his head in his hands. His journey to Long Island to warn General Washington of a plot against his life had resulted in naught save embarrassment. Not only was General Washington not there but the soldiers he'd spoken with had looked at Andrew as if he was daft.

"Surely you have spent too much time in the sun," one had said, laughing at Andrew's expense. "His Excellency is safely ensconced in Trenton now as we speak."

Later he had sought solace in a tankard of ale but there was no solace to be found anywhere on God's green earth. The truth was as plain as his own face in the glass each morning. His time was past. He could see that now. The torch had been passed while he dreamed, passed to men who were younger and stronger than Andrew. Men who were willing to fight the battles Andrew no longer understood.

A bitter laugh rose from the darkness of his soul. Indeed, it would be better if he lay dead on the sandy soil of Long Island. He had nothing left to give, nothing left to offer save a lifetime of regrets. Words he should have said, actions left untaken, the sad procession of mistakes made by a man who should have known better.

The ambitious young lawyer from Boston had been replaced by a patriot who no longer believed in the rebellion other men gave their life's blood to pursue.

None of it mattered any longer. He knew how it would all end. The patriots would be victorious. The Crown would become an ally. The sun and the moon and the stars would all remain in the heavens. And Andrew McVie would be alone.

He looked up at the lighthouse and shook his head at the absurdity of it all.

He'd never thought to set eyes upon the place again. Indeed, he had no understanding how it was he'd come to this particular spot on the New Jersey shore when he had been traveling toward Princeton. All he knew was that the need to be here had overtaken him, driving reason from his brain.

In truth, he should be sitting at Rebekah Blakelee's table at this very moment, eating her fine food and considering how it was his life had amounted to so little.

He had neither wife nor child, no home where he could lay down his head and rest his weary heart. The loneliness he had accepted as his punishment ofttimes rose up from the depths of his soul and threatened to choke off the very air he breathed.

Other men had friends to share a summer's night or warm a cold winter's afternoon. Andrew had nothing but regrets, and those regrets had grown sharp as a razor's edge these few weeks past, cutting him to the center of his being. For a little while this summer he'd rediscovered his heart and believed that happiness could be possible for him in this lifetime.

Emilie Crosse had come to him on a morning such as this, in this very spot, spinning a story about a big red balloon that had carried her through the centuries. At first he had thought her mad and vowed to grant her a wide berth but he soon found it impossible to turn a blind eye to her considerable charms.

She intrigued him with her fierce intelligence. She delighted him with her saucy wit. At times her independence enraged him and he found himself longing for the more docile women of his acquaintance but again and again he found himself drawn back to her side.

Andrew was not a man given to flights of fancy. He did not believe in ghosts or portents or a world beyond the one in which he lived. But on the day he had met Emilie Crosse in the cellar of the lighthouse he had had the unyielding sense that his life would never again be the same.

She was taller and stronger than the good women of his acquaintance and she carried herself with a sense of purpose he envied, but still it was more than those traits that had captured his imagination. It was the world she'd left behind. A world of wonders so miraculous his mortal mind could scarcely comprehend their scope.

She talked of flying through the air inside a shiny metal bird, of men leaving their footprints on the surface of the moon. In her time existed contraptions that could outthink a man of Jefferson's intellect or Franklin's invention. Music could be captured on a shiny brown ribbon and listened to whenever you wished. Indeed, entire libraries could be contained on an object the size of a saucer. The poorest of citizens possessed riches beyond Andrew's wildest dreams. Not even Fat George on his English throne could fathom the wonders of which Emilie spoke.

And still she talked of these things as if they were of little value, as if she cared not if she returned to her own time and place.

Not so the man she'd traveled through time with. Zane Grey Rutledge had no use for Andrew's world. He was a man of his own time and Andrew knew Zane would move heaven and earth to return there again with Emilie, to the world where they belonged.

And there was the rub.

To Andrew's everlasting dismay, Emilie had traveled backward through time with the man she'd once been married to. Andrew had watched helplessly as the couple had found their way back to each other, wishing with his entire being that he could be the man she loved. That she could somehow make him whole again in a way that neither rum nor revolution could accomplish.

But it wasn't to be. Emilie and Zane belonged together. In truth, Andrew had known it from the start, known it deep in the part of his heart that had died with his wife and child so many years ago. A man might say Emilie and Zane were bound by the past they shared, the world they'd left behind, but Andrew believed a force more powerful than commonality linked their souls together.

Had it been that way with his Elspeth? Andrew could not remember. Late at night, in those moments before sleep claimed him, he saw her beloved face, heard the sound of her voice, felt the satin of her skin beneath his hand, but what she had thought and wished for and needed still danced somewhere beyond his ken.

"Aye," he muttered, wishing for rum or whiskey to blunt the edges of his pain. He had made so many mistakes, directed so little attention to matters of true importance that now he was doomed to go to sleep each night and wake up each morning in a world that held nothing for him but the shadows of what could have been.

His wife and child were dead and buried. The woman who'd captured his imagination loved another man. Not even the battle for independence that raged all around him was enough to ignite the fires of passion inside his cold and weary heart. It seemed he existed to do naught but take up space, counting down the days until he breathed his last.

Mayhap that was his destiny, he thought as he rose to his feet and walked to the edge of the outcropping of rocks that overlooked the water. To live alone there on the rugged island with only his own despair for company, as useless as the lighthouse was without a flame burning from the tower windows to guide the way for other lost and lonely souls.

If the Almighty had other plans for him, Andrew couldn't fathom what they might be.

He stood there at the edge of land for a long time, scanning the horizon for a sign, something—anything—that would show him the wrongness of his thinking, prove to him that there was still a purpose to his existence. But he saw nothing, save an odd cloud cover drifting in from the Atlantic, vertical bands in shades of pewter that moved steadily toward him, casting shadows across the harbor and whipping the still waters into a froth.

The hairs on the back of his neck rose.

"''Tis naught but a storm gathering force," he said into the wind over the mournful call of the gulls. The Jersey coast was known for the unpredictability of its weather. A fortnight ago he'd heard a sailor at the Plumed Rooster weave a tail of a towering waterspout that had toppled his frigate and drowned half the crew. Surely a band of gray clouds was no cause for alarm.

Still the sight tugged hard at his memory, as if it held some significance he had forgotten. *Enough,* he thought, turning away. He had felt the need to see the lighthouse again and he had done so. Surely there was no reason for him to linger, not with a storm threatening. He would row back to the mainland, mount his horse, then reach Princeton before nightfall. Rebekah, the good wife of Josiah Blakelee, would provide a roof over his head and food for his rumbling belly. Tomorrow morning he would see Emilie and Zane, tell them about this foolish trip to the lighthouse and—

A spot of crimson caught his eye. He narrowed his eyes, focusing in on the billowy fabric floating atop the choppy waters.

A big red balloon, Andrew . . . that's how it happened. . . .

Beads of sweat formed at his temples and across his forehead. He could hear Emilie's voice as clearly as he had on that first day.

Where is that red balloon, mistress Emilie? he had asked, disbelief dripping from every syllable. *Where is the basket?*

I don't know, she had answered him simply. *We crashed into the water. I assume all was lost.*

He looked again but this time he saw nothing but the choppy water. Had the scrap of crimson been his imagination playing tricks upon his addled brain?

"No," he said aloud, gaining strength from the sound of his own voice. "'Tis there. It exists."

The cloud cover was settling itself around the island, obscuring the top of the lighthouse. A damp wind, too chilly for late August, stung his face with salt as a sense of destiny began to build inside his chest.

The sight of Emilie and Rutledge rowing toward the island from the mainland came as no surprise. They would help him find his way in their world as he had helped them in his.

A few minutes later Emilie embraced him. "Andrew! What on earth—?" Her face was taut with anxiety.

"I was on my way to the Blakelees'," he said.

"We were on our way to Philadelphia," said Zane.

Andrew and Rutledge clasped hands in the awkward way of men who shared more than either would admit.

"The cloud cover," Andrew said, pointing. "It seems most familiar to me but I cannot say why."

"Oh, God...." Emilie's face went pale and she sagged against Rutledge. "Please not now—"

"Why are you here?" Rutledge asked him.

Suddenly he knew beyond doubt. "Because there is no other place for me in this world."

"Let's leave," Emilie said, her voice holding a touch of panic. "We don't have to be here at all, none of us do. We can row back to the mainland before the storm hits." She started for the rowboats but Rutledge grabbed her by the wrist.

"Look," he said, pointing beyond the lighthouse.

Andrew turned slowly. His breath caught sharply in his throat as he saw the magnificent sight before him. A large basket danced lightly across the rocks, suspended by ropes attached to a crimson balloon so large it dwarfed even the lighthouse. "Sweet God in heaven," he whispered in awe. Despite its size the vessel seemed so fragile, so insubstantial, that he wondered how it was it had survived its amazing journey.

Rutledge swept Emilie into his arms. For the first time Andrew felt not the smallest pang of envy. She belonged to Rutledge and she always would. "This is our chance, Em!" Rutledge spun her around. "You said it wouldn't happen but it did. This is our chance to go back home where we belong."

Andrew heard the squeak of rope against wicker. "It's beginning to rise!"

Emilie pulled away from Rutledge. "This can't be," she murmured. "You just don't understand."

"We don't belong here, Em," Rutledge pleaded. "Let's—"

"Zane—" Her voice broke. "I can't... there are reasons I—" She tossed her embroidered purse to Zane but it fell to the ground at her husband's feet. Gathering up her skirts, she ran toward the lighthouse.

"Stay or go, man!" Andrew bellowed as the winds howled around them. That glittering world they had described was calling to him. "The chance may ne'er come again."

"You're right, McVie." Suddenly Zane smiled, a smile that could mean but one thing. "Damn right." With that Zane turned and went to join his wife.

The basket shuddered then rose higher. Somehow Andrew had never imagined braving the mysteries of time without his friends from the twentieth century. But there was no hope for it. He was sick unto death of struggle. The happiness others took for granted was not part of the Almighty's plan for him, but this grand adventure was and he'd be more than a fool to let this opportunity slip through his fingers. In the glittering world Zane and Emilie described he could lose himself in the wonder of it all and maybe—just maybe—forget that there'd been a time when he'd wanted more.

He reached down and scooped up Emilie's fabric purse and tucked it into the cuff of his leather boot.

"Stay or go," he said again. If only someone could prove that his existence here mattered, that one small thing he said or did lived on. But he was asking for the impossible. Hadn't Emilie said his name vanished from the history books, never to reappear?

Maybe the reason he vanished from the history books was that he vanished from the eighteenth century entirely. Maybe he had accomplished all he was meant to accomplish in this world and it was time to seek newer worlds to conquer.

And maybe he was as crazy as a mad dog baying at the full moon. Did any of it matter a whit in the greater scheme of things? When you'd already lost everything, not even death seemed too much to risk.

The world Andrew McVie had known since birth no longer seemed familiar. This was the reason he'd been drawn to this place, at this moment in time. Moments ago his future had seemed as bleak as the skies overhead. Now, in the blink of an eye, he found himself filled with hope for the first time in years. His life here was over and his new life in the future was about to begin. He prayed to God there would be a place for him there.

His dreams were of other times, and to deny them would be to consign himself to an early grave, and so he climbed into the basket just before it floated free of the earth's shackles and headed into the unknown.

The last thing he saw as the balloon rose into the clouds was Emilie and Zane silhouetted in the window. They were waving goodbye.

CHAPTER ONE

Somewhere Over New Jersey

"YO, MAN! LOOKIN' GOOD!" The dark-haired wench in the basket of the green dragon balloon waved at Andrew as she drifted by.

Andrew wasn't certain what manner of address she used, but he nodded politely and lifted his hand to salute in kind.

Was that the sixth person to address him thus, or the hundredth? He no longer remembered. Indeed, it seemed he had scarcely ascended above the clouds before he was joined by balloons in the shapes of houses and half-moons and oddities for which he had no name. And to make matters even more perplexing, each balloon held a basket and each basket held a passenger bound for the same adventure.

Emilie and Zane might believe they had lived a miracle, but they were wrong. Traveling through time was

18

as commonplace as riding the Post Road between Trenton and Princeton. They had said what happened to them was an act of fate, a once in a lifetime occurrence, but the evidence to the contrary was there right in front of his very eyes.

A balloon in the shape of an elongated dog drifted close. A man and woman waved to him from the bright yellow basket. "Party at the Forbes mansion at nine," the woman called out. "Champagne supper."

The man cupped his hands around his mouth. "Great costume! I have one like it at home."

No one had ever seen fit to comment upon his attire before. Andrew glanced down at his faded brown breeches and tobacco-colored waistcoat and found it to be a most ordinary outfit.

"What century would ye be from?" he called out, but the flames beneath his balloon roared, and with it the basket rose up and away. They had the look of the future about them, but for all Andrew knew they were farmers from the commonwealth of Pennsylvania.

All things seemed possible.

He peered over the side but the clouds obscured his view of the ground below. Save for one heart-stopping view of the lighthouse growing smaller beneath him, he had seen naught but clouds and more clouds. And now to discover that he did not make the journey alone . . . It was enough to make him wonder if he would find himself back at the point from which he had begun, an hour older and much wiser.

A huge striped balloon of green and white crossed his path but the occupants were too engrossed in conversation to pay him any heed. It would appear he was the only one on God's earth who found it unusual to sail above the clouds with nothing but the wind beneath him.

He wondered how it was that he would be returned to the ground below. Zane had suffered a broken arm when he and Emilie had come down from the sky. All that stood between Andrew and a painful death was the fragile basket that shuddered beneath him.

The magic fire propelling the balloon sputtered, hissed, then finally died. Andrew, heart thundering inside his chest, gripped the edge of the basket as it began to drop. As a child he'd imagined clouds to be soft pillows of down suspended in the air, but that was far from the truth. Each cloud hid an unpleasant surprise, rocking the basket to and fro, rattling him to his bones. He considered the wisdom of leaping to the ground but he had no idea how far away the ground might be or how many broken limbs such a feat might entail.

Gritting his teeth, he prepared to find out.

Shannon Whitney believed in three absolutes: the necessity for clean air, clean water and the Sunday *New York Times*. Or, more specifically, the crossword puzzle from hell that was tucked away in the magazine section each week and whose sole purpose was to drive sane people to madness.

Of course, there were those who would say doing the puzzle in ink was the first sign of incipient lunacy, and Shannon was among them. Still, that didn't stop her from uncapping her favorite pen every Sunday morning and spending more time than she would care to admit wrestling with six-letter words for crustaceans and eight-letter words for undergarments worn by seventeenth-century courtesans.

"Pantaloons...too long," she muttered, gnawing on the cap of her Bic. "Bloomers...too practical." She tossed the pen across the backyard and watched as it skittered along the flagstone path and rolled toward the pool. What was the point in trying to exercise her intellect when she could scarcely hear herself think over the rumble of propane tanks overhead?

Every year members of the blasted Central New Jersey Hot Air Enthusiasts club pleaded with her to allow them to use her land for their festival, and every year she refused. "We won't hurt a thing," their president claimed. "You have our word we'll leave your land exactly as we found it."

That, of course, wasn't the point but she didn't expect a man who spent the better part of his life flying around in a hot-air balloon to understand.

That was one of the many things wrong with the rich, she thought. The more money a man had at his disposal, the more ridiculous his toys. And what could be more ridiculous than flying over central New Jersey in a wicker basket suspended from a balloon filled with nothing but hot air.

She'd grown up in a world of privilege where polo ponies and private tennis courts were as common as guest rooms and finished basements, where grown men who should know better bet fortunes on the outcome of a chukker or the spin of a roulette wheel. People said that money couldn't buy happiness but Shannon wasn't convinced. Delinquent mortgages, bankrupt businesses, parents unable to pay their children's medical bills—money could do a lot more than gather interest in a Swiss bank account.

She tilted her head and listened as the rumble came closer. Whether or not the members of the club understood her reasons, she'd made her stand perfectly clear. She valued her privacy and wasn't about to compromise her stand on the issue just because some idiots liked to take to the air like Dorothy in *The Wizard of Oz*. If the wizard could give them brains she might rethink the position, but until then her land was off-limits.

Disappointment clogged Andrew's senses as he brushed dirt and twigs from his hair and clothing. The adventure of a lifetime had turned out to be another folly in a lifetime of abundant folly.

There was nothing exciting about falling through the branches of a silver maple tree and landing with a thud on the ground. In truth, he was fortunate to have escaped with his limbs intact but he took little consolation from that fact.

When the clouds had finally given way he'd been granted a clear view of the Raritan River and of a landscape most familiar to him, even from his peculiar vantage point. He sailed over the roof of a house identical in form and size to the houses he'd left behind. The only unusual sight was the rectangular pond behind the dwelling. He'd heard sailors speak of the turquoise waters of the Caribbean but he had never thought to encounter such a thing.

He wasn't in the glittering world of the future Emilie and Zane had beguiled him with. He wasn't even in another colony. He was still in New Jersey, perhaps no more than a few miles from where his journey had begun.

The basket had come to rest upside down in a thicket, while the deflated balloon dangled from the branches of a towering silver maple. There was no sign of the contraption that fired the mechanism that kept the balloon aloft. Whatever it was, it had been lost in the plummet to earth.

"'Tis of no consequence," he said, heading for the footpath that led to the house. His chance to leap forward through the centuries had passed him by. He tried to tell himself it was not meant to be, but the words held cold comfort.

He would inquire of his whereabouts, partake of a cool cup of water, then be on his way. If he put a good foot under him, he might be able to reach the lighthouse before nightfall. He had much he wished to discuss with Emilie and Zane.

There was an odd smell to the air, he noted as he made his way along the path. The wet, rich smell of rotting leaves and earth mingled with something heavy and sharp, something he'd never smelled before. Smoke? The tang of pine teased his nostrils but not the sting of burning wood. This was something different, something that made his eyes feel scratchy and his throat ache.

He glanced up through the canopy of trees. Indeed, the sky held a yellowish tinge that was unfamiliar to him. He was not a man who spent time contemplating the wonders of the natural world, yet even he could see that all was not as he knew it should be.

The balloons, he thought. Fires had propelled them into the air. Surely those fires were responsible for the strange yellow haze that blanketed the sky. He felt a surge of relief that a logical answer could be found to explain the occurrence.

The path narrowed as he neared the house. The hedgerows were neatly trimmed along this section of the path and he noted bundles of firewood stacked equal distances apart. Only a person of great personal wealth would lavish such care on the back end of his property. Andrew found his gut twisting with suspicion. Persons of great wealth invariably found themselves on the side of the British, and he prepared himself for a confrontation.

He had no doubt that the owner would greet him with questions he couldn't answer... and a loaded musket.

Shannon dangled her feet in the swimming pool and waited. The balloon had gone down somewhere on her property and she knew it was simply a matter of time before the hapless pilot made his way to the house in search of something cold to drink, a trip to the john and a comfortable place to wait for the spotters to show up. She knew the drill as well as she knew her own name and she dreaded it.

The fact that she was alone at the house didn't disturb her, although she supposed it should. Mildred and Karl, the couple who took care of things, had the summer off and, for a welcome change, the safe houses Shannon maintained for battered women and their children were vacant. Of course, that was a temporary condition. In the next day or two another terrified woman would stare down her fears and take that first step toward an independent life, same as Shannon had more than three years ago.

Walking out the door and leaving the violence behind was how it had begun for Shannon. Facing her husband across that crowded courtroom and speaking the truth for all to hear had freed her from the last of her fears and she would let no one and nothing intimidate her ever again. Not even the fact that Bryant had been paroled six months ago was enough to rob her of her independence.

If only it was that easy to conquer the aching loneliness deep inside her heart.

Every now and again she managed to convince herself that she'd grown accustomed to being alone, to being satisfied that what she had was all she'd ever need. But then she would see a man and woman walking hand in hand or hear the soft laughter of lovers and she'd be struck anew by how the best part of life continued to elude her.

And probably always would.

A difficult truth but one she could no longer deny. She was almost thirty. She had been married and divorced. She had learned firsthand that when it came to the rest of your life you didn't settle for anything less than the man of your dreams.

The fact that the man of her dreams existed only in her imagination was proof positive that she'd end her days alone. She wanted a man of strength and character. A man who could take charge of a situation without losing sight of her needs and desires. A man who would love her above all else and recognize the gift she gave when she loved him in return.

All in all, she might as well pray for Aladdin's lamp and three wishes because that was the only way she could ever conjure up such a paragon of masculinity.

She heard a rustle of branches, then turned toward her right. A man stood in the shadow of the silver maple tree.

"Took you long enough," she commented as he moved into the waning sunshine. "I was about to give up on you."

He strode across the lawn toward her as if he owned the property and everything on it. He was clad in a scruffy version of some old outfit from the Revolutionary War period: faded brown breeches, a rough shirt of tan cloth, a leather waistcoat and worn boots. As costumes went it was almost painfully authentic. She found herself wishing for a touch less realism and a bit more theatricality.

He stopped some ten feet away from her and stared down as if he'd never seen a woman before.

"Doesn't anyone in that blasted balloon club of yours understand the concept of private property?"

His gaze moved from her face to her breasts and belly and for an instant she wished she was wearing a sedate maillot. She rose to her feet and threw back her shoulders, daring him to challenge her right to make the rules for her own land.

The lass was nearly naked. She stood there with the stance of a warrior, almost daring him to look at her. Had she no modesty? The sight of her body, barely covered by the narrow strips of yellow fabric, enflamed him with desire unlike anything he had ever known. Heat, dark and dangerous, threatened to overcome years of civilized behavior and turn him into a rutting stallion.

May the good Lord forgive him, but he wanted nothing more than to strip the lass of her garments and have her right there in full view of God and man.

Where Emilie had been tall and strapping, this woman was small and finely made, but he sensed that she was not a woman easily bested in any way. This was a woman a man courted, not one you lay down with then forgot come the morrow.

With great difficulty he tore his eyes away from the splendor of her ripely curved body and glanced at his surroundings, and what he saw made his heart beat even faster. That wasn't a pond as he knew ponds to be. Not only was it a perfect rectangle filled with bright blue water, but a long wooden board extended out over one end. White stripes were faintly visible beneath the water.

"Haven't you heard a single thing I've said?" the almost-naked lass snapped. He looked back at her and felt a new rush of desire that rattled him to his bones. "Will your spotters be able to find you?"

Spotters? What in bloody hell was a spotter? "Nay, mistress," he said with deliberate caution. "I come alone."

She tilted her head to the right at the sound of his voice. "A Scotsman, is it?" A long and lovely sigh floated on the air toward him. "I suppose no one told you this property was off-limits."

He nodded. Agreeing with her seemed the wisest course of action until he knew what she was about.

Something was obviously wrong with the poor man. He seemed incapable of stringing more than a handful of words together at any one time and, truth to tell, he was beginning to look a bit the worse for the wear.

"You're pale as a ghost," she said. "Did you hit your head when you landed?"

"I have no wish to cause you alarm, mistress. If you would show me the direction to town I will bid you a good night."

He rolled his *r*'s like a refugee from an old Hollywood costume drama. She'd known a Scotsman or two in her life and they certainly didn't sound like him. Or look like him, for that matter.

"I'm nowhere near town," she said carefully. "You just flew over my house. You should know that."

"A post road, then," he persisted. He looked up at the sky. "Enough daylight remains to cover considerable ground once I find my way."

The poor man *must* have struck his head. He might even have a concussion. She hated to think he was merely dense. "I think you'd better come inside," she said. She'd give him something cold to drink while they waited for his pals to track him down.

No response from him. Why on earth should that surprise her? The man was silent as the tomb. She turned around to find him squatting next to the chaise longue. He was staring at the sections of the Sunday *Times* scattered about the way primitive man must have stared at fire.

She started to say something flip and funny but the words died in her throat. Dear God, but he was magnificent in his own way. His thick brown hair was pulled back into a ponytail and tied with a strip of leather. His face was craggy, his features rough-hewn. It was the face of a man who had braved the elements and more than one man's wrath. He wasn't handsome by anyone's standards. Still, he was the most compelling male she'd ever seen. His eyes were hazel with flecks of gold, unspectacular as eyes went, but there was something else at work, some indefinable something that stole her breath. He was of no more than medium height but he had about him an aura of such solidity, such strength, that deep inside her heart an ache began that felt much like yearning.

My life will never be the same after today. The thought came to her full-blown, as clear as if she'd spoken the words aloud, and she didn't know whether to laugh or cry. *This is the man you've dreamed about. There is no one else like him in the world.*

She pushed aside the ridiculous thought, the same way she'd learned to push aside her fears. What an overblown, ridiculously romantic notion. The man had fallen out of a hot-air balloon—and gracelessly, at that. He wasn't a knight on a white charger come to rescue her from her lonely life. Obviously she'd watched *Ghost* and *Sleepless in Seattle* one time too many.

It was time for a dose of reality.

They'd go inside, he'd make a phone call, drink some cold water, then he'd be on his way.

And Shannon's life would go on same as it had before he walked out of the woods and made her remember how it felt to want something she could never have.

CHAPTER TWO

THE EVIDENCE WAS THERE in front of Andrew's eyes. Printed across the top of each page of the newspaper were the words Sunday, August 29, 1993.

He was not a man given to great emotion, but his hands trembled as he put the paper back down. *Done,* he thought. *The deed has been done.*

The world he knew was naught but a memory, a relic consigned to a chapter or two in a dusty history book. General Washington. Thomas Jefferson. He paused as a huge lump formed in his throat. *Emilie and Zane.*

Gone, all of them, vanished into the mists of time.

For one powerful moment the enormity of what he'd done swept over him, filling him with a sense of loss that threatened to be his undoing. But then his eye was caught by a picture in the lower left-hand corner of the first page of the newspaper. The words beneath the picture made no sense to him: Shuttle Blast Success. Astronauts Eager. But the picture...good God in heaven, what artist had imagined such a sight? A towering structure that proudly angled toward the skies, leaving a trail of fire in its wake.

It was indeed a world of wonders even more heart-stopping than those Emilie and Zane had described. And now he was part of it all.

The last of his doubts vanished in a surge of elation that sent his spirits soaring higher than the balloon that had carried him through two centuries to this place and this time. It mattered little that he had seen other time travelers making similar journeys. All that mattered was that he had accomplished the impossible. He had seized opportunity with both hands and wrought a miracle, and his life would never again be the same.

He sensed the dark-haired woman's gaze intent upon him and looked up. Indeed, she watched him openly, her aqua eyes wide, her expression most curious. Suddenly he felt the need to keep his method of travel to himself, although he could not say why. Despite the evidence to the contrary, Emilie and Zane had been of the opinion that traveling through time in a balloon was an uncommon occurrence. Better to keep his own counsel until he knew the situation in which he found himself.

Would you believe me, lass, he wondered, *or would you mark me for a fool?*

"Did you say something?" Shannon asked.

"Nay, mistress."

"I'm sure you did."

"Nay," he said. "'Tis your imagination."

"No," she replied. "You said something. I heard you."

He said nothing.

You're losing your mind, Shannon thought. *Look at the way he's watching you, as if you were certifiable.* She slipped into her terry robe and pulled it close to her body, though she didn't know why she bothered. The Scotsman made her feel exposed in a way that had little to do with bare skin. There was no accounting for the odd sensation that had gripped her at the first sight of him striding across the lawn as if it was his name on the mortgage instead of hers.

The accent, she thought. *If he didn't have that accent I would've sent him packing.* She'd always been a sucker for a man with a burr.

"You can bring the paper inside with you," she said in a dry tone of voice, meant to hide the rapid thudding of her heart. "I don't mind."

"'Tis most interesting," he said, straightening up.

"Apparently so." She noted the way he clutched it close to his chest. "I don't suppose they have anything like the *Times* where you come from."

"Nay, mistress. We have naught to compare."

"What on earth is with this 'mistress' bit, anyway?" She felt suddenly contentious. "A bit archaic, don't you think?"

Again that look of uncertainty, which was so much at odds with the aura of raw masculinity that he projected with so little effort. "I have no knowledge of your Christian name."

She couldn't hold back a soft laugh of surprise. "Shannon Whitney."

"Andrew McVie." He inclined his head. "Would you be married, lass?"

"I have to hand it to you Scotsmen. You certainly don't waste any time."

He looked at her blankly.

She felt her cheeks flush with color. "I was married. I'm not any longer."

"A widow."

"No," she said, "a divorcée."

"'Tis an epidemic."

"What is?"

"Divorce," he said, shaking his head. "Mistress Emilie and Rutledge were torn asunder by the malady. How is it that marriage has fallen into such disfavor?"

"Welcome to the nineties," she said, again struck by the feeling he was unlike any man she would ever know. "Half the marriages in this country end in divorce."

"Such a thing is not possible."

"Good grief, McVie. What rock have you been hiding under? I can't believe it's that different in Scotland."

"How is it you believe I know of life in Scotland?"

"You're certainly not from New Jersey."

"I was born north of Boston."

"I know Boston accents and that isn't one of them."

"I speak the truth."

She sighed. "I'm sure you do, but why is it I have the feeling we're having two separate conversations here?"

"Mistress?"

She waved her hand in the air between them. "Never mind." The man had crashed into the trees a few minutes ago. Was it any wonder his conversation didn't quite track? "Let's get you a chair and something cold to drink." With a little luck his people would spot the balloon and come to fetch him before nightfall.

"Aye," he said. "'Twould be most agreeable."

The man was a bundle of opposing forces. One second she was certain he was coming on to her and the next he was bemoaning the prevalence of divorce in America. He was as solidly built as an oak tree, yet she sensed a vulnerability in him that touched her in a way little else ever could have.

All of which was patently absurd. She didn't know the slightest thing about him, save for the fact that he was one of those hot-air balloon enthusiasts who drove her nuts every summer like clockwork. So what if he had a delectable accent? So what if he was built like a powerful oak tree? If anyone knew the utter unimportance of externals it was Shannon, and she'd be doing herself a favor if she kept that fact uppermost in her mind.

"The necessary," he said. "Where would it be?"

"The necessary?"

"The privy, mistress."

"The bathroom. Why didn't you just say so? There's one down the hall near the kitchen."

A privy inside the house, near the kitchen? Andrew's stomach roiled at the thought.

Surely the lass had misunderstood him. He followed her along the stone path to the door at the side of the house. A wooden structure that looked a great deal like a privy stood not far from the striped pond with the bright blue water. He started to say something to mistress Shannon, then remembered the wonders Emilie and Zane had told him about and he held his tongue. Mayhap there were more miracles to be discovered.

The dark-haired woman's hips swayed in a most agreeable fashion as she walked and Andrew didn't find it difficult to remember how she looked beneath the short white robe. Her fingernails were painted a soft shade of pink and to his amazement he saw that her toenails were painted thus, as well.

Was this how it was in the future, then, where even something as unimportant as a woman's toenails received an artist's attention? And, even more astonishing, he wondered if there were people in this world who made their living providing that attention. He tried to imagine himself kneeling before a woman, paintbrush in hand, but the concept was more lustful than practical and one best put from his mind.

"The back door is broken," she said over her shoulder, "so we'll have to go in through the kitchen. The bathroom's right there."

He was surprised that such a big house didn't have a separate building for the kitchen. No man of wealth would welcome the stench of singed chicken feathers wafting through the parlor. Indeed, it was a most average house, no more or less imposing than the ones he had known in Boston and New Jersey. Made of stone and brick, the house stood two stories high. Three chimneys graced the roofline and a pair of dormer windows looked out toward the woods beyond the pond. The windows were six-over-six, the sashes painted white and in need of some repair.

Andrew felt it difficult to contain his disappointment.

Thus far, except for the rectangular pond and the newspaper tucked under his arm, his surroundings were much as he remembered them. The house he'd shared with Elspeth had boasted a large backyard with a stone wall blocking off the vegetable garden, same as mistress Shannon's.

Mistress Shannon opened the side door then pressed her hand against the wall. Instantly the room was flooded with the light of a dozen suns and Andrew stepped back in alarm.

"Sweet Jesus!"

The woman looked at him. "Are you okay?"

"'Tis bright as midday."

She gestured toward the ceiling. "Recessed lighting."

He leapt onto a ledge and placed a hand against the ceiling. It felt cool against his palm. "Where would the candles be placed?"

"Get down from there, you colossal idiot!" Her voice rose in agitation. "Get your filthy feet off my counter *now*."

He ignored her. "'Tis a most clever device, but I am of a mind to find the candles."

"And I'm of a mind to call the police if you don't come down from there." She looked around the room as if searching for something to beat him with.

He did as the lass bid. His boots left clods of dirt behind and he brushed at them with his arm. The reddish brown dirt fell to the shiny white floor. She looked angry enough to strike him, and by all that was holy he could not fathom why.

She pushed a chair toward him and motioned for him to sit down. "If you didn't look so dreadful I'd throw you out on your ear," she said. "Sit down while I pour you some iced tea."

The chair was a shiny silver metal, bent into a curving shape that pleased the eye but baffled the mind. He wondered what silversmith had accomplished such an enormous job, for there were five more chairs exactly like it surrounding the matching table. Attached somehow to the metal was a cushion covered in a fabric he'd never seen before. It was slippery to the touch and shiny yellow in look, and when he sat upon it the squeaking noise it made was most astonishing.

She crossed the room and swung open a white door, revealing a closet, also bright as day, that held all manner of foodstuff.

"O.J., milk, there's the iced tea." She removed a big green pitcher then poured the liquid into a tall glass. "Drink this," she said, handing it to him.

He gulped some down then drank some more. "A pallid brew," he observed, "but cold." He wondered how that state had been achieved.

"A simple thank-you is sufficient."

He studied the glass, then the half-filled pitcher. "I see no evidence of tea leaves. Perhaps that is the problem."

"Awfully picky for a trespasser, wouldn't you say? If I were you, I'd drink the tea and keep the opinions to myself."

"'Twas not my intent to criticize, mistress."

The look she gave him brooked no argument. "If you need the john, now might be a good time."

"John?" Thus far he had seen no evidence of a man.

"The bathroom," she said, sounding exasperated. "The privy, as you called it."

He brightened. At last, something he understood. They both spoke English but the variations within the language were extraordinary. He refused to believe she had an indoor privy and pointed out the window. "The wooden structure beyond the blue pond?"

"Very funny, Mr. McVie. That's the cabana." She pointed down the hallway. "Second door on your right."

"You are one very strange man," Shannon murmured as Andrew disappeared down the hallway. You'd almost think he didn't know what a bathroom was. She'd been to Scotland twice. They had bathrooms over there and overhead lighting and everything else the twentieth century had to offer. Her unexpected visitor acted as if these things were brand-new inventions.

She heard the bathroom door open then close behind him. At least he understood the concept of privacy. When he had leapt up on top of the counter she hadn't been sure civilization had quite reached his rung on the evolutionary ladder.

She looked out the window in the direction from which he'd first appeared. Dusk was washing over the tops of the trees and there wasn't a sign of life except for a blue jay squawking his loud displeasure. You'd think McVie's spotters would have found him by now. In the past it hadn't taken more than ten minutes for wayward balloonists to be retrieved. *Cheer up,* she told herself. Maybe they were collecting his gear at this very moment and would come traipsing across her backyard any minute in search of their cohort.

Of course, there was also the possibility that he'd been fool enough to go up without any backup system at all, in which case she'd just call him a cab and he could worry about his blasted balloon and gondola in the morning. It wasn't like her to let a stranger into her home, especially not when she was alone. From the moment she'd heard him land in her trees her reactions had been completely skewed, as if she were being ruled by her emotions rather than her brain.

Her eyes strayed toward the telephone. Maybe she should call Dakota and let her friend know what was going on.

The idea had some merit and she was about to reach for the receiver when the telephone rang.

"I should've known it would be you," she said as Dakota's familiar voice greeted her. "You do this all the time."

"It's one of the problems with being psychic. My phone bill takes a beating." Dakota laughed. "Is everything okay? I was meditating and kept hearing your mantra."

Shannon, who was not a believer in mantras and things that went bump in the night, cut to the chase. "There's a man here."

"I know," said Dakota. "I could feel it in my bones. Is he friend or foe?"

"Neither. He's a weird Scotsman. If I didn't know better, I'd say he's not part of this century."

"Maybe he's not," said Dakota, who believed in just about everything. "Where did he come from?"

"My backyard," Shannon said with a slight laugh.

"I mean, how did he get there?"

"His hot-air balloon went down in the woods."

Dakota sounded almost disappointed. "One of those guys from the festival?"

"I suppose so." She wished she sounded more certain. The man was in her house, for God's sake, and she hadn't had the brains to ask for identification. What on earth was the matter with her? She was usually a hell of a lot smarter than that.

"Do you want company?" Dakota asked. "I could drive over."

"I'm fine," Shannon said. "But thanks for—" She tilted her head to the side and listened.

"Shannon? What's going on? Are you still there? I'm picking up some very strange vibes."

"He's flushing the toilet. What on earth is the matter with the man?"

"Flushing the toilet is a *good* thing," Dakota said. "It's leaving the seat up that drives me crazy."

"Nobody flushes five times in a row."

"Maybe he's sick."

"Again! That makes *six* times! I don't care if he did hit his head. He can wait for his damn friends in the woods."

"Shannon, maybe—"

"I'll call you later."

She hung up the telephone, her heart pounding double-time. Colorful was one thing. Crazy was another. Normal people didn't flush toilets as if they were playing a Las Vegas slot machine.

Quietly she stepped into the hallway and listened. It sounded as if a plumbers' convention was going on in the guest bathroom. Water ran full blast. The toilet flushed continuously. And above the racket came McVie's exuberant "Bloody hell!"

"Enjoy it while you can, buster," she said, marching toward the drawer where she kept her gun, "because you've flushed your last commode."

*   *   *

It was a miracle, that's what it was. A bloody miracle. Water everywhere and on command! Andrew crouched on his hands and knees and peered into the white marble bowl. A veritable whirlpool of icy cold water swirled about then vanished, to be followed by another whirlpool at the tug of the brass handle.

Then there was the waist-level basin that provided an endless stream of water so hot it caused mist to form on the looking glass behind it. And there wasn't a fire anywhere to be seen. To make matters even more fantastical, the entire wall was a giant looking glass where he saw himself grinning like a jackanapes as he watched the water swirl about the marble bowl.

Nothing Emilie and Zane had told him had prepared him for this surprise. He felt beneath the bowl and touched the cold tubes of metal that disappeared into the wall. Did the water come through those tubes or did it make its exit thusly? And why was it necessary to force water into a room from so many places? What went on in here that required so much water of so many different degrees of heat?

She'd called it a privy but it was not like any privy he'd seen or imagined. There was a seat attached to the white marble bowl and its purpose was obvious, but that splashing water and the loud noise it made had him reluctant to put it to use.

Besides, there was the question of the waist-level basin. There were only so many things a man could do in a privy and none of them had anything to do with looking glasses or fresh flowers displayed in glass bowls.

He opened the doors beneath the basin and stuck his head inside the small cabinet. It smelled of cedar and more roses and he sneezed at the combination. His hand fell upon a container and he withdrew it, holding it up to the fading sunlight at the window. Air Freshener, it read in bold type. The words held no meaning for him. He turned the receptacle over in his hand. Make Your House Smell Like An English Garden. Most peculiar. He sniffed at the container and caught the scent of roses again. He tapped the metal cylinder against the floor but nothing happened. Then he spied the words Press Here on a ridged button at the top.

He did so, sending a cloud of sickeningly sweet flower scent into the room. "Great God in heaven!" he roared. "'Tis a stink unlike any I've known."

His eyes watered as a mist of scent settled across his head and shoulders, and he stood and plunged his head into the warm water flooding the basin. At that moment the door swung open and, through the water streaming down his face, he saw the mistress Shannon standing before him with a pistol pointed straight at his heart.

CHAPTER THREE

"'TIS A SMALL GUN," Andrew McVie mused, "but I fear it is more deadly than the firearms I knew."

Shannon gripped the pistol with both hands. "Over there," she said, motioning toward the wall. "Put your hands against it and spread 'em."

"A strange request to make of an innocent traveler."

"I'll show you strange. Now spread 'em."

"The words are familiar but the usage is not."

"Oh, for God's sake. Don't you watch cop shows in Scotland?" It had always worked for Angie Dickinson in *Police Woman*.

He looked at her with the blank expression she was coming to know.

"Put your hands against the wall and spread your legs so I can frisk you."

A broad smile spread across his craggy face, making him almost handsome. "Mistress, I am your humble servant."

He did as told. There was something intimidating about all of that raw maleness that was hers for the taking. Not that she wanted to take anything, but still, the whole situation was exciting in a bizarre way.

She stood there, gun in hand, staring at his bold, extremely masculine form. She'd seen Crockett and Tubbs frisk suspects a thousand times on "Miami Vice" reruns, but the thought of doing so herself was daunting.

You have to do something, idiot. Pat him down, at the very least.

Holding the gun in her right hand, she quickly patted him across his shoulders and down his back. She doubted her nerves could take much more. His musculature was impressive, to say the least, and she knew without asking that those muscles weren't the result of pumping iron in front of mirrors in some fancy health club. He'd got them the old-fashioned way—through hard work.

The question was, what kind of hard work?

"Empty your pockets," she commanded. Not terribly original but it was a start.

"Is that part of frisking, mistress? Thus far it has been a pleasurable interlude."

"Just do it!"

"I have nothing of consequence to show."

"That's absurd. You must have something."

He reached into the pocket of his waistcoat and removed a quarter, a cambric kerchief and something he quickly slipped into the waistband of his breeches.

"What was that?"

"'Tis nothing of importance."

"I'll be the judge of that."

He handed her a laminated card. She turned it over. A photo of a pretty, red-haired woman looked up at her. Emilie Crosse, it read, followed by a New Jersey driver's license number.

"What on earth are you doing with this?" she asked, almost afraid of the answer. Maybe he was a carjacker and this was the only piece of evidence that could link him to his hapless victim.

"Return that to me," he ordered.

"I want an explanation."

"I have none I wish to offer."

"Where is Emilie Crosse?"

He said nothing.

She aimed the gun. "I want some answers, McVie, and I want them now."

"You are a comely lass," he observed, "but most unwomanly in demeanor."

She didn't know whether to laugh or shoot him. "I'm standing here with Emilie Crosse's driver's license and it's pretty damn obvious you're not Emilie, so either you start talking now or I'm calling the police."

"You have a sharp tongue, mistress. 'Tis no wonder you and your husband are no longer wed."

"You're really pushing it, mister."

He took a step toward her.

She held her ground.

He took another step.

"I'm an expert marksman," she said. "I hit what I aim for."

"'Twould be a sorry thing were you to miss at such close range."

"You're not funny."

"It is not my intention to be so."

"I'd like to give you the benefit of the doubt but you're making it impossible."

He lunged for the pistol, knocking her right hand to her side. Her fingers flexed open and the gun clattered to the floor. They both dove for it but Shannon threw herself on top of the pistol, trying to ignore the way it dug into her ribs when McVie landed on top of her.

He was strong. Too strong. She felt the sharp teeth of panic as memories crowded against her, but she refused to acknowledge their power. *Take a deep breath,* she commanded herself. *You can handle this.* Three years of self-defense training had to be good for something.

She forced herself to go limp.

He hesitated.

She bucked her pelvis sharply, knocking him off balance, then flipped him onto his back and straddled him, pressing the gun against his Adam's apple.

"This is my home," she said, her voice taut. "I will not let you or anyone else take that away from me. Tell me what you're doing here or I swear to God I'll shoot you from here to kingdom come."

Andrew had no wish to meet his Maker at the hands of mistress Shannon, but neither did he wish the moment to end. The white robe had fallen from her shoulders, exposing her golden body to his roving eyes. Her breasts, covered only by that strip of yellow fabric, rose and fell to the rapid tempo of her breathing.

The delectable curve of her waist was plainly visible, as were her flat belly and womanly hips. Her most secret self was shielded by naught but a band of cloth. And—sweet Jesus!—her naked thighs grasped his hips, so tightly he could feel her muscles straining with the effort.

'Twould take naught but the slightest movement to topple her and regain mastery of the situation, but no man worth his mettle would willingly forgo such a glimpse of paradise.

But there was the look in her wide aqua eyes to consider. This was her home, her land. She deserved the truth even if in the telling he put himself at risk.

"Emilie Crosse was a friend, mistress, and a good wife to the man she loved."

"What are you doing with her driver's license?"

"She has no need of it." *Do not ask more, mistress, for I do not know what that driver's license is about.*

"That's what I was afraid of."

"Nay, mistress, 'tis not a cause for worry."

"Is she dead?" Her voice cracked on the last word.

He considered the question for a moment. In truth, he could but say that Emilie no longer walked this earth, but following that line of reasoning, it should not be possible for him to be drawing a breath in the year of our Lord nineteen hundred and ninety-three. "She was well and contented the last time I laid my eyes upon her."

The lass's relief was obvious. "I don't want to think the worst of you, McVie, but you're making it difficult to get to the bottom of this. All I know is that there was a hot-air balloon festival today and you dropped onto my property. If there's anything else, I'd like to hear about it."

A festival? Was it possible the balloons were used for more than traveling through time? "'Tis a simple explanation," he began slowly, "but I am uncertain if you will accept it with ease."

"Try me." How was it a woman so finely made could sound as forbidding as a man twice her size?

"I am not part of your world."

"Tell me something I don't know."

He frowned, unable to discern her meaning. "I detect a note of irony but fail to understand its source."

This from the man who flushed toilets for entertainment? If he'd spouted Kierkegaard, Shannon couldn't have been more surprised.

"You already told me you're not from Scotland." She swallowed hard. "So where are you from?"

His hazel-gold eyes met hers. "My last home was in New Jersey."

"This is New Jersey."

"I passed much of the summer on a farm near Princeton."

"Princeton isn't far from here."

"Nay, mistress, the Princeton I know is long gone."

Let him talk . . . you know he's telling you the truth, Shannon. . . . Don't be afraid. . . .

His expression darkened, yet still she felt no fear. Strangely enough, her courage did not come from the gun but from some inexplicable sense of connection she felt with this stranger.

"When I awoke this morning, it was the year of our Lord seventeen hundred and seventy-six."

A buzzing began in her ears and she shook her head to dispel it. "I must be going crazy," she said with a short laugh. "I thought you said 1776."

"Aye, mistress, 'tis what I said."

The buzzing grew louder and she started to tremble, as well. "That's not possible."

"I am proof that it is."

"You're not proof of anything. You don't look more than thirty-five."

He winced. "Thirty-three the fifth of May last."

"No," she said, beginning to laugh. "If what you're telling me is true, you're two hundred and fifty years old."

"That does not bear closer consideration."

She stopped laughing as abruptly as she'd begun. "Are you telling me you found Emilie Crosse's New Jersey driver's license in eighteenth-century Princeton?"

"Aye."

"Do I really look that gullible?"

"I have no knowledge of that word nor do I wish to upset you, but in truth, mistress Emilie and her husband came back to my time in a hot-air balloon."

"Right," she said, beginning to think of things like rubber rooms and straitjackets. "And you jumped into the same balloon and flew it right into my backyard?"

His face was transformed by his smile. "'Tis the way it happened."

"Give me a break." She stood, making certain to keep the gun pointed in his general direction. "You expect me to believe you used a hot-air balloon like some kind of time-traveling cab service?" *He's telling the truth... the unvarnished, unbelievable, undeniable truth....*

"Believe as you will, mistress. I can do naught to convince you, save present the story as it is."

She considered him for a long moment. "Why would anyone in his right mind come to our time?"

"Mistress Emilie's husband described a world of wonder and riches."

"For the fortunate few."

"He said man has walked on the surface of the moon and traveled toward the stars."

"Did he tell you about homeless families sleeping on the streets or old people living alone and in squalor?"

"In the United States of America any man can amass a fortune if he is willing to work hard for it."

He said it with such conviction that her heart seemed to turn over inside her chest. The last time she'd heard such starry-eyed optimism it had been from the Korean grocer in town, who still believed in the American dream. "True in theory but the reality is less rosy."

"You live in splendor," he said, gesturing toward the artwork on the walls, the soft carpet on the floors.

"But I'm not happy."

The words hung in the air between them. To Andrew it seemed as if they had not only sound but form and substance, as well.

"Why not, mistress?" he asked softly. "'Twould seem you have all a lass would need for happiness." If a woman needed more gifts than beauty and wealth and intellect he could not imagine what they might be.

"I don't know why I said that." She turned away from him. "Forget you heard it." The robe she'd used to cover her form dipped low on her shoulders and as she moved to pull it back up he saw a crescent-shaped scar.

He moved toward her. "A knife wound," he said. "How is it you suffered such an injury?"

She adjusted the collar on her robe but kept her face averted. "An old story and a boring one. I'd rather hear more about you."

"Someone hurt you."

"I don't want to talk about this."

"I wish to know."

She turned to face him, a defiant glare in her eyes. "Why don't you call someone? It's time you were on your way."

"'Tis no one to call to, mistress, but I will take my leave if that is your wish."

She felt his words pulsing through her body.

She was wary and he had no stomach for being the cause of her discomfort.

"Tell me," she said, voice low and urgent. "Level with me just once and I'll help you. Don't tell me this nonsense about traveling through time—"

"I can tell you no story but the truth and you must choose what it is you wish to believe."

"It's not that I don't want to believe you," she said. "It's just that I'm finding it difficult."

"I cannot believe man has walked on the moon, yet I am willing to accept it as fact."

"It's not the same thing."

"Mayhap it is."

She shook her head. "'Mayhap.' I really wish you'd stop saying things like that. Nobody talks like that."

"As you wish." He started for the door. *I would not hurt you, Shannon. Not in this life or any other.*

His words pulsed their way through her body, leaving a trail of fire behind. She'd heard his thoughts as clearly as if he'd spoken them out loud. *I would not hurt you ... not in this life....* She refused to acknowledge them. Trust and danger lived side by side.

Instead she stood perfectly still, arms wrapped across her chest, and listened to the sound of his heavy footsteps as he headed for the door. *Don't go,* she thought, surprising even herself.

He stopped, hand on the doorknob. "Mistress?"

She looked up and met his eyes. "I didn't say anything."

"I heard your voice most clearly."

"I don't think so."

He swung open the door.

Please stay.

He hesitated. Her heart slammed into her rib cage.

"Damn it," she said finally. "You can sleep in the cabana." She noticed the expression on his face. "The structure beyond the pool."

"You have nothing to fear, mistress. I will not harm you in any way."

"Don't go reading anything into this," she warned in that fierce, warriorlike tone of hers. "It's getting dark, you fell into the trees, I'm just being a Good Samaritan. If you try anything funny, you'll find yourself staring at my gun."

"I have no wish to be funny," he said, confused by her choice of words to describe what was happening between them. "I will take my leave at daybreak."

Too soon.

"Nay," said Andrew. "Not too soon at all. The early morning is the best time to feel the road beneath you."

She stared at him, her face white as a sheet. He'd heard her words but she hadn't spoken them out loud.

Or had she?

"Have it your way," she said, turning away. "Good night."

CHAPTER FOUR

"EVERYTHING'S FINE," Shannon told Dakota for the third time in as many minutes. *Except for the fact that McVie and I are hearing voices.* "The crisis is over."

"I've been sitting here by the phone for an hour. I ate a pint of ice cream. You should've called."

"I *did* call," Shannon pointed out. "Besides, you should've known I was fine. You know everything else before I do."

"That's what had me worried. The vibes were skewed."

"I beg your pardon?"

"I don't know how else to put it. Every time I tried to concentrate on you, I came up blank."

There is a God, Shannon thought. She was having enough trouble sorting out her own emotions. She didn't need her best friend inside her head, sorting them out for her. "You're not picking up anything at all?"

53

"Zip," said Dakota.

"Nothing about Mr. McVie?"

"Not since we last talked. Total blank."

A weird sensation rippled up Shannon's spine and she shivered. "Has that ever happened before?"

"Just once," said Dakota after a moment. She hesitated, then she added, "Maybe I should come over there and check this guy out. Something's weird. I can feel it in my bones."

"No!" Shannon realized she'd overreacted and tried to step back from it. "I mean, there's nothing to check out. He's gone."

"His spotters came for him?"

"Not exactly."

"What exactly?"

"He's out in the cabana."

"The cabana?"

"There's nothing wrong with the cabana. Running water, a toilet, a chaise to sleep on."

"Why didn't you call him a taxi?"

"You're the psychic librarian. You tell me."

"Very funny," Dakota said, sounding huffy. "I'm worried about you. So shoot me."

"Look," Shannon said, "I appreciate your concern, but I'm fine."

"Right," Dakota said. "I'll call you in the morning."

Shannon hung up the telephone, feeling a weird combination of affection and annoyance. Dakota meant well but she had to realize Shannon was perfectly capable of dealing with whatever life threw her way.

She'd proved that the day she filed charges against Bryant and didn't back down, not even when it grew as ugly as their marriage had been. Not that she'd realized how ugly their marriage was. It took months before she understood that what he passed off as loving attention was really a dangerous obsession. One that had left its marks on her body and on her soul.

She went upstairs and stripped off her bathing suit then slipped into an old pair of jeans and an oversize T-shirt. She wandered back down to the kitchen, moving through the room in a daze, running her hand along the bleached wood countertops and across the shiny lip of the stainless steel sink.

This is a good life, she thought as if trying to convince herself. She had security, solitude and the satisfaction that came from helping other women discover that being alone wasn't the worst thing that could happen to you.

It should be enough.

So why was it she felt a gaping emptiness in her chest where her heart used to be each time she thought about the future and came up blank?

She stood in the solarium and looked out the still-broken French doors at the backyard. It was dark outside now and the temple lights that lined the perimeter of the pool glowed softly against the blackness of the summer night.

He was out there. She couldn't see him but she knew he was there. Maybe Dakota couldn't sense his presence, but Shannon registered it in every nerve and fiber of her body. She carried the sense memory of him in her thighs, the way his powerful body had felt beneath hers, the strange smell of him as they'd rolled together on the floor of the hallway, locked in strange and exciting combat.

Maybe she was going insane. Maybe the reason Dakota couldn't sense his presence was that he didn't really exist. Maybe she'd conjured him up out of her own loneliness and need, created him to fill an empty summer's night.

She caught the slightest movement next to the pool. He stood there, legs apart, hands on hips, looking back at her as she stood in the doorway, watching her watching him. It was like those endless reflections in a series of mirrors where reality and fantasy flash by so quickly that you can't tell where you begin or end.

A crack of lightning illuminated the sky, followed moments later by a clap of thunder. A soft rain spit against the glass.

He doesn't even know enough to come in out of the rain, she thought. He could go into the cabana and be safe and dry. He didn't have to stand there staring at her as if she was the Super Bowl or something. *So what are you going to do? Make him stay out there like a German shepherd that isn't quite housebroken yet?*

She opened the door and motioned for him to go around to the front and come inside.

"Were you going to stand out there in the rain all night?" she asked as he stepped into the house. "You could have gone into the cabana."

"'Tis different from the rains I know."

"Rain is rain."

"As I would have said but twenty-four hours ago."

"How is it different?"

"The taste," he said. "The smell of it. Indeed, the way it falls upon the skin."

"God help me, but I almost believe you."

"I have no wish to deceive."

"Who are you?" she asked, voice rising in agitation. "One last chance to tell me the truth."

"I am Andrew McVie," he said, his voice echoing in the quiet sun room, "and I have told you the events as I know them to be."

"I don't know why I should believe you."

"Nor do I, mistress."

"You can sleep in here," she said, pointing toward a chaise longue in the far corner. "You already know where the bathroom is."

"Aye." His solemn face split once again in a wide grin and, despite her misgivings, she found herself smiling back at him. "You possess all of your teeth," he observed with a nod of his head.

She started to laugh. "What did you say?"

"Your teeth," he said, gesturing. "They are white and symmetrical and you still possess them all."

"You're serious, aren't you?"

"Mistress Emilie possessed all of her teeth and she was one score and ten. A most wondrous thing in a woman."

"Well, I am almost one score and ten as well, and I not only have all of my teeth but most of them have no cavities."

"And to what magic do you attribute such a thing?"

"Good genes," she said with a shrug. "That and Pepsodent."

"Pepsodent?"

"Toothpaste." She groaned. "I hate it when you give me that blank stare." Was she really going to explain toothpaste to a man who might be pulling the biggest stunt since "Candid Camera"? "Stay here. I'll be right back."

* * *

She grew more beautiful with familiarity. Andrew could detect no signs of artifice about her person, simply a most pleasing combination of face and form, designed to delight a man's eye. Although he had been disappointed to see she no longer wore the skin-baring yellow costume, she looked most appealing in men's trousers and a billowy shirt.

The first time he had seen Emilie she had been wearing tight-fitting black trousers that hugged her in a most indecent fashion. Walking behind her had been an enlightening experience. She had explained to him the freedom of dress available to women in her century but Andrew had found it impossible to believe such outfits existed . . . until now.

He paced the huge and airy room, taking note of the spare white furniture and the way it seemed to hold the faint smell of her skin at its heart. He had believed that knowing Emilie Crosse Rutledge would prepare him for the twentieth-century woman, but he had been wrong.

Mistress Shannon had the delicacy of form with which he was familiar, but she also possessed a strength of body that astounded him. And, as if those opposing traits were not puzzling enough, she spoke with Emilie's disturbing bluntness yet he sensed shadows lurking behind her beautiful aqua eyes that had not clouded Emilie's vision.

"A mistake in the offing," he muttered as he picked up a silky coverlet from the back of the long chair. He had not come forward in time to find love or companionship. The coverlet also carried with it the scent of mistress Shannon's perfume, and he quickly replaced it atop the long chair. He was not a foolish man. He recognized danger when danger was about and he would do well to keep temptation at bay.

Loneliness made a man think with his heart and not his head. For a brief time last summer he had believed himself in love with Emilie when, in truth, he had fallen under the spell of the world she'd left behind.

He would not make that mistake again.

The dark-haired woman glided back into the room. "A toothbrush and some toothpaste." She handed him a flexible metal tube and a long-handled brush with tiny bristles.

He unscrewed the white top of the tube and watched, fascinated, as a roll of some sweet-smelling white substance oozed slowly out as he applied pressure.

"You put that on the bristles," mistress Shannon said, "then use the brush to clean your teeth." She frowned. "You do know how to clean your teeth, don't you?"

"Aye," he said indignantly. "Soft twigs and a good washrag achieve much the same results."

"Apparently not," she said. "If it did you wouldn't be so surprised to see that I have all my teeth." She stepped back toward the door. "I'll leave you to get some sleep."

"I will see you to your chamber."

She smiled briefly. "That won't be necessary."

"Aye, mistress, 'tis the proper thing to do."

"Now I know you're not from this century," she said, her smile reappearing. "There isn't a man on this continent who'd do that without an ulterior motive." She narrowed her eyes. "You don't have an ulterior motive, do you?"

"Naught but the desire to give you safe passage through the house."

He means it, Shannon thought as he followed her through the hallway and into the kitchen. He was determined to see her safely to her bedroom. She was charmed, despite herself.

She checked to make certain the kitchen door was locked then fastened the chain, aware all the while of his intense scrutiny. "I'm going to set the alarm," she told him as she punched in the code. "You'll hear a loud—"

A high-pitched wail filled the room and McVie swore in surprise.

"A loud noise," Shannon finished.

"What in bloody hell is that?" he demanded.

"A security alarm."

"I do not understand."

She pointed to the device, wondering why she was explaining the system to a man who might—just might—be as much a product of the twentieth century as she was. "There are units at all of the windows and all of the doors. If someone tries to break in, an alarm sounds and the police are called automatically."

"There is danger abroad? A war in progress?"

"Not the way you would think," Shannon said, "but most home owners take special care these days."

He grew silent. She could see the consternation in his eyes.

"You need a man's protection," he said at last.

"No," said Shannon. "That is the one thing I don't need at all."

He followed her into the living room and watched as she checked the alarm at the window. "No child's toy can provide safety."

She marched into the foyer and set the alarm at the front door. "I don't expect it to provide safety. I expect it to alert me to trouble." She met his eyes. "My gun will do the rest."

"And what if a man wrested the pistol away from you?"

"I doubt if that could happen."

"It can and will happen, mistress. You are strong but slight of frame. You can be overpowered."

"Like hell," she snapped. "You couldn't do it before."

"I did not try."

"Right," she drawled. "You just like having pistols jammed into your Adam's apple."

"Trust me in this regard, mistress Shannon."

"I'm a brown belt in karate."

"I have no knowledge of belts. I only know that you are at a natural disadvantage."

"If I felt like it, I could throw you to the ground before you drew your next breath."

He laughed in a most infuriatingly male fashion. "A most unlikely possibility."

She darted toward him, off balance in her eagerness to show him exactly who was boss. Three years of training went right out the window as she tried to topple him to the ground without the proper leverage, concentration or control.

Basically it was like trying to topple an oak tree with her bare hands.

"Damn you!" she panted in frustration. "Fall down."

He gripped her by the forearms and forced her to meet his eyes. *I can best you,* his look said, *but I choose not to.* There was no denying his strength or his mastery of the situation, yet she felt no fear.

He held her tightly enough to make his point but at no time did he cause her even the slightest pain. For those few moments she was completely under his control and he was man enough not to take advantage of the situation.

A sense of elation gathered inside her chest as she felt the tension and anger drain from her body.

"Your actions were untoward, mistress," he said, releasing her.

She nodded. "I know that now."

The expression in his eyes shifted and she found herself drawn to him against her better judgment.

"You will have no need of screaming boxes this night," he stated as if it were any of his business.

"I don't understand."

"I will protect you against danger."

She stopped breathing. Literally stopped. Her heart pounded so violently at his words that it hurt to draw air into her lungs.

"Mistress?"

She struggled to regain her composure. "Th-thank you," she finally managed to say.

He followed her through the quiet house, up the staircase, then down the hallway to her bedroom. "Good night," she said, stepping inside.

"I bid you a good night." He inclined his head toward her.

She had the insane urge to curtsy in return, but nodded instead, then closed the door behind her.

Andrew stood in the hallway in front of mistress Shannon's closed door, listening to the sound of her soft footsteps as she moved about the room.

What manner of world was it when women lived alone in fear, forced to rely upon a screaming box for protection? Had she no family or friends to see to her safety and well-being, no one with whom to break bread?

He paced the narrow hall, considering his options. He could go back downstairs and explore this strangely familiar modern house. There was all manner of oddities to discover. He was certain he could pass the night uncovering one miracle after another, until his brain spun with new sights and sounds and possibilities.

But he had made a promise and he was, above all things, a man of his word.

Who hurt you, mistress? he wondered, leaning against her door and closing his eyes. *And why are you alone in this world?*

CHAPTER FIVE

DAKOTA WYLIE WORKED as a librarian at the New Jersey Historical Society in Princeton. The library itself was tucked into a corner of the campus near McCarter Theatre. On Monday mornings she usually performed as a tour guide, leading Girl Scout troops and senior citizen clubs through the restored Colonial mansion on Stockton Street that housed the museum.

She wasn't sure if it was serendipity or part of a larger plan, but on that particular Monday morning the museum was closed for repairs and nobody expected her at the library until noon.

Not that anything as insignificant as her job would have stopped Dakota. She'd tossed and turned all night, thinking about Shannon and the unexpected visitor and wondering why on earth she couldn't get a fix on the situation.

Bits and pieces of conversation...the spine-tingling sense of the unknown...the certainty that destinies were being played out right that very minute and Dakota couldn't quite figure out who and where and why. Once she even flashed on a lighthouse and George Washington, two peculiar thoughts that didn't bear contemplation.

By the time the sun finally came up she was a frazzled mass of nerve endings.

Something wasn't right. She couldn't put her finger on exactly what it was, but she'd learned a long time ago to trust her instincts and follow her hunches, no matter how outlandish they might be. Shannon needed her. You didn't pick up vibes about a person one minute then lose them the next, and that was exactly what had happened last night. One minute the whole thing had been as clear as the quartz crystal she wore around her neck, then the next minute her mind screen went blank.

The last time that happened had been with Cyrus Warren from Lawrenceville. She'd been doing a reading for him behind the stacks in the library when his aura had disappeared just like that. That night Cyrus choked on a chicken bone in T. G. I. Friday's right under the placard describing the Heimlich maneuver.

So of course she'd read Shannon's cards over morning coffee then checked the runes just to be sure. Each time all seemed as it should be. Long life. Good health. Wonderful family. But the one thing that didn't quite make sense was when and where this was going to happen.

Try as she might she couldn't pick up a time frame or a setting for the events that would transpire, and she had the strongest sense that it had something to do with the man who had dropped into Shannon's life from a hot-air balloon.

*　　*　　*

Shannon woke up with a start. Dakota was leaning over her bed, eyes wide with excitement.

"It's about time!" Dakota tossed her the robe that had been draped over the rocking chair. "I was beginning to think he'd slipped you a mickey."

"What on earth—?" Shannon twisted around to get a glimpse of the clock on her nightstand. Somehow the notion that Andrew McVie stood guard on the other side of her door had been as exciting as it was comforting, and dawn was on the horizon by the time she'd finally fallen asleep. "It's not even seven o'clock. Have you lost your mind?"

Dakota, psychic but not subtle, paid no attention. "Get up! I want to meet him."

Shannon stifled a yawn and swung her legs from the bed. "He was right outside the door all night."

Dakota gestured toward the hallway. "Well, he isn't there now."

"What about the alarm? Why didn't it go off?"

"Don't ask me," Dakota said with a shrug. "I came in through the French doors in the back."

"Those doors are broken."

"They aren't anymore."

Andrew.

Shannon darted toward the window and looked out toward the backyard. The surface of the pool was calm. The lounge chairs were undisturbed. There was no sign of life anywhere. A sudden sense of despair threatened to overwhelm her and she could do nothing to keep it at bay.

"He's gone," she whispered, pressing her cheek against the glass. Somehow she'd believed he would be there, seeing her safely into the new day.

"Where did he go?" Dakota asked.

She aimed a sharp look in her friend's direction. "I was hoping you'd be able to answer that."

"Not me," said Dakota. "I can't get a bead on that man, no matter how hard I try." She tilted her head slightly to the right. "He was in this room, though. I can feel him."

"You must be wrong," Shannon said. "He never came inside."

"Yes, he did," Dakota persisted. "I'm picking up some very definite vibes."

"Then you're picking them up from me because he never crossed the threshold."

The look on Dakota's face said otherwise, but Shannon chose not to pursue the issue. Had he watched her sleep? Instead of annoying her, the thought sent a charge of excitement up her spine. There was something unbearably intimate about the image, something both erotic and tender and too tempting for her own good.

"You look different," Dakota said. "Are you okay?"

"Tired." She'd been reluctant to give herself over to sleep. Knowing he was a heartbeat away from her had felt so intoxicating, so *right,* that she'd wanted to savor the moment as long as she could.

"It's more than that. You look . . . enthralled."

"Good word," Shannon said dryly. "I don't think I've ever been enthralled in my life."

Dakota peered out the window. "Maybe he's in the woods looking for his balloon."

"Or maybe he's gone."

Dakota shook her head. "He's not gone. Not yet."

She looked at her friend. "You don't think so?"

"Absolutely not. His business here is far from complete."

"You make him sound terribly mysterious," she said, forcing an awkward laugh. "He's just some guy from one of those hot-air balloon clubs."

"I don't think so."

Shannon's heartbeat accelerated. "Don't let your imagination run away with you, Dakota. He veered off course and his spotters lost the trail. There's nothing more to it than that."

"You don't believe that any more than I do."

"Gimme a break," Shannon muttered, forcing herself away from the window. "I'm going to go downstairs and start the coffee."

"I'll start the coffee. You get dressed."

"No!" With great difficulty Shannon tried to modulate her tone. She felt a strong and illogical need to protect Andrew McVie, even from her closest friend. "I've tasted your coffee," she said with a quick smile. "I'll do it."

Dakota followed her downstairs, chatting the whole while about auras and vibes and whether or not the New York Yankees would go all the way. Typical Dakota Wylie conversation, and Shannon found herself relaxing. *He's still here,* she told herself as she started the coffee. Dakota had picked up his vibes and, despite her general distrust of all things psychic, she had a grudging and mystified respect for Dakota's abilities. Besides, didn't most people believe exactly what they wanted to believe, no matter what common sense had to say about it?

"Your countertop is filthy," Dakota remarked, drawing her index finger through a layer of reddish brown dust. "What did you do, repot your geraniums in here?"

"It's a long story," Shannon said, pouring them each a glass of orange juice.

"I'm not going anywhere."

She handed Dakota a glass. "He jumped up on the countertop last night."

Dakota's big brown eyes widened behind her granny glasses. "Any particular reason?"

"He—there was something wrong with the recessed lighting."

"So he's a balloonist and an electrician, too? What a guy."

Shannon glared at her friend. "Will you stop it?" she snapped. "The man's weird, okay? Case closed."

She busied herself taking the milk from the refrigerator and finding two clean cups in the cabinet. Dakota wandered over to the back door and looked out toward the pool.

"We have company," Dakota drawled after a moment.

Shannon raced to the door in time to see Andrew McVie dragging a gondola and a deflated crimson balloon from the woods.

"Stay here," she said, wiping her hands along the sides of her robe. "I'll go help him."

She darted out the door, hoping against hope that Dakota would stay where she was.

"Good day, mistress Shannon!" Andrew called when he saw the beautiful dark-haired woman hurrying across the yard to greet him. She wore a filmy, flowing gown and cloak and looked much like the women of his acquaintance...except for the fact that her limbs were plainly visible through the sheer fabric. "'Tis a fine summer morning, is it not?"

"Go away!" she said, her words at distinct odds with the friendly smile upon her lovely face. "Go back into the woods and wait for me to call you."

"I am in need of a place to store these objects," he continued, assuming her greeting was perfectly normal for the year 1993. "It would be most unlikely that I should need them again, but they may help another one day hence."

"I don't give a damn about that blasted balloon," she said in a tone of voice more heated than before. "Just go *now!*"

He looked over her shoulder and saw a woman of medium size running toward them, and he felt his mouth gape open in surprise. She wore a long, flowing skirt in a brightly colored print, a frilly white blouse, heavy black boots that were better suited to a shipbuilder, and a tiny pair of spectacles that Ben Franklin would have favored. Huge earbobs of shiny silver dangled from her lobes, and around her neck and wrists she wore clanking chains of silver and gold. Each of her fingers was encircled with a ring of varying style. Her black hair, what there was of it, was cut close to her head, framing her face in soft curls that were short as a child's. Yet it wasn't the strange hairstyle or the display of jewelry that most amazed him; it was the tattoo of a heart on her right shoulder.

He turned to mistress Shannon. "A tavern wench?"

Shannon groaned out loud. Not even seven-thirty in the morning and already the day had the makings of a disaster. "That's my friend Dakota. She's going to ask you a lot of questions. Don't answer them, McVie, not if you know what's good for you. If people find out, your life won't be worth a plug—"

"Introduce us, Shannon!" Dakota stopped right in front of Andrew. "I'm dying to meet your new friend."

Shannon grimaced. "Andrew McVie. Dakota Wylie." She turned to Dakota. "Don't you have to go to work?"

Dakota smiled guilelessly. "Not until noon."

"Damn it," Shannon murmured under her breath.

Dakota extended her right hand. "A pleasure."

McVie looked skeptically at Dakota's hand, then at Shannon, who nodded.

"An honor, mistress Wylie."

Dakota's eyebrows lifted toward the sky.

Oh, God, thought Shannon. She could almost see Dakota's psychic antennae going up.

McVie clasped Dakota's hand in greeting and Shannon watched in horror as Dakota crumpled to the ground in a heap.

Andrew reacted more swiftly than Shannon. He scooped Dakota up into his strong arms and carried her into the house, while Shannon brought up the rear. *This is a nightmare,* she thought. He had no idea what his life would be like if news of his two-century balloon ride got out.

The tabloids thought they had a gold mine with Charles and Di. Shannon could only imagine what they'd do with a real live Early American with a grudge against the Crown.

Not that Dakota would ever deliberately do anything to harm another living soul. It was just that Dakota was a slave to her emotions, prone to outbursts of psychic gossiping that left mere mortals gasping for air.

"She is unwell?" Andrew asked as he set her down on the living room sofa.

"It's the heat," Shannon offered. "Would you bring me a glass of cold water?" He stood there unmoving. She turned and saw the look of puzzlement on his face and her heart went out to him. "The glasses are in the cabinet to the right of the window—" She stopped abruptly. This was all well and good but it didn't explain how to find the cold water. There wasn't time to detail the inner workings of the refrigerator. "The sink in the bathroom," she said at last. "Turn the handle to the right and pull up for cold water."

He vanished down the hall. Shannon looked down at her friend and wondered what it would take to make Dakota vanish that easily.

A lighthouse with its tower dark... a tall, red-haired woman and a man of size and stature... a sense of danger everywhere, but that danger was mingled with a deeper sense of commitment to a cause... but what cause?

Dakota felt herself pulled back into her body. She fought it the best she could but the force was stronger than her will to resist and her eyes flew open as she struggled to sit up.

"You're not pregnant, are you?" Shannon asked, handing her the glass of cold water.

Dakota took a long sip. "No, I'm not pregnant. You need a man to get pregnant." She met Shannon's eyes. "It was him. His touch."

Andrew McVie stepped into her line of vision. "I am not always aware of my own strength, mistress. I offer my most humble apology."

She glanced at Shannon. "He's not joking, is he?"

Shannon looked decidedly uncomfortable. "We're not accustomed to good manners here," she said to McVie by way of explanation.

Dakota finished the glass of water, then wiped her mouth with the back of her hand. She glared at Shannon. "You know darn well what I'm talking about. It's him. Something isn't right."

McVie tapped his temple with a forefinger, then turned toward Shannon, who looked as if she was barely suppressing laughter.

"She's not crazy," Shannon said. "She just has an overactive imagination."

McVie nodded, and Dakota had the overwhelming urge to knock their heads together just to hear the sound their skulls made.

"I'd like to know what the two of you are up to," she said, bristling with indignation.

"You know I'm only teasing," Shannon said with a smile.

"I don't know anything," Dakota shot back, "except the fact that there are some damn strange vibes around here."

"Vibes?" McVie came closer. "Say again. I am not familiar with such a word."

"I know you're not," Dakota said, "and I intend to find out why."

CHAPTER SIX

"FRIEND OR FOE?" Andrew asked as Dakota slammed the front door behind her.

"Friend," Shannon said with a sigh. "Strange, psychic friend."

"Physick?"

"No, no. Psychic. She can see the future."

"My mother had second sight," Andrew said in a matter-of-fact tone of voice.

"Dakota has more than second sight," Shannon continued. "Sometimes I'd swear she can read minds."

He fixed her with a steady gaze. She tried not to notice the burnished gold flecks in his hazel eyes. "You chose not to reveal the details of our acquaintance. If she can read thoughts, that should not have deterred her from obtaining the truth."

"I know," said Shannon ruefully. "I'm still working on that one." And thanking her lucky stars for the reprieve.

"Why is it you wish to keep such knowledge for yourself?"

"Because it's a cold, cruel world out there, McVie, and they'd eat you alive."

"I do not understand your meaning."

"People today thrive on gossip," she went on, pacing the living room. "If it got out that you were from another century, you'd be pulled apart by television producers, movie directors, reporters from all around the world. You'd end up a prisoner of your own miracle." And why any of this should matter to her was beyond her.

A smile broke across his craggy face. "You believe I am of my own time, mistress?"

She sighed. "I believe, Mr. McVie. God help me, but I believe."

The fact that she believed him should not have mattered to Andrew. Her belief in his story altered nothing. Yet he knew deep in his soul that with her words "I believe," everything between them had changed.

"Mark me well, I have no wish to be a burden upon you, mistress Shannon. I need only to be pointed toward the town of Princeton."

"You need more than that."

His brow lifted. "Explain yourself."

"Look at you." She pointed toward his garments. "If you went out on the street dressed like that, you'd be arrested for vagrancy."

"In my time the mistress Wylie would be pilloried for her attire." He dared not discuss the wanton yellow outfit mistress Shannon had worn the previous day.

"Then you understand what I'm saying."

He looked down at his clothing. "There is nothing wrong with my choice of garments."

"They're two hundred years old."

"They provide warmth and coverage."

"They're beyond shabby."

His brow lifted higher.

"They are," Shannon continued, spots of color staining her cheeks. "And they don't smell that great, either."

"Mistress, 'tis a difficult task to remain spotless in the woods."

"I understand, but if you intend to make a life in my time, you're going to have to make a few changes." She wrinkled her nose in a comic fashion. "Preferably beginning with your wardrobe."

She was a most disarming lass, even when she was criticizing his person. "I know only one way of dress."

"What about your friend who came from the future? What kind of clothes did he wear?"

"I do not recall in detail, mistress, but that tells me the difference between us was not great."

She squared her shoulders. "And that tells me it's time we begin introducing you to the twentieth century."

"I am most eager to learn."

"There's no time like the present."

"Aye," he said. "Wherever the present leads you."

Thirty minutes later they sat down to breakfast on the patio, and the first lesson began.

"Your table manners are atrocious," Shannon said bluntly. "Don't shovel your food into your mouth."

He looked up from his plate of eggs and ham. "I eat with dispatch and efficiency."

"You eat like a pig."

"This is not Fat George's table laden with silver and china," he observed. "'Tis a common table and I eat like a common man."

"Well, not here you don't. We don't hold our forks that way any longer. You look like you're mining for gold."

He leaned back in his chair and folded brawny arms across his chest. "Show me then how it is, since you hold the key to such wisdom."

"You're right," she said, dabbing at the corner of her mouth with her linen napkin. "I will." She speared a tiny piece of egg with her fork and raised it to her mouth, then made certain to chew at least thirty times. She swallowed, then offered him a dazzling smile. "That, Andrew McVie, is how it's done."

"A man's meal would be cold as ice before it passed his lips."

"A gentleman wouldn't comment on such a thing."

"Hot food should be eaten hot," he observed.

"Agreed," said Shannon, "but you don't have to look like a slob when you're eating it."

"A slob?"

"A pig," she explained. "An untidy person."

He lifted another forkful of eggs and ham. "Do all people comment thusly upon the dining practices of others?"

She thought of Miss Manners and laughed. "Some people even make their living doing so."

"'Tis a strange world," he said.

"Stranger than you know." She rested her fork on the side of her plate. "I think a trip to the mall is in order."

He frowned. "A mall is a public promenade in the center of town."

"It's more than that today." She told him about the collection of enclosed stores and restaurants that comprised Bridgewater Commons.

"Such an enterprise is beyond my ken."

"Mine, too," said Shannon, who had given up power shopping with her marriage. "But there's no hope for it. We're going shopping."

After their morning meal Andrew watched as Shannon stacked dishes in a kitchen cabinet, poured liquid soap into the same cabinet, then closed the door. He was about to ask why she didn't put the dishes to soak in the big sink beneath the window, but she pressed a few buttons and a horrific grinding noise and the sound of rushing water filled the room.

"What in bloody hell—?"

"A dishwasher," she said. "It automatically washes the dirty dishes."

He nodded as if a dishwashing cabinet were an everyday occurrence. A dishrag, hung from a peg, caught his eye. "And then you dry them with a rag."

"No," said Shannon. "The dishwasher dries them for me."

"That cannot be." He crouched in front of the infernally loud dishwashing cabinet. "There are rags inside the cabinet?"

"Hot air."

"Say again, mistress."

"I'm not a mechanical genius but I think hot air circulates through the dishwasher and that dries the dishes after they've been cleaned."

"'Tis a miracle."

"No," she said, "'tis everyday life."

"You mock my speech, mistress?"

"Never that." Her lovely face seemed lit from within by her smile. "Your speech is delightful."

"You have no wish to change it?"

"I thought you were a Scotsman," she said, still smiling. "I imagine others will make the same mistake. Besides, there's great diversity in this country. You'll blend right in."

"You need not be so solicitous of my needs, mistress. I am most resourceful and will make my way through your world."

"Your friends who traveled back to your world," she said, smile fading. "Didn't they need your help?"

"A revolution is being waged," he said. "Danger is afoot everywhere. I did only what I deemed necessary to afford them safe passage."

"I can do the same for you. We're not in revolution, but I guarantee my world is more dangerous than yours could ever be."

He thought of smallpox and influenza, of childbed fever and the losses of wartime. Nothing Emilie and Zane had described to him could surpass those horrors, and he strongly doubted that mistress Shannon could show him anything that would alter his thinking.

"You can open your eyes," Shannon said. "The worst is over."

"Nay, mistress." Andrew's eyes were still tightly closed. "I think not."

"I merged onto the highway and we're going along in our own lane now." He had accepted the existence of her car with remarkable aplomb. Merging onto Route 287 with an eighteen wheeler jockeying with her for position was another story entirely. "There's nothing to be afraid of."

The poor man looked positively green. Her heart went out to him as he slowly opened his eyes and looked around. *You're incredible,* she thought, drawing her own gaze back to the road. She wondered if she would exhibit one-tenth McVie's courage if the situation was reversed.

"We move with great speed," he observed, color returning to his face. "Is such rapid movement the norm?"

She gazed at the speedometer. The needle rested firmly on fifty miles per hour. "Actually, we're in the slow lane. That guy in the red Porsche's probably doing seventy."

"I have no understanding of porshuhz or doing seventy."

She checked her side mirror and moved into the center lane. "I can go faster if you want to see what doing seventy is all about." What was a speeding ticket compared to showing off for a spectacular man?

He shook his head. "I see no benefit to moving faster."

"Most men would tell me to go for it."

He met her eyes. "I am not most men."

Oh, God, she thought as her heart seemed to slide into her breastbone. *He has no idea how true that is.* Not in appearance or demeanor or the overpowering sense of strength that seemed to emanate from every pore.

"I find myself wondering how it is you begged me stay."

"I didn't beg you to do anything."

"I heard the words clearly, mistress, from your own lips. *Don't go. Please stay.* Said in a tone of entreaty."

Was it truly possible that he'd heard her thoughts as clearly as she believed she'd heard his?

"Maybe we should forget the mall and take you to a doctor." She tried for a light and breezy tone of voice, but failed miserably.

"I am not in need of a doctor's care."

She moved back into the right-hand lane as they neared the exit to Bridgewater Commons. "Suggesting you stay on a little longer and begging are two vastly different concepts."

"There was deep emotion in your tone."

"What about you?" she asked, tires squealing as she took the exit faster than normal. "It's not like I tied you to a chair to keep you prisoner."

"There was logic to your reasoning. Common sense told me to heed your suggestions."

"Hah!"

"You mark me a liar?"

"You mark me for a fool if you think I'm going to believe that."

"You are a suspicious woman, Shannon Whitney. A most undesirable trait in a female."

"Now there's something that needs work," she said as she stopped for a red light in front of the mall. "That patronizing, paternalistic attitude of yours stinks."

"I am a man," he said. "And I treat women as women."

"In this century men treat women as equals."

"Women are not equal to men."

"The hell they're not."

"Your strength is inferior to mine."

"And my brain is superior to yours," she shot back. "It all evens out."

"We have not tested our intellects to know such a thing."

"Simple logic would bear me out," she said, falling back on male tactics. "My world is more advanced than your world. I am a product of my world. Therefore I am more advanced than you."

"I am a graduate of Harvard," he said.

"Sure you are," said Shannon, heading toward the parking lot.

"And I practiced law in Boston."

She drove the car up onto the curb then dropped down again with a thud. "Right," she said. "And I'm a nuclear physicist."

"You do not believe me."

"A lawyer?" She swung into a parking spot, then looked him full in the face. "Do all lawyers dress the way you do?"

"I have not practiced law since my—" He stopped abruptly.

"Go on," Shannon urged. "You can't drop a bomb like that and not give me the details."

"The details do not matter any longer," he said, his voice gruff.

"I'd like to know."

"My past is dead. I look to build a new life here, in this time and place."

She thought of her own past, the painful details of her marriage, and something inside her gave way. *I've been there,* she thought. *I know how you feel.*

She checked her lipstick in the rearview mirror, then summoned up her best smile. "If you're looking to build a new life, you've come to the right place, Andrew McVie. There's nothing more American than the mall."

Andrew had the profound sense that he had just managed to elude danger. Not the type of danger that broke bones or drew blood, but danger of a more subtle and deadly kind. How close he had come to unburdening himself upon mistress Shannon, telling her of Elspeth and David, letting the endless parade of his mistakes march past her until she knew his soul the way she knew her own face in the glass.

Nay, he thought, casting a glance at her lovely profile. To reveal himself to her would be a mistake of colossal proportions. One he did not intend to make.

He managed to unsnap the bonds that held him in his seat, then pulled the silver handle that opened the door. Zane had done an admirable job of describing an automobile. He remembered the night Rutledge had drawn a picture in the dirt of a square box that rested atop inflatable wheels. Accepting that as a possibility had not been difficult, but then Rutledge had gone on to tell him that the box, called a car, was not drawn by a team of horses but powered by a series of sustained explosions deep within its own self.

"Does everyone own one of these cars?" he asked, taking in the endless rows of such things lined up in the open field behind the enormous building called a mall.

"Almost everyone." Shannon shut her own door.

"How can you find your own amidst the crowd?"

"It's not always easy."

"There are no horses?"

"Sure there are." She started walking toward the mall and he fell into step with her. "But it's expensive to keep a horse."

"And it is not expensive to drive a car?"

"Depends on the car and the driver and the insurance."

"Insurance?"

"Against accidents."

He thought of the thing she had called a truck and the damage it could have inflicted upon his person had they collided. "I do not wish to hear any more, mistress Shannon. I have seen many a serious carriage accident in my time. I can but imagine the result among cars."

He heard a sound behind them and turned to see a group of children of perhaps sixteen laughing and looking in his direction.

"See what I mean?" said Shannon, glancing sternly in their direction. "Those clothes have got to go."

Andrew stopped in his tracks and watched the children pass. "Surely such attire as theirs is not commonplace in this world."

"Biker pants, tank tops, Doc Martens," said Shannon. "Just your average everyday teenagers."

He was not familiar with the word *teenagers*, but its meaning was clear. The only thing about their attire that made him feel comfortable was that the boys wore their hair in much the same fashion as Andrew himself.

"I will not wear those trousers," he said, walking again toward the mall.

"I promise I won't ask you to." They approached the wall of glass doors leading into the mall itself.

"You're going to see a lot of strange things, Andrew. I'll do my best to explain them all to you, but it would serve us both well if you let me do most of the talking."

"'Tis not natural for a man to let a woman lead the way."

"And it's not natural to sail through the centuries in a balloon. You're in my world now. Let me help you."

Her words were based on good common sense but they went against the grain. She had seen him in a way no woman should see a man, needful and uncertain. He was accustomed to dominating situations, not looking to others for direction. He was a man, and as a man it was his lot in life to lead.

But thus far not in this world.

And not with this woman.

Which were two of the many reasons he must get about the business of establishing a new life in this new world in which he found himself.

CHAPTER SEVEN

ANDREW MADE TO PUSH OPEN the door, then leapt back, astonished, as it swung open of its own accord.

"Electronic eyes," Shannon said with a groan. "I forgot to tell you about them." She pointed up toward the red light overhead. "It senses your approach and signals for the door to open."

"How?"

"Don't ask me," she said as they stepped inside. "Some of it amazes me as much as it amazes you."

Good grief, what other everyday wonders did she take for granted that could throw McVie for a loop?

Like the crush of people lined up in front of the movie theater to see *Jurassic Park* for the umpteenth time.

"What is it they wait for?" Andrew asked.

"You're not ready for movies yet," Shannon said briskly. Especially not movies about man-eating dinosaurs with major attitude. "Let's get you dressed first."

"Nay, mistress." He walked toward the railing and leaned against it to stare at the skylights overhead. "'Tis an amazing sight, trees growing within a building and reaching for the sky."

"I suppose it is amazing," she said, glancing down at the tiny grove of trees planted in the rock garden. "I never really gave it much thought."

"These are the things Emilie and Zane told me about." He was like a kid let loose in a toy store. He wanted to see and touch and understand everything he saw. "Everywhere I look I see abundance."

They paused in front of a pricey jewelry shop and looked at the diamond rings and Rolex watches.

"You adorn your person with jewels," he commented, looking at her diamond studs and tennis bracelet. "And Emilie arrayed herself in gold and silver. The king of England could not ask for more."

"The *queen* of England," she corrected with a smile. "And, trust me, she can put us all to shame."

"'Tis beyond my ken," he said as they strolled past a card shop, toy store and two more jeweler's establishments. He gestured toward two older women chatting in front of Sam Goody's. "They glitter like foreign princesses. How can it be the average citizen can have such wonders at her command?"

"Now I know why you came forward in time," she said dryly. "You're an eighteenth-century yuppie."

"Emilie had called me thus but I do not remember its meaning." He frowned. "I believe it was not a good thing."

"A yuppie is a thirty-something consumer whose greed outstrips his income."

"You offend me, mistress."

"I didn't mean to." She tried to steer him toward one of the men's stores but he seemed transfixed by the display of maternity bras at one of the women's shops. "It's just if you're looking to understand what we're about, you have to look past the glitter and get to the heart of it."

She started for the escalator then decided that was asking for trouble.

"We can take the stairs," she said, "or—" She stopped. Where was he? A second ago he'd been right next to her, staring at nursing bras. *Think,* she told herself. Where would a man go?

The combined smells of pizza and hot dogs and chow mein wafted down toward her. The food court, she thought, dashing across the corridor. Chinese, Italian, Greek and all-American deli foods, stall after stall of them, there for the asking. How could he possibly resist?

She checked from one end of the food court to the other. She asked counter clerks, customers and the security guard. Nobody had seen an oddly dressed man of medium height who looked as if he'd never seen a mall before in his life.

"Go downstairs to mall information," the security guard suggested. "They'll make an announcement through the P.A. system."

Great idea, Shannon thought as she raced for the down escalator. Great idea for anyone except Andrew McVie, who didn't know a P.A. system from a hole in the ground and might think he was hearing the voice of God at the Bridgewater Commons mall.

*   *   *

Andrew watched as three women with babies walked through an open door, then disappeared. Once a long time ago at a tavern near Boston he'd seen a magician make various items disappear in an amazing display of legerdemain. A lady's kerchief. A half-crown piece. A pack of cards. He had been suitably impressed by the man's talents, but not even that had prepared him for this.

He approached the door. An older woman, arms laden with parcels, waited by the door, as well. Her eyes widened as she took in his apparel, then she looked away. In truth, she looked quite peculiar to his eyes. He had never seen such a display of naked flesh on a woman of such advanced years. Her legs were bare and he could see each and every vein as they coursed up and down her muscular calves. She wore a short pair of men's trousers, a top garment without sleeves or collar, and enough paint on her face to cover the side of a barn.

Madam, he thought with a shake of his head, *wouldn't you be better served at home, tending to your grandchildren?*

Tearing his gaze away from the painted woman, he noticed the numbers above the door and the way they seemed lit from within. The highest number lit up and the doors slid open. A gaggle of children burst forth, followed by their mothers, and two men in strange dark garments that were almost mirror images, each of the other. If Shannon intended for him to dress in such ridiculous attire he would tell her in no uncertain terms how he felt about the matter.

He motioned for the older woman to cross the threshold before him. She seemed surprised but did as he bid her. Two girls of perhaps sixteen entered, as well. Their lanky bodies were clad in tight-fitting trousers of faded blue and half-sleeve shirts that bore the messages U2 and Virginia Is For Lovers. Neither girl had been blessed with bosoms that merited notice but one was slightly more endowed than the other. Beyond that they were as twins, even down to the tiny earrings that glittered at their lobes.

So when the doors closed and the two girls fell upon each other in a heated embrace Andrew was so shocked by their actions that it took him a moment to realize the room he stood in was dropping down in space while music blared from some unknown source.

"Sweet Jesus!" Andrew exploded. "What in bloody hell is happening?"

"Vulgar display," sniffed the older woman next to him, gesturing toward the kissing couple. "Necking in public . . . dreadful. Simply dreadful."

"Why don't you both chill?" said one of the girls, whose deep voice proved her not a girl at all. "All you old people got a problem with sex."

His companion giggled. "Maybe it's because they're not gettin' any."

"Yeah," said the boy, moving toward the older woman. His arm shot out and some of her parcels tumbled to the floor of the moving room. "Don't think this chick's gettin' any, do you?"

Rage filled Andrew's gut. He stepped forward, wedging himself between the boy and the woman. "You will tender an apology to this good woman," he said in a voice that brooked no argument.

"You and who else're gonna make me?"

Andrew grabbed the child by the scruff of his neck and lifted him off his feet. "You will apologize *now*," he roared, "or you will have breathed your last."

"Don't let him threaten you, Mike!" the girl cried out. "If he hurts you, you can sue him for every penny he's got."

The boy's eyes flashed fire.

Andrew's grip upon him grew stronger. "Say it," Andrew commanded in a low voice. "Say it now before us or say it before God at heaven's gate."

"S-sorry," the boy managed. "J-just havin' some fun."

The moving room came to a stop, the doors opened, and Andrew fairly tossed the boy from him. The pair vanished into a crowd of people.

"You are a brave man," said the painted lady as he bent to retrieve her parcels. "He could've had a knife. Not many people would have come to my aid the way you did."

"That is difficult to believe," said Andrew, helping her from the moving room. "There was naught to do but offer my assistance."

"Such a lovely accent," the woman said with a smile. Her teeth were white and straight and all there. Another miracle. "Are you from Scotland?"

"Aye," said Andrew with an answering smile. "I am."

A loud voice seemed to fill the mall. "Will Andrew McVie please return to the information booth. Andrew McVie, please return to the information booth now."

His eyes widened. "Sweet Jesus."

The painted woman looked up at him curiously. "Are you Andrew McVie?"

"Aye."

"And you don't know where the information booth is, do you?"

He shook his head. "'Tis a fact I do not." *Nay, madam, and in truth I do not know* what *it is.*

She linked a bony arm through his. "Then let me have the honor of escorting you. It's the least I can do after what you did for me."

"It's only been three minutes, ma'am," said the woman manning the information booth. "It's a big mall. I'm sure your friend will be here any time now."

"I'm not," said Shannon, turning away. Andrew McVie was a strong and independent man, but even he was no match for what the late twentieth century could throw at him. The sheer size of the mall itself must seem daunting to him. He could have fallen down an escalator and broken a leg. He might have wandered outside and been hit by a car.

She buried her face in her hands and groaned as another awful thought presented itself. What if he'd strolled into Lord & Taylor, seen something he wanted and tried to stroll right out again with it tucked under his burly arm? Not only didn't he have any money, the only identification he had was a driver's license belonging to Emilie Crosse who, as far as Shannon could tell, was alive and well in 1776.

A familiar voice caught her attention and she peered between her fingers. Andrew was striding toward her. A sixtyish woman strode right along with him, chattering up a storm. Relief came close to buckling her knees.

"Well, here's your missing friend," said the woman, obviously reluctant to part company with Andrew.

"You make sure he tells you what he did back there on that elevator." She reached up and pinched his rugged cheek. "You hang on to him, miss. They don't make men like this anymore."

The woman bustled away and Shannon met Andrew's eyes.

"So, what did you do back there on that elevator?" she asked.

"'Twas nothing another man wouldn't have done in similar circumstances."

"A few more details would be appreciated."

A frown pleated his forehead. "A simple thing. I reminded a boy that elders are deserving of respect."

"How strongly did you remind him?"

"I struck no blows."

"I'm glad to hear that," she said dryly. "I don't know how it is back in your time, but this is a litigious society. Sneeze wrong and you'll find yourself on the receiving end of a lawsuit."

"The girl threatened to pursue such an avenue."

"This is a less . . . physical world in some respects," she said, trying to ignore the rampant violence that was part of everyday life in so much of the country. "We handle our disagreements with words, not blows."

"You may wish to make that speech to the boy who threatened harm to the elderly woman." He wheeled right, then started walking away.

"McVie!" Shannon tried to catch up with him but he managed to stay a few lengths ahead of her. On purpose, no doubt. "Where are you going?"

He continued walking.

"McVie!" she shouted. "Stop!" *Have you gone mad, Shannon? Don't run after the man. It's his life . . . and he'll only complicate yours. Let him go.*

But he was alone in the world and lonely. You didn't give up everything you knew and travel to a distant world if you were happy with your life. He didn't realize it, but he was a babe in the woods here. One wrong step and he'd be gobbled up by the twentieth century and forgotten.

She couldn't let that happen.

He was heading toward the exit near First Place. She broke into a run and grabbed him a few yards from the door.

He shook her off and kept walking.

"Andrew!" She darted in front of him, almost daring him to stomp right over her. "Please."

He stopped. "I have no wish to argue with you, mistress."

She prided herself on the fact that she never cried, yet found herself blinking back hot tears of frustration that confused as much as they embarrassed her. "What's wrong? Why are you so angry?"

She looked up at him with aqua eyes wide with emotion and he wondered how it was those emotions had grown so strong, so quickly.

"Andrew?" She rested her hand on his forearm. "Tell me."

"I do not know what to tell," he said, struggling to control the battle of opposing forces inside his chest. "I am a stranger here."

A quick smile lifted the corners of her mouth. "You just realized that?"

"Yes," he said slowly. That moment of near violence in the moving room made it all real to him in a way nothing thus far had.

"You won't be a stranger for long," she said, drawing her index finger beneath her right eye in a quick motion. Was it for him she cried?

"I believed it to be a difference in language and ease," he said, "but there is more to understand than that."

"Poor Andrew McVie," Shannon whispered, meeting his eyes. "Are you wondering if you made a mistake when you came forward to our brave new world?"

"Nay, mistress—" He caught himself. "No, Shannon," he said, pushing the eighteenth century into the shadows. "This is not a mistake. This is where I am meant to be."

She smiled but remained silent and in her silence he read something akin to sadness.

CHAPTER EIGHT

DRESSED IN his eighteenth-century attire, Andrew had been an intriguing figure.

Garbed in upscale twentieth-century clothing, he was devastating.

While he would never be a handsome man in the classic tradition, his strong-boned face and powerful form commanded attention, and Shannon experienced a jolt of pure jealousy as the register clerk at the pricey men's store turned on the charm for Andrew, who was now wearing soft brown trousers, a cream-colored silk shirt and Italian loafers. He had expressed serious misgivings about the loafers, convinced they would flop off with the first few steps he took.

The clerk's eyebrows lifted when Shannon whipped out her American Express gold card to cover the purchases, and Shannon's elation was overshadowed only by the look of discomfort in Andrew's eyes.

96

"You'll get used to it," she told him as they exited the store with their purchases. "I promise you the shoes will stay on. Indians got along fine in their moccasins, didn't they?"

"'Tis not the shoes," he said in a gruff tone of voice. "My indebtedness to you increases each hour."

"Believe me, I have more money than I can spend in a lifetime," she said with a careless wave of her hand. "Don't give it a second thought." Surely her ex-husband never had.

"This is not what I am about," said Andrew, apparently unwilling to let the subject drop. "I have always made my own way in the world."

"But this isn't your world," Shannon countered gently as they walked toward the restaurant. "This is *my* world and until you understand the rules, you'll need someone to help you."

Andrew said nothing until they were seated in a booth. He seemed not to notice the half dozen TV screens that broadcast different sporting events day and night.

"I will pay for the meal," he stated after she ordered hamburgers, fries and Cokes for them.

"With what?"

He reached for the bag that held his old clothing. "This." He withdrew an old pocket watch from within and pushed it across the table.

Shannon held it in the palm of her hand. "It's gold, isn't it?"

He nodded. She noted the way a muscle on the left side of his jaw tightened. She turned it over and squinted to make out the tiny, faded script etched into the case.

"From Elspeth." She looked at him curiously.

"My wife." Such simple words, but the sadness in his eyes was anything but. "On the occasion of the birth of our son."

"Gold?" she said again, her voice rising on the word.

"There was a time when I need not beg for money, Shannon."

"Oh, God," she whispered handing back the watch. No man should have to sacrifice his past in order to obtain a future. "Have I made you feel that way?"

His expression softened. "'Tis the situation that makes me feel this way. I did not intend to be a burden to others in this world. I thought—"

"You're not a burden. You're my—" She stopped. What on earth had she been about to say? *You're my destiny.* Pathetic. Truly pathetic.

"I will leave you tonight."

"No!" The word exploded with the force of years of loneliness behind it. "You can't."

"I must."

She felt angry. She knew it was unfair but the emotion overwhelmed her. "If you believe you have a debt to repay, then repay it." A thought struck her and she seized it eagerly. "You repaired the back doors this morning, didn't you?"

He nodded. "A simple thing. I am surprised you did not see fit to have it done a long time ago. You are not a poor woman, as you told me yourself."

"I have many other things to do with my money," she said. More important things. "But the windows do need to be repaired and painted and the cabana needs a new floor. You could work off your debt and—"

"Done. I will stay until all is completed."

The waitress served the hamburgers, openly eyeing Andrew as she did so, and Shannon barely resisted the urge to kick her hard in the shins.

"There is fire in your eyes," Andrew noted over the French fries.

"It's your imagination."

"Nay, Shannon, I see it quite clearly."

She leaned back in her seat. "I think that waitress likes you."

He followed Shannon's gaze. "She was most attentive," he said with a wicked grin. "Back home a wench such as she would do well."

"Don't get any ideas," Shannon snapped, appalled by her jealousy. She'd never felt that way about Bryant. "Sexual harassment doesn't go over very well these days."

"Men and women draw their own battle lines and those lines are never the same twice."

Again she felt that strong stirring of the blood, a deep yearning toward him that defied her understanding. She took a sip of soda then leaned across the table. "I suppose this is as good a time as any to set some battle lines, as you put it, for us. I mean, since we'll be living under the same roof we should—"

"You have nothing to fear from me, mistress. I have never taken by force something that should be freely given in trust."

She looked down at her hands, clasped on the tabletop, and took a deep breath. "I wish my ex-husband had felt as you feel."

Andrew's gut knotted at her words. All along he'd sensed a deep sorrow about her, a wariness that belied the generosity she had thus far shown him. She was strong and brave, it was true, but those virtues had been won in battle.

"He was harsh with you, mistress?"

"Harsh?" Her laugh held no mirth as she touched the side of her face. "He broke my jaw on our wedding night. Said I had spent too much time dancing with my brother-in-law." She laughed again. "Can you imagine that? My brother-in-law."

Bile filled his throat and he reached for the sweet-tasting brown liquid to wash it away. "No sign of such treatment remains."

"Ah, the wonders of modern surgery," she said lightly. "One thousand and one ways to keep a family's secrets a secret."

"There is more?"

"More than you need to know."

"I wish to hear it."

Her look held a challenge. "Nobody wishes to hear it, Andrew. Not my mother, not my father, not any of my brothers or sisters."

"I do," he said. "I will listen."

"There's nothing much to tell," she said in a flat tone of voice. "I wanted a husband. He wanted another possession to put on a shelf." She moved her hair off her forehead in an impatient gesture. He noted the diamonds and rubies glittering on her slender hand. "I tried to walk out on our wedding night but he told me he was sorry...he swore he would never do it again...that he'd had too much to drink." Again that impatient gesture. "I loved him," she said simply. "And I wanted to believe him."

"Your family," Andrew said, aware of the way his heart beat fiercely inside his chest. "Why did they not intercede on your behalf?"

"Because Bryant came from a good family. Because he was powerful." She glanced away toward the window. "Because they figured he was the best thing to ever happen to my family, and my little problem was a small enough price to pay for all he would do for us. We had money but he had connections."

"Bloody bastards," he said, slamming his fist down on the wooden tabletop.

"Yeah," said Shannon with a quick smile. "Bloody bastards about says it all."

"Did you never try to escape?"

She nodded. "Once I made it to the check-in counter at the airport." She held her thumb and index finger a hairbreadth apart. "I was that close to freedom when Bryant burst through the doors and swept me out of there."

He couldn't bring himself to ask how she had paid for her attempt at escape but she told him anyway and he knew her words would stay with him until he breathed his last.

"He beat me in the back of the limousine," she said, a faraway look in her aqua eyes. "Punched me again and again.... He was careful not to hurt my face this time...punched me in the shoulders, the breasts, my belly.... The driver kept looking in the rearview mirror but he didn't do a thing. He just kept watching."

His gaze strayed to her shoulder.

"Yes," she said, voice strong. "The knife wound you saw was from Bryant."

A red mist of rage threatened to devour Andrew as he imagined an ugly death for the man who had caused her such untoward pain.

"But you are divorced," he said when he could again speak. "How is it you came to break free?"

"The last time I tried to leave Bryant hired a hit man—someone who hurts people for money—and the police got involved." Her voice gathered power as she spoke, as if in the telling, the story was losing its hold upon her soul. "The hit man was an undercover cop—policeman—and they offered me a deal. They would help me to fake my death, then lead Bryant into a trap.

"It was dicey, but it worked. I found out they weren't as interested in helping me as they were in arresting Bryant for his involvement in some drug-smuggling scheme out of the Bahamas. They needed to get him out of circulation so they could break down the chain and put them all out of business. He plea-bargained it down to five years and was paroled the beginning of this year."

"He walks free? I would have consigned him to a cold and lonely grave."

"It doesn't much matter," she said. "I'm safe now."

"How is it that you can say with certainty neither he nor another in his employ will threaten your person?"

She hesitated. "I became a different woman."

"I do not understand."

"I did what you did, Andrew. My old life no longer fit and so I found a new one."

"You left your home?"

"I left everything. My home. My family. My friends. I even left my old identity."

"You are not Shannon Whitney?"

"I am," she said, her voice strong with certainty. "I am more Shannon Whitney than I ever was the woman I used to be. Katharine Morgan doesn't exist any longer and I'm not certain she ever did."

He felt himself wishing he could find the man who had hurt her and rip the man's lungs from his body. His own body ached with her pain. The image of her laid low by a man's hand was enough to drive all reason from his brain and send him out in search of blood.

"I hear all that you have told me and yet, despite all, you opened your home to me. It is beyond my understanding that you would find it in yourself to trust a stranger."

She met his gaze full on. "It's beyond mine, too, yet I feel that we are . . . connected in some way."

"Aye," he said slowly. "'Tis nothing I want or need, yet I cannot bring myself to leave."

Her hands rested together on the tabletop. His right hand lay mere inches away.

"You don't have to leave," she said in a soft voice. "Not until you're ready."

He covered her hands with his and for a moment he felt whole again and hopeful, the way he had when the world was young and his whole life stretched out before him, all shiny and new.

No one in the restaurant thought it strange when Shannon paid the bill for their lunch. Andrew had felt most uncomfortable when she reached into her purse and produced the same shiny gold rectangle she had used to pay for his clothing. The serving wench took it and the bill and disappeared into the back.

"I believe that rectangle is some form of currency," he said, "yet it is returned to you unaltered each time you give it away."

Shannon smiled, and it was good to see the light of humor in her sad eyes. "It is a form of currency," she said, "but not in the way you think." She went on to explain a system of credit that seemed to put a great store on faith among strangers.

"And all of this is accomplished using the post?"

"Sounds unbelievable, doesn't it?"

"The post in my time was most unreliable. A letter might take seven days to travel from Philadelphia to New York."

"Still does." Her eyes twinkled. "Some things never change."

Her good humor should be of no consequence to him. She was neither wife nor lover. Their acquaintance was too new to call her friend. Yet the sight of Shannon, face aglow with laughter, lit a fire deep inside his soul that would not be extinguished. He wondered what it would take to keep her thus all the days of her life.

More than you could ever provide, he told himself as they walked outside to her car. She was from a world of ease and wealth, a world he wished to call his own one day. But until the time came when he could walk through that world as an equal in privilege she could be naught but a dream.

He began to cough as they made their way toward the place where they had left the car to rest.

"'Tis something most disagreeable," he said, rubbing at his scratchy eyes. "Never have I encountered air with such characteristics."

"Pollution," said Shannon, jingling the keys she held in her right hand. "I never notice it here, but when I go up to Manhattan I can't breathe without coughing."

"What is the origin of this pollution?"

"Something called the Industrial Revolution."

"I have not heard of that particular uprising."

She laughed, but not unkindly. "It isn't an uprising, Andrew. It's more of a result than anything else. When we get home I'll sit you down at the computer and let you do some exploring."

"Emilie remarked once about a cum-pyoo-turr. It is an object that thinks like a man but has not emotion nor intellect."

Her eyes widened. "I'm impressed. What else did Emilie tell you?"

"About metal birds that carry men through the skies and talking boxes and pictures that move and have sound and music."

"She covered a lot of territory, didn't she?" Shannon muttered. For a moment he thought he saw a flash of jealousy and his heart soared, but that was absurd.

Shannon opened the doors to her car and Andrew was about to climb inside when she motioned for him to stop.

"Look!" She pointed toward the sky. "You're about to see one of those metal birds your pals told you about."

He craned his neck and looked up, squinting into the bright sunlight. He saw muted blue sky and some cloud cover and little else.

"Do you hear that noise?" Shannon asked. "That's the plane. It'll probably break through the clouds any minute."

He watched and waited, heart pounding in anticipation, and then when he was about to give up he was
rewarded with a glimpse of something silvery and
sleek, moving majestically across the heavens. It
seemed a thing apart from man, as if it had sprung
wholly from imagination and needed no help to stay
aloft.

"Probably heading for Newark," Shannon said,
watching him. "It's a 747."

"What is that?"

"A huge plane that became popular in the late sixties, early seventies. It carries three hundred people."

"That cannot be."

"I should take you to the airport," she said. "Hundreds of planes take off and land every day of the
week."

"Such an adventure must be only for the wealthy."

"Not at all," said Shannon. "I'd bet most men and
women in this country have flown at least once."

That statement was beyond his comprehension, and
when the plane vanished into the clouds he climbed
into the car feeling acutely aware of how little he knew
about this world.

It was devilishly hot in the car and he grimaced as
the metal buckles on the seat strap burned his fingers.
He wondered how a strap could save his life in the
event of catastrophe but decided to cast his lot with the
future and hope for the best.

"It's a beautiful day outside." She inserted a key
beneath the wheel and the car came to life. "We could
go home if you like, but I thought there might be some
place you'd like to see." She hid her eyes behind shadowed spectacles. The urge to pull them from her face

was strong but he resisted. "The airport, maybe, or Philadelphia."

He considered her suggestion. "I believe you said Princeton is not far."

"Ten miles or so."

"I would like to see it." So much had happened near Princeton. In his mind he could see the Blakelee farm, the spot in Milltown where he and Emilie and Zane had spent a night. So much of his life was tied into that small parcel of New Jersey land.

"Sure," said Emilie. "I'll show you Nassau Hall and Morven and Bainbridge House—"

"I'd like to see Princeton," he said again, "but not today."

She lifted the glasses and rested them atop her head. "Why not?"

"There are windows to be repaired and other chores to do," he said, "and if I am ever to be free of debt 'tis time I started."

He needed to remind himself that he had come forward in time to find purpose for his life.

And not to fall in love.

CHAPTER NINE

DAKOTA SMILED at the young girl with the green-and-white-striped socks and triceratops T-shirt. "You'll find everything you ever wanted to know about the New Jersey Devil in our folklore section in the east wing." She handed the girl a flyer. "Our map will help you find the right section."

The girl scurried off with her mother, a woman who was obviously at the end of her summer-with-kids rope. It happened every year like clockwork. Only the most dedicated researchers visited the historical society from June to August 15, then bam! Parent after parent trooped their offspring through the society's hallowed halls in an attempt to amuse children who had overdosed on summer fun.

As far as Dakota was concerned, you didn't need to be psychic to recognize a lost cause when you saw it.

You either loved history or you didn't. For some people the sweep and romance of the past was as dead as yesterday's newspapers. They didn't hear the music or feel the passion or understand the fluid nature of time itself.

Dakota did. For her the past, especially the revolutionary war past, lived side by side with the present, turning her days into a rich blend of what was and what had been.

Which was why she'd spent most of the afternoon up to her elbows in documents dating back to the summer of 1776.

Not 1775.

Not 1777.

Seventeen hundred and seventy-six.

And she wasn't reading about the Declaration of Independence or any of the things most people associated with that time period.

She was looking for anything she could find on Andrew McVie.

"You're losing it," she muttered, reaching for another huge volume of town records from the time. *You meet a perfectly normal man—if you don't count the way he talked—and suddenly you're convinced he's a time traveler.*

Dakota believed in the energy of crystals, the power of runes, and that being a Gemini gave you license to change your mind as often as you liked. She saw auras. She read minds. And now and again she had the unshakable feeling that just because she was born in the latter half of the twentieth century, that was no reason to believe she belonged there.

But real, live time travel? That was pushing the edge of the envelope, even for her. When you started playing around with the laws of physics, the logical side of her brain—underappreciated though it was—kicked in and yanked her back to reality with a thud.

She was too much her parents' child. Her father was a professor of physics, cursed with a brain that saw the inherent logic in everything from mathematics to MTV, while her mother adhered to the chaos theory of existence: sooner or later something incredible was going to happen and she intended to be ready to enjoy it when it did.

The four Wylie children were an odd mix of 4.0 grade point averages and enough ESP to turn the world on its ear. Frederick Wylie had been telling his children to plan for the future since they were old enough to understand the words *bank balance* and *career.* Ginny Wylie had just smiled and told them bedtime stories about Atlantis and spaceships to Mars. "Life is short!" Ginny had exhorted. "When adventure comes knocking, fling open the door."

So what was Dakota doing searching for McVie's name in every yellowed, mildewy old book she could find?

"Because I've lost my mind, that's why," she said out loud.

"Ms. Wylie!" Dr. Forsythe, head of the museum, glared at her from across the room. "Shh!"

Shh? I'm twenty-six years old and you're telling me to shh?

She hadn't been shushed since seventh-grade study hall. No wonder Forsythe's aura was so gray and forbidding. The man had the soul of a bureaucrat. Auras were funny things. Most people didn't believe they existed, but they did. And they were as individual and precise as fingerprints. All Dakota had to do was see an aura once and—

That's it, she thought as her heart rate doubled. *Auras.* Or the lack of them. That's what had been bothering her since she'd first seen McVie dragging that red balloon across Shannon's backyard.

She closed her eyes tightly and reconstructed their morning encounter. She conjured up the rugged face of Andrew McVie and studied his features one by one. Nope. No aura. Not even a glimmer of one. She would have settled for a faint hint of gold, a touch of pale blue, the slightest wash of red, but there was nothing.

Her heartbeat speeded up yet again. And that wasn't the half of it. The man had a force field around him that wasn't to be believed. Talk about the thunderbolt. He'd clasped her hand and she had felt as if she'd been hooked up to a major source of electricity and all of that power was zapping its way through her.

You'd think power like that was sexual but it wasn't—at least, not with her. It was something different, something harder to define, as if the entire chain of history had followed him to this time and place.

"Ms. Wylie!"

She started at the sound of Dr. Forsythe's nasal voice next to her left ear.

"Good grief," she said, hand to her throat. "Did you have to sneak up on me like that?"

"I asked you the same question three times, Ms. Wylie. Have you located the master directory of casualties under General Mercer during the Battle of Princeton?"

"No—I mean, yes." She shook her head to brush away the cobwebs. "I mean, I'll find them for you."

His bushy gray brows knotted together in a disapproving frown. "We don't pay you to daydream, young lady."

She scowled back at him. *And you don't pay me enough to live on, either.* If it wasn't for working the psychic fairs on the weekends and private parties on Monday nights, she'd be living in Shannon's cabana along with Balloon Boy.

She rummaged through the tower of papers on her desk and found the information Forsythe was looking for. Being psychic helped a lot when you thrived on disorganization, chaos and a deep-rooted love of the unexpected. She tucked the papers under her arm, then marched into his office.

"Here you go," she said, tossing them down on his meticulously clean blotter. "I'm going home for the night."

He glanced at the eight-day clock on his credenza. "It's only four forty-six."

"I have a headache," said Dakota, which wasn't that far from the truth. "I want to go home and take care of it."

Ten minutes alone with Andrew McVie—without Shannon hovering around like a too-protective mother hen—should do it.

"I thought you'd be more surprised by the radio," Shannon said, vaguely disappointed, as the last strains of "Surfin' USA" by the Beach Boys faded away.

"Emilie told me about such things."

Shannon made a face. "And I suppose she taught you the words to 'Doo Wah Diddy' in her spare time?"

"In truth, she did. 'Twas part of the plan to save General Washington."

She looked over at him. He wasn't smiling. "Are you pulling my leg?"

"Nay, mistress. My hands are nowhere near you."

"I mean, are you...making sport of me?" A phrase directly out of an old costume drama on cable television. *Okay, Hollywood, let's see how good your research is.*

"I tell the truth." He started to sing the words to the old sixties rock song and Shannon slammed on the brakes. All around her on the highway horns blared and tempers flared.

"Sweet Jesus!" Andrew roared. "Is it death you're courting?"

Embarrassed, she signaled then moved over to the slow lane. "Warn me the next time you decide to do something like that." She wondered if her heartbeat would ever return to normal. "Do you have any more surprises like that up your sleeve?"

He launched into a rousing version of "Jingle Bells" that soon had her laughing out loud.

"You're a man of many talents, Andrew McVie."

"Aye," he said with that grin she was coming to know, "but those talents did naught for the cause. His Excellency was already departed when I reached Long Island."

"His Excellency?" She signaled again to exit the parkway.

"General Washington."

"You called him 'His Excellency'? Good grief, I thought the whole idea of the Revolution was to get rid of royal titles and everything that came with them."

"I can say naught that will explain such a thing to you."

She rolled to a stop at a red light. "I can't believe I'm having this conversation, but what happened when you got to Long Island and found Washington had already left?"

"I went to the Grapes and Ale and downed three tankards."

She started to laugh. "Really?"

He nodded. "Aye."

The more things change... "So what happened with Washington? Did someone really try to kill him?"

"You have little knowledge of history," he observed.

"Guilty. It was never my favorite subject." Although it was beginning to take on dimensions she'd never dreamed.

"The people of Crosse Harbor believed me a hero for saving His Excellency's life but 'twas Zane who did the deed."

"Well, so what?" she said with a snap of her fingers. "Who cares what it says in some stuffy old history book? Nobody pays any attention to them, anyway."

"You do not worry about your place in history?"

She laughed as she turned onto the street that led to her house. "My place in history? I won't even be a footnote, Andrew. This world's a much bigger place than the world you left behind. Most of us will live and die and the world won't even know we were here."

A harsh observation, perhaps, but better he knew what he was dealing with.

For some reason Andrew seemed surprised to find the balloon and gondola still on the lawn in Shannon's backyard.

"Did you think it was going to reinflate and fly away?" she asked, casting him a curious look. "That's where you left it this morning."

"This is not the way it was for Emilie and Zane." He began gathering up the balloon into a manageable parcel. "It vanished when they crashed into the water."

"Obviously it didn't vanish permanently," she said, "or you wouldn't be here."

"There is something different about it," he said, staring down at the billowing crimson fabric. "It seems . . . paler. Faded."

"Wouldn't you look faded if you'd traveled across two hundred years?"

"'Tis more than that," he said, obviously disturbed. "We were gone but part of the day and the change is noticeable."

She inspected what she could see of the balloon and shrugged. "I don't see any difference."

"Aye," he said. "The difference is there, Shannon, but the meaning is beyond my ken."

Without the balloon he was trapped there forever. Her elation made her feel almost guilty. "Nothing about this entire situation makes any sense. Why should this be any different?"

"Because it is," came a third voice.

They both turned around to find Dakota leaning against the weeping willow tree.

"Don't you ever knock?" Shannon asked in exasperation.

Dakota rapped three times against the trunk of the tree. "So, are you guys going to come clean or do I have to get down on my knees and beg?"

"You're not going to start again, are you?" Shannon's hands itched to wrap around Dakota's throat.

Andrew continued to calmly fold the balloon into a neat package as if the end of life as they knew it wasn't rapidly approaching.

Dakota moved closer to Andrew. She was openly staring at him, her psychic antennae all but flapping in the breeze.

"Dakota." Shannon's voice sounded a warning.

"You don't have an aura," Dakota said to Andrew. "It took me a while to figure it out, but that's what bothered me when we first met. It isn't every day you meet someone without an aura."

"I do not know what an aura is, mis—"

"You must excuse Andrew," Shannon said, feeling like a guilty rat for holding out on her closest friend. "He's not from around here."

"I picked that up pretty quickly," Dakota said with a short laugh. She leveled a sharp look at Shannon. "If you tell me he's from France, I'll brain you."

"He's from Scotland," Shannon said, once again realizing just how easy it was to lie.

"I don't believe you," said Dakota. She turned back to Andrew. "Okay, so you don't know about auras. I can handle that. Half the people I work with don't know about auras. But the way you talk, this faded balloon—"

"You see the difference?" Andrew asked. His intensity was almost visible. "You see that the color has faded?"

"Of course I see the difference," Dakota said with an impatient gesture. "How can you *not* see the difference? It was a lot darker this morning."

Andrew looked as if he wanted to sweep Dakota into his arms and kiss her. "It is not a product of my imagination," he said to Shannon.

"I never said it was your imagination." She glanced uncomfortably in Dakota's direction. "The sun was strong today. It faded the fabric. Things like that happen."

Dakota ignored her and focused on Andrew. "Take my hand," she ordered him.

"Don't," Shannon said to Andrew in a clipped tone of voice. "Pay no attention to her."

Dakota held out her hand. The multitude of silver and gold rings on her slender fingers glittered in the sunshine.

"Please, Andrew," Dakota said. "I need to know."

Shannon stepped between the two of them. "There's plenty of room in the garage for the balloon and the gondola," she told Andrew. "Put it wherever you like."

He looked relieved to escape Dakota's intense scrutiny and quickly vanished.

"What on earth is wrong with you?" Shannon snapped as soon as he was out of earshot. "Have you lost what's left of your mind?"

"You're hiding something," Dakota persisted, not in the least bit cowed by Shannon's rising anger. "This is your funky, embarrassing, New Age-psychic-librarian best friend you're talking to. I can't help you with trust funds or charity galas, and now that there's finally something I *can* help you with, what do you do but push me away with both hands. I know he's not from this time. I know—" Dakota drew in a deep, shuddering breath and began to sway on her feet.

Again? Shannon thought. *How can it be happening again? She didn't even touch him!* She grabbed Dakota by the shoulders and steadied her.

"I need a diet Coke," Dakota managed.

Shannon started to laugh. "Diet Cokes stave off fainting spells?"

"I didn't faint," Dakota protested. "I swooned. There's a difference."

"Nobody swoons," Shannon said, leading her friend off toward the house. "I don't think anybody has actually swooned since hoop skirts went out of style after the Civil War."

"Bingo," said Dakota with an evil grin, "although it's an earlier war I have in mind. So, tell me, why am I swooning now?"

"Because you're a nut."

"I resent that."

"Okay," said Shannon. "You're an eccentric."

"A visionary," Dakota amended. "I come from a whole line of visionaries on my mother's side and I know visionaries are always misunderstood. Trust me when I tell you I'm picking up definite vibes from another time and place."

Shannon motioned her through the French doors.

"He did a good job with these," Dakota said, glancing about.

They'd been broken all summer. But the doors weren't the only things to change since Andrew McVie arrived, Shannon thought.

"You were born under a generous star," Dakota said as they entered the kitchen. "With my luck a plumber would drop out of the skies into my backyard and he'd tell me he didn't work on Sundays."

Shannon opened the refrigerator and pulled out two cans of soda. "Still having trouble with the kitchen sink?"

Dakota rolled her eyes. "The kitchen sink. The bathroom sink. The bathtub. The heating system." She popped the top on the soda can. "That's what happens when you live in an old house."

Shannon sat down at the kitchen table. "My offer still holds," she said, meeting her friend's eyes as Dakota sat down opposite her.

"I'm not going to let you pay for repairs to my house."

"Why not? I have more money than I know what to do with. Why can't I spend it on my friends?"

Dakota took a sip of soda. "You're spending it on him, aren't you?"

Shannon's brows lifted. "The clothes?"

"Don't look so surprised. Did you really think I wasn't going to notice? Suddenly the guy looks like he stepped out of the pages of *GQ.*"

Shannon smiled innocently. "I did think that shirt was particularly attractive."

"You paid for all of it."

"What makes you say that?" *Don't flirt with danger, Shannon. You know she'll catch you every time.*

"How could he pay for it?" Dakota countered. "He doesn't have any money."

"He has money."

"Yeah, but it's not from this century."

"You really do have a one-track mind, Wylie."

Dakota put her can of soda down and met Shannon's eyes. "This isn't going to last."

Shannon felt as if someone had her stomach in a vise grip. "What isn't?"

Dakota's gesture encompassed the house and beyond. Her eyes were dreamy behind the tinted lenses of her granny glasses. "Him. You. All of this. I just don't see him here for long."

"You're not making any sense."

Dakota leaned forward and placed a hand on Shannon's forearm. "Sooner or later he's going to have to make a decision, and when that time comes you'll have to let him go."

"Let him go? He's not an indentured servant, Dakota. He could leave right now if he wanted to."

"But you don't want him to, do you?"

That vise grip on her stomach tightened. "It doesn't much matter to me either way."

"Baloney it doesn't. You've fallen in love with him."

Shannon leapt to her feet, overturning the soda can. "Oh, damn it! See what you made me do."

Dakota pushed a napkin across the table to mop up the spill. "Falling in love is nothing to be ashamed of."

"The man's a stranger, Dakota. He dropped into my backyard less than twenty-four hours ago. I'd have to be insane to fall in love with someone I don't even know."

"Maybe so," said Dakota with maddening calm, "but the fact is you're in love with him and he's not going to stay around. You know it. I know it. And sooner or later he's going to know it, too."

Shannon felt her control begin to crack. She thrust her shaking hands into the pockets of her linen trousers and met her friend's eyes. "Stay out of this, Dakota. I love you dearly, but this time I'm asking you to butt out."

"I'd do anything in the world for you," Dakota said with a sad smile, "but that's the one thing I don't think I can do. Like it or not, we're in this together."

CHAPTER TEN

THE GARAGE WAS a large enclosure with room enough for at least three cars such as the one Shannon drove.

Andrew quickly found a place for the balloon and wicker basket in a stall to the left of Shannon's car. A sense of unease tugged at him as he pushed the entire contraption up against the back wall and covered it with a large white cloth he found on a shelf. Why had the balloon not vanished from his life the way it had with Emilie and Zane? Shannon's friend seemed to believe there was meaning to all of these events and he was not above wondering if that might not be so.

In truth, it had thus far been a most disturbing day. The glittering world he'd imagined did indeed exist, but there was a darkness at its heart that threw a shadow across the landscape. He had been surrounded by splendor that all else took for granted and yet in the midst of that splendor he had encountered

the sharp blade of violence, as senseless as it was unexpected.

And still no one seemed surprised. Not the painted
lady at the mall to whom it had been directed, nor
Shannon who had suffered the effects of such violence
within the sacred bonds of her marriage.

The world he came from lacked much in the way of
luxury but at least a man knew who his enemies were
and where they might be found.

There was a sense of defeat about everything and
everyone, a curious lack of the commitment that propelled a man or woman to right the wrongs of the
world. They took the wonders of their time for
granted, as if flying through the air or owning a king's
ransom in jewels was their right and not the miracle it
truly was. It was as if the endless string of wars had
extinguished the flames of righteousness and left only
bitter spoils.

Shannon had said it to him in plain and simple
words—that the average man stood little chance of
making his mark on the world, and no chance at all of
influencing history. How had such a thing happened in
two short centuries?

Their trip to the mall had taught Andrew that the
time had come for him to take charge of the situation
and adapt himself to this new century with as much
dispatch as he could muster. He had always been master of his own fate, willing to rely on no man for direction.

How difficult it must have been for Zane to be thrust
back in time to a world that did not easily recognize his
worth. Not only was his currency worthless, so were his
credentials. And that was a bitter pill to swallow.

During his time at Harvard Andrew had learned that knowledge was power. He was an intelligent man. He had chosen to travel forward in time of his own free will. Now he must make it his business to learn to function in this world as swiftly and efficiently as possible or resign himself to being a leech upon others for the rest of his days.

At first he had not understood Shannon's insistence that his story remain a secret between them, but today at the mall her fears suddenly made sense. There was a hunger in this world that he'd not seen or felt anywhere before, a need that he could not define but felt as a persistent vibration in the very air he breathed. What could they want, he wondered, when miracles were the stuff of everyday life?

He spent much of the afternoon at work repairing the windows of the structure Shannon called a garage. He wielded the hammer like a weapon. With every nail he pounded into place he pictured the supercilious clerks he'd encountered at the mall, all of whom had found great amusement in his dependence upon Shannon.

Apparently even in the year 1993 it was the man's place to provide clothing and sustenance for the woman. He'd felt a fool and worse each time she reached for that shiny rectangle she used to obtain credit from the shopkeepers.

A gold card, Shannon had called it. A most apt name for an object that served as gold's equivalent. If only other objects were so aptly named. The room that moved up and down was called an elevator, while the silver stairs that carried you up of their own volition went by the odd name escalator. Men's trousers were called pants or slacks. Shoes no longer came with buckles. Hair could be long or short or anywhere in between and there was not a powdered wig in sight.

In general, people seemed to wear as few items of clothing as they could, and Andrew doubted he would ever grow accustomed to seeing a woman's nipples looking back at him through the sheer fabric of her bodice. And then there were cars and trucks and the flying metal birds called airplanes.

He knew he must make an effort to adapt to his new situation. He would no longer say "mistress." When he did not understand a reference he would wait and cobble together its meaning with bits and pieces of other information and clues. He would find a way to make a place for himself in this world, even if it was bigger and faster and more dangerous than he'd ever imagined possible.

"What manner of food is this?" He looked askance at the triangle of dough covered in a red sauce and melted white cheese.

"Pizza," said Shannon, eating it with her hands in a most disconcerting—yet appealing—fashion. "It's Italian."

"Italian? Is such foreign fare common?"

She wiped the side of her mouth with a square of soft paper. "As common as hot dogs."

"Sweet Jesus!" He stared at her in alarm. "Has it come to that?"

She looked at him and burst into laughter. "I don't mean the four-legged kind, Andrew. It's—" She stopped. "Actually, it sounds pretty disgusting, but it's ground-up meat pushed into a casing and boiled. We serve it with mustard and sauerkraut."

"Aye," he said. "'Tis a vile concoction you describe." He took a bite of the pizza, struggling with a long, stretchy string of the mild white cheese. "This, however, is most agreeable." He took another bite then looked across the table. "This came in a box?"

"That's how they deliver it," Shannon explained. "I called in my order and thirty minutes later they brought the pizza here to me." She reached for a strange-looking object, roughly the size of a woman's shoe, then pulled a long rod from its depths.

He watched, mouth agape, as she touched her finger to the center of the object in quick movements much like playing the piano. Grinning, she handed it to him.

"Put it to your ear," she ordered, then laughed. "No, not that way. Turn it around."

He did as told and heard an odd ringing noise, then a human voice, clear as day, talking right into his ear. "Good afternoon, everybody. At 6:05 the temperature at Newark Airport is eighty-five degrees and—"

Andrew dropped the object to the tabletop. "There is something unnatural about such a thing."

"It's a telephone," Shannon said, obviously amused by his reaction. "Probably one of the most important inventions the world has ever seen."

"'Tis a foolish invention," he said. "How can you judge the worth of a man if you cannot look him in the eye?"

"You wouldn't think it a foolish invention if you were talking to someone in England, would you?"

He picked up the telephone and turned it over in his hand. "How can this object make conversation possible across the ocean?"

"I know it has something to do with fiber-optic cables and satellites and all sorts of things."

"All of that so a man can have strange food delivered in a box."

"If you want to put it that way, yes," said Shannon.

"People make a living that way?"

"A good living," Shannon said. "Fast foods are big business."

"Does no one sit down at the family table and partake of a normal supper?"

"This is a normal supper these days, Andrew. Families are on the run during the week. It's a rare clan that has the opportunity to sit down for a meal at the same time."

"Where do they run?"

"They work late, they go to night school, soccer practice, Little League, Girl Scouts, Pop Warner, you name it, they're out there doing it." She sprinkled red flakes on top of her pizza. "And when they're not out there, they're at home watching TV."

"The moving pictures on the small glass window?"

She nodded. "If you don't feel like going out to see the world, TV brings the world into your home." She considered him for a moment. "If you want to learn about this strange place you're in, TV is one of the best ways to start."

"Have you no books?"

"Thousands of them," she said. "Finish your pizza and I'll show you the library."

He's like a kid in a candy shop, Shannon thought as Andrew devoured *Timetables of American History.* He hadn't moved from his spot near the window. His torso was curved over the book, almost as if he were protecting it from harm.

Her heart went out to him. Talk about culture shock. The poor man was racing through the pages, flying from the minuet to the Virginia reel to rap without a parachute.

She recognized in him a need to know all there was to know, to absorb as much information as he possibly could in order to arm himself against the unknown. Dakota's warning repeated in her brain. *Temporary... this is only temporary.*

Shannon wasn't a fool. She knew the time would come when he moved on. You didn't travel through more than two hundred years of time and space to content yourself with a small town in central New Jersey. *Or with one very lonely woman.*

Where on earth did that thought come from? She was alone but she wasn't lonely. Not really. She had Dakota and the people who ran her shelters, not to mention the women and children who passed through them on their way to happier, better lives. And, God knew, she had a social life other people would envy. An endless array of society functions and charity balls and luncheons that would gobble up as much of her time as she would allow. Her picture was a staple in local society columns.

She wasn't looking for a relationship with a man. She didn't need a man to make herself complete. *Are you sure of that?* the same small voice asked. Wasn't there one small part of her heart that still yearned for home and family, for someone to share her days and warm her nights? She'd trained herself not to wish for the impossible and it annoyed her to fall prey again to those old longings.

Dakota is right, she thought, struggling to shake off the melancholy mood she'd fallen under. There was nothing permanent about any of this. As soon as he grew comfortable with twentieth-century ways, he would be gone. Men like Andrew McVie weren't meant to spend their days lounging by the side of a swimming pool, sipping margaritas and listening to baseball on the radio.

He was a dynamic man from a dynamic time and sooner or later he'd be looking to make his mark on the world in which he found himself.

And she would be left behind, sitting alone in her fortress, safe from anything that could cause her harm . . . including love.

Valley Forge. The terrible winter at Morristown. The War of 1812. Abraham Lincoln and the unimaginable horrors of the War Between the States. The pain of Reconstruction. The Spanish-American War.

As he read on, Andrew felt as if he were being pummeled from all sides, battered and bruised by decades of struggle. Aye, there were triumphs along the way — the westward expansion, the Industrial Revolution — but it seemed to him that each of those triumphs was offset by strife.

World War I and its legacy of shell-shocked veterans whose nerves were permanently damaged by something called mustard gas. His gut knotted as he read on, unbelievably to World War II where millions of people were slaughtered cold-bloodedly for their religion or nationality or choice of friends. Try as he might he could not comprehend an entire world engulfed in the flames of warfare.

In 1950 warfare had erupted again in Korea, an island on the other side of the world, and then in Viet Nam, and the Holy Land, and Arabia and—

He flung the book at the far wall and rose from his chair.

"The wonder of it all is that the world still exists," he roared as he paced the empty library.

Shannon appeared in the doorway. "It's a bit much to digest in one sitting." She handed him a cold drink.

He gulped it down and wished for rum. "How is it that life continues?" he asked, knowing there could be no answer. "The weapons of destruction are everywhere. How does a man build a life knowing it can be destroyed in the blink of an eye?"

"Optimism," she said with a shrug of her slender shoulders. "Stubbornness. Wasn't it the same in your day? Life has always been an uncertain proposition. We just make the best of it while we're here."

"'Tis not the way I thought it would be," he muttered.

"And isn't that just too bad," she snapped with a harsh edge to her lovely voice. "If you were looking for something easy, McVie, then you've come to the wrong time and place."

"Aye," he said. "I am quickly learning that."

"What did you want?" she asked, moving toward him. "What on earth did you think you could find here that you couldn't find where you were?"

The word leapt forth of its own accord. "Purpose," he said. He had meant to say both wealth and ease, and the truth of his statement surprised him.

Her expression softened and he had the sense that she understood his meaning in a way few others of this time or any other ever could.

"I hope you find it, Andrew McVie." Her voice caressed him. "Life isn't worth a damn without it."

"You have purpose?"

She considered his question. "I do," she said at last, "but purpose and happiness don't always go hand in hand."

"Happiness is a fool's errand. A man is more well served by a sense of purpose."

"Said by a man who once held happiness in his hand."

"You have no knowledge of that, mistress Shannon."

Her eyebrows lifted. "Mistress? I thought you had put that aside."

He ignored her comment. "How is it you believe you know so much about me? Have you skills like your friend Dakota?"

She shook her head. "I'm not psychic, if that's what you mean. I simply remember the way you looked when you showed me the watch Elspeth gave to you."

Emotion gripped him by the throat, making it difficult to speak. "As a husband I was a grave disappointment."

She said nothing, simply leaned against the doorjamb and watched him with those big aqua eyes.

"I had but one goal," he continued. "The pursuit of the almighty shilling. All else paled by comparison."

"You'll find little has changed. Many men and women make the same mistake each and every day."

"'Tis a sorrow to hear that. I would wish no man the grief I knew when Elspeth and David were lowered into the ground." *They're in the arms of Jesus,* the good Reverend Samuels had said as Andrew stood silently next to the grave, cold as the December winds blowing across the cemetery. *They'll never hurt again.* If only someone had been able to say that about him.

She moved closer, so close that he caught the sweet scent of her skin, felt the warmth of her body near his. "I'm sure they knew you loved them."

"Love is not always enough for a good woman to warm herself with on a winter's night."

"Your wife was unfaithful?"

"Nay," said Andrew, "although I gave her just reason to seek comfort with another. The law was wife and mistress and child and all else walked behind. Elspeth lived a life of loneliness in a town that was not her home and she did it to help serve my own purpose."

"What happened to Elspeth and David? How did they—?"

"Fire," he said bluntly. "I was on my way back from Philadelphia. They died just hours before I reached them." His voice broke and he looked down at his feet, strange to him in the low-slung leather shoes. "That was when I left the practice of law and took up the cause of rebellion."

The words tumbled from his mouth like so many marbles through a child's fingers. He told her of the spy ring, of the chances he took, the praise he received for risking his life. "I had no right to such praise," he said, wishing for the sweet oblivion to be found in a bottle of rum. "A man who risks his life when his life is a thing of value does a praiseful thing. A man who risks his life when death holds strong appeal deserves naught but scorn."

She placed her hand on his forearm and for a moment he thought his battered and weary heart felt whole again. *'Tis your imagination. What you feel is but a man's need for release.*

Her cheeks flushed and he looked at her sharply. Had she somehow heard his innermost thoughts? The notion both pleased and alarmed him in equal measure. He'd always held his emotions on a tight rein in the belief that a man did not acknowledge anything that spoke of weakness.

Yet this woman had seen him stripped of all wealth and power and knowledge—reduced to learning how to survive in a strange new world—and still she viewed him as a man of worth.

"I am not what you think, Shannon," he said, his voice gruff with emotion.

"And you are not what *you* think, either," she whispered. "Let it go, Andrew. Get on with your life."

He looked down at her hand resting against his forearm. Seeing where his gaze lingered, she gave him a brief smile and made to deprive him of her touch, but he placed his hand over hers.

She met his eyes.

He reached out with his other hand and let her dark hair drift through his fingertips. So soft...so silky...so sweetly perfumed. A man could grow drunk on such sweetness.

Dame Fortune did me an honor when she brought me to this place, mistress.

"I am pleased you think so, Andrew."

He jerked back in surprise. "I said nothing to warrant a reply."

"You did. I heard you quite clearly."

"I did not speak aloud."

"Still," said Shannon, "I heard your voice and it's not the first time. . . ."

"The world is a strange place," he said. "There are many things we are not given to understand."

"I don't want to understand this. Magic doesn't need to be understood."

The urge to draw her close against his body was growing more difficult to ignore. "From the first moment I have felt a sense of destiny, as if all things in my life have led me to you."

"Oh, God," she whispered, resting her forehead against his chest. "When you stepped out of the woods I felt as if my life was just beginning."

He cradled her head between his hands and lifted her face to his. Her eyes were wide. Her lips parted slightly on a sigh. He knew if the Almighty called him home at that very second he would have died already knowing the face of paradise, for he could wish for no greater reward than the taste of her mouth against his.

CHAPTER ELEVEN

THIS CAN'T BE HAPPENING, Shannon thought, even as her eyes closed for his kiss. *Things like this don't happen in real life.*

"They do happen," he said, his breath warm against her skin. "We are the proof of it."

He knew her thoughts before she gave them voice, the same way she knew his. There was a connection between them, inexplicable though it was, and she was powerless before it. But not frightened. This was surrender of a sensual kind, the kind of giving over of control that promised even greater rewards. Something deep and real and forever.

He brushed his lips across hers, lightly at first, as if taking her measure. She inhaled the scent of his skin, reveled in the delicious sensations awakening within her body. His fingers were callused and rough against her face but his touch was so gentle, so tender that she wondered if you could die from feeling cherished.

134

She'd never felt cherished before, never felt as if her pleasure mattered. And it would with Andrew. She knew it instinctively, the same way she knew that they were moving toward something that would change her forever and in ways she couldn't imagine.

She wanted to crawl inside his heart and ease his pain. She wanted to slip into his mind and know his secrets. But, dear God, more than anything she wanted to hold him deep inside her body and spend the night in his arms.

And a night would be enough. She would make it be enough. Nothing lasted forever. Not youth or beauty or riches. Certainly not happiness. But she would rather grow old knowing that she'd followed her heart this once than knowing she'd let a chance for happiness slip through her fingers like so many grains of sand.

He deepened the kiss, drawing her breath from her body on a shuddering sigh of longing. She felt drunk with it, so intoxicated with the smell and touch and sight of him that she thought she was hearing bells.

Unfortunately she *was* hearing bells.

"Someone's at the door," she murmured against his mouth.

He kissed her again—thoroughly—and it took a great display of willpower on her part to leave his embrace.

"You are expecting visitors?" he asked, smoothing back her hair with a gesture of such affection that her knees threatened to buckle beneath her.

She shook her head. "Whoever it is, I'll tell them to come back tomorrow."

"That is a sound idea."

She grinned, feeling young and flirtatious and filled with hope. "I thought you'd like it. I'll be right back."

She floated down the hallway toward the front door in a romantic haze. The doorbell rang again just as she unfastened the dead bolt.

"I was beginning to wonder if you were home," said the attractive African-American woman who waited on the doorstep. "I rang twice."

"I was in the library." She hugged the woman and ushered her into the foyer. Karen Naylor was an attorney, an advocate for battered wives, and one of Shannon's favorite people in the world. "Business or pleasure, Karen?"

"Business, unfortunately. We're going to have a full house tonight in the old building."

Shannon reached for the notebook she kept in the basket by the door. "How many?"

"Six," said Karen. "Mother, grandmother and four children. The mother is being seen by the doctor right now and then Jules will bring them over in the van."

"How old are the children?"

"Eleven, eight, five and eighteen months."

"Do we need the crib?"

"Not a bad idea. The little one has some sleeping disorders."

"Why doesn't that surprise me?" Shannon muttered. So many women stayed in an abusive marriage for the sake of the children, only to find the children scarred by the endless cycle of physical and emotional abuse. "Did you call Dakota? She'll want to stop by tomorrow after work and see to the kids." Dakota's crusade was literacy and she'd taught many a young mother and child about the joys of reading.

"I left a message," Karen said, "but I think Monday is psychic party night. You might want to try her again in the morning."

"I'd better check the guest houses and make sure everything's in order," Shannon said, her mind shifting into high gear. "I have a stack of new magazines, some videotapes and some really terrific kids' clothes." She looked up at Karen. "Are any of the kids girls?"

"Three of them," said Karen. "You'll be in your glory."

Shannon scribbled a few hasty notes then glanced at her watch. "What on earth are you doing out so late? You could've called to tell me this."

"I know," said Karen, "but I have some papers I wanted to drop off for you to read, so I figured why not do everything at once?"

Shannon's interest was immediately piqued. "My updated will?"

Karen nodded. "That and the new modules for the trusts."

Shannon rolled her eyes comically. "Both will make wonderful bedtime reading, I'm sure."

"Just make sure you *do* read them," Karen warned. "This is important stuff. I need to make certain you know what you're signing."

"I told you what I wanted, you say you've delivered it. What more can I ask? I trust you."

"Don't trust me," Karen said, rolling her eyes. "Double-check everybody."

"Words to live by," said Shannon with a wicked grin.

Karen considered her carefully. "You look like the cat that ate the canary."

"Do I? I can't imagine why."

Karen gestured toward the doorway. "Could he be the reason?"

Shannon spun around to see Andrew, arms folded across his chest, watching them.

"So, introduce us, girl." Karen beamed a smile in Andrew's direction. Then, sotto voce to Shannon, "Where have you been hiding him? He's adorable."

"He's an old friend," she said, motioning for Andrew to join them. "He, ah, he just dropped in the other day and I've asked him to stay awhile."

He's not smiling, Shannon noticed as he walked toward them. If anything, he looked annoyed.

Karen thrust out her right hand. "Karen Naylor," she said, hanging on to her smile.

Andrew ignored the outstretched hand, and Shannon groaned inwardly. Darn Dakota and her swooning spells. The poor man would probably be afraid to shake hands for the rest of his life. She considered the wisdom of giving him a poke in the ribs to urge him forward but decided against it. With her luck Karen would tumble over in a dead faint and they'd have someone else to worry about. Karen was a literal, intellectual type. If Shannon told her Andrew had dropped in from the eighteenth century, Karen would arrange to have them both committed.

She cleared her throat.

Karen's smile faltered but her hand remained outstretched.

Shake her hand, she thought. *You're embarrassing the daylights out of me.*

Andrew looked down at her, a puzzled expression on his rawboned face. With obvious reluctance he reached out and clasped Karen's hand for a nanosecond then backed away.

"Andrew McVie," he said.

"What a wonderful accent," Karen said, a flicker of embarrassment in her chocolate brown eyes. "Where are you from?"

"Boston," said Andrew.

"Scotland," said Shannon at the same time. "I mean, first Scotland, then Boston."

"Ahh," said Karen, her gaze darting from Andrew to Shannon then back again to Andrew. "So what brings you to New Jersey?"

"He's taking a sabbatical," said Shannon.

Andrew's brows lifted.

So did Karen's.

You're making a mess of this, Shannon, she berated herself. *Let the man answer for himself.*

"I'm taking a sabbatical," said Andrew.

Karen's mouth twitched as if she was holding back a laugh. Who could blame her? This was worse than Abbott and Costello's *Who's on First?*

"What is he taking a sabbatical from?" Karen asked Shannon.

"Very funny," Shannon said, then fell silent so Andrew could answer for himself.

"The law," Andrew said.

Karen's eyes widened. Shannon wished the floor would open up and swallow her whole.

"You're an attorney?" Karen asked.

"I am," said Andrew.

"I've always wanted to meet an attorney from the U.K.," Karen said, zeroing in on him. "Now, are you a barrister or a solicitor or a lawyer?" She laughed. "Or have I totally botched it all up?"

"I am a lawyer," he said in a tone of voice Shannon hadn't heard before.

"So how is that different from a barrister?"

"I do not know."

"Well," said Karen, turning back toward Shannon, "I have to get home." She reached into her leather tote and removed a large white envelope. "Read the papers and we'll set up a time for you to come into the office and sign everything."

Karen gave Shannon a quick embrace, then, with a nod for Andrew, she said good-night and left.

Shannon turned on him in a fury unlike any he'd seen before.

"What in hell is wrong with you?" she roared. "How dare you be so rude to Karen."

"I did nothing untoward," he said, bristling.

"You treated her abysmally."

"I answered her questions."

"You had no intention of shaking her hand."

"Aye," he said. "'Twas not my intention at all."

"Why in hell not?" she continued, her anger increasing. "You shook Dakota's hand."

"And you are aware of the results."

"But that's not it, is it?" she persisted. "It's because she's black."

He could not deny it.

"Bigot!"

He glared at her. "I come from a different world. Black slaves do not embrace their owners."

"You jerk! Slavery's been dead for over one hundred years. For your information, Karen's a lawyer, same as you."

The notion was so preposterous he laughed out loud. "You speak nonsense."

"I speak the truth, Andrew. Karen is a lawyer."

"I do not believe you."

"She graduated Harvard law."

"You make that up to goad me into an argument."

"What bothers you more—that the lawyer's a woman or that she's black?"

"In truth, I find both impossible to believe."

"You're honest," she said. "I'll grant you that. But that doesn't make your opinions acceptable."

"Is there but one way to think in 1993?"

"No, there are many ways to think, but when it comes to the basic rights of others, there is only one way that is acceptable to decent, caring human beings."

"You believe me to be uncaring."

She lifted her chin. "In this regard, yes I do."

"Elspeth and I did not hold slaves."

"How wonderful for you," she drawled. "But did you do anything to convince others to release theirs?"

"'Twas not my business to tell others how to live their lives."

"Even if the way they lived their lives kept other lives in bondage?"

"Most slaves were well cared for."

"Oh, please!" She raised her hands in disgust. "Care to explain the Civil War to me, or didn't you get that far in your reading?"

"There were reasons beyond the existence of slavery for the War Between the States." He had read the story that very evening and the facts were clear in his mind.

"But none more important."

"You act as if I bear the weight of slavery upon my shoulders."

"You do," she said with righteous fury. "All of you who allowed such a system to continue. You had the chance to eradicate it with the Declaration of Independence and you let it slip right through your greedy fingers."

"There is little time to debate such things when you are fighting for the future of your country. I know of this declaration and I know of how it was wrought. There would be no United States of America had Jefferson and Adams not bowed to the needs of the Southern gentlemen present."

"An easy answer," Shannon said, "but I don't buy it. There had to be another way."

"Much of life is compromise," he said. "Have you not learned that yet?"

"Of course I have, but I find myself wondering if you've mastered the art."

"Do not hide your meaning, Shannon. Tell me straight."

"You still don't get it, do you? Think of me, Andrew. Those same attitudes toward blacks carried over toward the treatment of women. How did you view Elspeth? Was she your property? Your partner? Your slave?"

"She was my wife and all that entailed." The words sounded apologetic. He didn't mean them to be. Why was she asking him to defend something that needed no defense?

"I'll tell you what that entailed. Up until this century being a man's wife meant being his property. And up until a very few years ago a man could do anything he wanted to his property, including destroy it. A man could beat his wife, rape her, even kill her and no-body—nobody!—would say a word.''

He wanted to pull her into his arms and soothe her fears but knew that would be the wrong thing to do. It wasn't his touch she needed, it was something much harder for him to give.

"On God's oath, I never struck Elspeth nor wished to cause her harm of any kind," he said. "Nor would I harm another woman in any way."

"I know," she said, her voice a whisper. "I believe that."

He felt the need of her touch and took her hand in his. "Then what still troubles you that you look at me in such a manner?"

"Many women come through my life, Andrew, and they all are in need of help."

"I understand you feel a kinship with the other good wives who have suffered unjustly."

"I do," she said, squeezing his hand. "And those wives and women and children come in all shapes and sizes and religions and races. If—if you are to be here...with me...then you must accept them as your equal and mine."

"'Tis a great deal you ask of me."

"I know it is," she said, "but you are a good man."

His mouth quirked upward in a smile. "You presume a great deal upon limited acquaintance."

"I know what I know." She touched his face with a gentle hand and he felt as if he'd been blessed by God. "You are a better man than you realize, Andrew Mc-Vie, and I believe you can learn to accept Karen and others like her."

"I cannot say with certainty if that will prove true."

"I can."

"It is not possible for you to know things that I do not know about myself."

"I've learned to rely on my gut instincts." She faced him full on, that warrior-woman stance he'd been taken by on first acquaintance. She saw in him something that he'd thought long gone, a finer self he would sell his soul to believe still existed. "You will try, won't you?"

He nodded. "I will try."

Her smile was brighter than the sun and it warmed him to the marrow. "It's a start."

"Aye," he said. "'Tis a start."

Where it would end he could not say, but he hoped with all his heart that the end would be a long time coming.

CHAPTER TWELVE

THE SHELTERS WERE a short distance away, located at the other side of the woods that were part of her property. Originally they'd been intended as guest cottages by the privacy-loving first owner of the estate, but the second Shannon saw them she knew they were destined to serve a much more important purpose.

With Andrew's help she loaded the trunk of her car with supplies and magazines and baby gear. She hadn't asked for his help. The fact that he thought to lend a hand touched her deeply. Their discussion had been painfully frank—for both of them, she would imagine. She'd half expected him to turn and walk away from her, and the fact that he didn't, that he stayed to help, meant more than she could say.

When she climbed behind the wheel he took his place in the passenger's seat. "We won't be back for a while," she said as she started the engine. "Sometimes it takes a few hours to get everyone settled in."

"Aye."

She backed out of the driveway, then turned onto the dirt road that led to the cottages. Minutes later she pulled up in front of the tiny house that served as one of the shelters.

"They're not here yet," she said. "That'll give us a chance to open the windows and put the food away."

Andrew inspected the front door with a critical eye. "'Tis in need of repair."

"Karl isn't much for repair work," Shannon said with a shake of her head.

"Karl?"

"Karl's my handyman. He and Mildred take care of things for me."

"I have seen naught of Mildred and Karl."

"Vacation," she said. "They've gone to visit relatives in Sweden."

"The window sashes are in sad condition." He looked at Shannon. "How is it you continue to employ a man who does so little to earn his salary?"

Shannon hoisted two bags of groceries and headed for the kitchen. "I'm what's known as a soft touch," she said over her shoulder as Andrew followed her through the tiny hallway. "Karl and Mildred worked for the previous owner. They're practically at retirement age. I doubt if anyone could've let them go."

They barely had time to unload the trunk before Jules's van rattled its way up the dirt road and rolled to a stop behind Shannon's car.

You never get used to it, Shannon thought as they watched the two women help the children from the van. If you did, you were a poor excuse for a human being.

"Gonna have a full house," Jules said as the grand-mother gathered up the baby blankets from the back seat. "I've got two more pickups."

"Two more? What on earth's going on?"

"Full moon. Hot weekend. Your guess is as good as mine."

"Any more babies?"

"Teenagers this time. Two in one family, one in the other."

"We'll need more food," she said. "As soon as I get everyone settled in, I'll go home and raid the pantry."

"I will go for you," said Andrew as Jules set off to collect the next two families.

"I admit you've adapted amazingly well but I'm not about to let you drive."

"I have no need of your car," he said. "I will walk."

"It's pitch-black outside. You'll never find your way there and back."

"Tell me what you require and I will see you get it."

She named a few staple items, told him how to by-pass the alarm system and where to find the pantry. Then she crossed her fingers that he'd manage to find the house before another two hundred years had passed.

In truth Andrew would have walked from there to kingdom come if it meant escaping the sorrowful eyes of the women and children.

He had seen terrible things in his lifetime. He'd held a young boy's hand as he lay dying on the village green near Lexington, victim of a Redcoat's musket. And he'd carried home the boy's meager belongings to his mother, who had already buried two sons before him.

But nothing had prepared Andrew for the sight of the two women who had come to Shannon for help. The older had the look of defeat about her person, visible in the slumped shoulders and fearful expression, as if she expected danger to leap from behind the trees or drop from the skies. It was the younger woman, however, who had borne the burden of some man's anger. Heavy bandages hid her left eye from view, while purple-and-black bruises ringed the right. A stepladder of what appeared to be tailor's stitches angled across one cheek, each stitch a testament to the horror she had sustained at the hands of the man to whom she'd pledged her life.

He made his way through the woods swiftly, relying on skills he'd thought would be unimportant in this world. A man did not need a road to find his way. A formation of trees, the stars overhead, all could be used to guide a man if he understood how to use them. There were differences, however, that made the exercise difficult in a way he hadn't foreseen.

Darkness did not fall with the same finality in Shannon's century as it did in his. He was accustomed to an all-encompassing blackness, a blackness so dark and deep the stars shining above seemed close enough to touch. But here there was a grayness to the night, as if a scrim separated him from the sky itself.

And the quality of the silence continued to confound him. Even now, alone in the woods, there was a constant noise he could not identify. Instinct told him it was not the noise of the wind or some strange insects or animals but something unnatural.

The back of Shannon's property was brightly lit, almost as if the afternoon sun shone down upon the land

and reflected in the blue depths of the rectangular pond. Electricity made these miracles possible, harnessing the same power that split the skies during a summer storm. Was that the source of the ever-present hum that hovered at the edges of his mind day and night? In truth, he wished for just an hour of the deep silence he had taken for granted.

He followed Shannon's instructions and entered the house without causing the box on the wall to scream.

"A small triumph," he muttered as he headed toward the pantry. He wondered if the rest of his life would consist of small triumphs that amounted to nothing at all.

Fifteen years ago, on the day after their college graduation, Pat Conner married Jack Delaney. Everyone said they were the perfect couple. Jack was poised at the starting line, about to enter an executive training program, while Pat was eager to start a family, something they accomplished with dispatch on their honeymoon.

They bought into the whole American dream: kids and career, the beautiful home in a trendy suburb, station wagon and golden retriever, the endless parade of expectations that could never be met.

Not by them.

Not by anyone.

"He'll find us," Pat said as she sipped warm broth through a straw in the kitchen while the kids wolfed down hot dogs. "He said if I ever tried to run, he'd find me and he'd find the kids and he'd kill us."

Pat's mother, Terri, looked up from her cup of coffee. "He was killing us anyway, honey, day by day."

She met Shannon's eyes and Shannon tried not to notice the bruises along the older woman's jaw. "Tell her this was the right thing to do, miss. Tell her he can't find us here."

"You're safe," Shannon said, reaching across the table to squeeze Pat's trembling hand. "Nothing can happen to you here."

"You don't know Jack," Pat said, glancing nervously toward her children. "He's a powerful man. He has friends everywhere."

"So had my husband," Shannon said.

Pat looked up in surprise. "You?"

"Me," said Shannon with a small smile. "I've been there, Pat. I know how it feels."

"But you— I mean—" Pat gestured broadly to encompass the estate. "I didn't think it could happen to someone like you."

"You thought wrong," Shannon said. "Abuse cuts across all social classes and all economic backgrounds."

"I pushed her into this," Terri said, looking down at her cup of coffee. "Last night when he— If he lays a hand on my baby or my grandbabies one more time, I'll kill him."

"Don't say that, Mom!" Pat's voice quavered with emotion. "He's my husband."

"He's a no-good bastard."

"You don't understand." Pat looked toward Shannon for support but Shannon kept still. "He doesn't mean to hurt us.... It's just—he's under so much stress at work. His job is shaky and..." Her voice faded and she took another sip of soup.

"See?" said the mother. "First she says he wants to kill her, then she's feeling sorry for him. I didn't know what to do. I figured this was our only hope."

"You live with them?"

"Since February. My—my husband died and Pat took me in."

"You made the right choice," Shannon reassured her. "The important thing is that you got her out of that house before it got any worse."

"I can make my own decisions." Pat spoke up. "I just want to give Jack a chance to rest." She looked toward her kids as they polished off the hot dogs and moved onto the ice cream. "It's hard for him. The kids make a lot of noise and they need so many things—" Her voice broke as she started to cry.

"It's okay," Shannon crooned, putting a comforting arm around the woman's shoulders. "Nothing can happen to you here. You're safe."

"I'm s-so scared," Pat said through her sobs. "I don't know what I'm going to do, where I'll go—"

"First things first," Shannon said. "The six of you need a good night's sleep. Tomorrow morning is soon enough to start planning your future."

Andrew moved deeper into the shadows. He'd seen the look on her face, heard the infinite tenderness in her voice, and it occurred to him that she was the finest person he'd ever known.

In times of war ordinary men and women rose to greatness with acts of heroism that were the stuff of history. But in truth it was easy to be heroic when the situation demanded it.

Heroism in the face of everyday trials was a rare thing indeed. Something Shannon possessed in great measure. She saw pain and she tried to ease it. She saw inequity and she tried to remedy it. He could not imagine many men or women who would open wide the doors of their home and take in strangers in need.

Take heed, a voice inside his head warned. *'Tis her way to lend comfort.* To read anything but human kindness into her behavior was to mark himself a fool.

"You were great with those kids," Shannon said a few hours later as they rode the short distance back to her house.

"They are angry," Andrew said.

"Is it any wonder? Their father beat the hell out of their mother and turned a gun on the two of them. That's enough to make anybody angry."

"'Tis more than that. Much of their anger is aimed at their mother."

Shannon glanced at him as she pulled into the driveway and hit the garage door opener. "Did they tell you that?"

"It was not necessary for them to tell me. It was there for all to see."

"I didn't see it."

Andrew shrugged his powerful shoulders. "There are things you see about women that are invisible to me."

She shut off the engine and turned to face him. "So what you're saying is it's a guy thing."

His forehead wrinkled. "A guy thing?"

"You know." She gestured broadly. "Male bonding, all that sort of stuff."

His frown deepened. "Male bonding?"

"I'd give you a copy of Robert Bly but I have the feeling you'd grab your balloon and go back home if I did."

"Speak plain, Shannon. Your words make no sense."

She sighed, struggling to find a way to explain self-help books, television talk shows and making peace with your inner child. "Many Americans spend a lot of time thinking about their lives," she said, "and a few very clever Americans make a lot of money writing books that help the others think better." He was looking at her so strangely that she had to laugh. "Of course, if you don't like self-help books you can always go to a therapist."

"I do not know that word, *therapist.*"

"A world without Freud? It sounds like heaven." She searched about for a definition. "A therapist is someone you pay to listen to your problems."

His mouth literally opened in surprise. "You pay someone to listen to your problems?"

"Well, yes," said Shannon. "And then the therapist offers solutions."

A funny smile lifted the corners of his mouth. "A few tankards of ale shared with friends at the Plumed Rooster accomplished much the same."

"I suppose it would," said Shannon as they got out of the car and walked across the side yard to the house. "The only problem is we don't have time for friends these days. We're too busy working three jobs in order to pay the mortgage, the baby-sitter, taxes—"

"Aye," said Andrew with a groan. "A man could work half his life in payment to the Crown."

"Well, we don't have to worry about the Crown these days, but Uncle Sam is more than happy to take his share."

"I thought you were not in communication with any of your family."

"Uncle Sam isn't really my family. He's everybody's family." She explained how it was a quasi-affectionate name for the American government. "He's a tall man with white hair and a beard and he wears very strange red, white and blue clothing that looks suspiciously like our flag."

"The same colors as the flag of England," he said, sounding quite indignant about the choice.

She unlocked the door and they stepped into the kitchen. "I don't know how to tell you this, Andrew," she said, turning on the lights, "but England is our staunchest ally and closest friend."

"And is she still the most powerful nation on earth?"

"No," she said. "Actually, we are."

"In truth?"

"In truth."

"'Tis been a most enlightening day."

"Yes," she said, thinking about the remarkable happenings of the past twenty-four hours. "'Enlightening' just about says it all."

Their eyes met and a fine tingle of anticipation began to buzz against her breastbone and move up the length of her spine.

"Well," she said, straightening her shoulders, "it's late and I have so much to do tomorrow at the shelters." She flipped on the door alarm, then started toward the hall. "I'll see you in the morning."

He fell into step beside her. "I will see you safely to your room."

She nodded. It felt good and right and she loved him for thinking it necessary.

They climbed the stairs together, not speaking. It was only the second time they'd climbed those stairs, yet she felt as if it were part of a shimmering chain of events that bound them to each other. Which, of course, was romantic nonsense, but still . . .

"This house has seven bedrooms," she said when they reached her door. "Feel free to use whatever one you like."

"I will be here, as I was last night."

She felt heat rush to her cheeks. "You don't have to do that, Andrew. I'm perfectly safe. Please sleep in comfort."

He didn't answer, just watched her with those beautiful hazel eyes of his, watched her until she thought she would dissolve into a pool of longing.

"Well, good night," she said, hand on the doorknob. Her heart thundered so loudly she could barely hear the sound of her voice. "I'll see you in the morning."

Still he said nothing, and the heat building inside her body rose another degree. *Why are you looking at me like that? Are you going to kiss me?*

"Aye," he said, drawing her close. "I am."

She inhaled the smell of his skin.

He cupped her face in his hands.

She thought she would die of anticipation.

He wondered if pleasure could kill a man.

It was a simple kiss, as kisses went.

Their lips met.
Their breaths mingled.
It wasn't enough . . . yet it was everything.
And the miracle of it all was that they both knew it.

CHAPTER THIRTEEN

ANDREW WAS REPAIRING the window of the guest bathroom the next morning when the Negress lawyer arrived.

"Good day," the woman said, not extending her hand to Andrew. "Is Shannon around?"

"She is at the house with the women," he said, not looking up from his work. He felt uncomfortable and did not like feeling thus.

She ran her dark hand along the sash. "Nice work you're doing." He sensed that she was smiling at him in a most friendly fashion, but chose not to acknowledge it. "Is carpentry your hobby?"

He nodded, wielding the scraping implement across the peeling layer of paint.

"I'm into running," she said.

An odd statement and one for which he had no reply.

"You don't like me very much, do you?" she asked.

157

"I did not say that."

"You didn't have to, Mr. McVie. Your silence pretty much says it all. I'm going to go find Shannon. Have a good day."

Andrew waited until the sound of her car died away, then tossed the tool to the ground. There was nothing deferential about the woman. She neither courted him nor treated him as her inferior. In truth, she spoke to him as if they were equals before both man and God, and that unsettled him more than anything she could have done.

He thought of his days at Harvard, then tried to imagine a woman walking those hallowed halls in search of knowledge. The image simply would not come clear for him. The fact that the woman in question was a Negress made it all the more impossible for him to comprehend.

Shannon believed him a bigot in matters of race. He chose not to label himself that way. It was understood in his time that the division between slave and master was absolute. Even when a slave was released into freedom, that freedom bore a great similarity to all that had come before.

Such was not the case today. The descendants of slaves—men and women alike—were lawyers and doctors. Successful in their own right and on their own terms.

And in a world that Andrew had once considered his for the asking.

He wondered if there could be room enough for every man and woman to find power and success or if some fell by the wayside and were forgotten.

Nothing was as he'd imagined it would be. His dreams had been of a world where men lived like kings, where women stayed beautiful into their fourth decade and beyond, where he would instantly find meaning to a life that had long ago lost its sense of purpose.

"And where are you now, Andrew McVie?" he muttered. Repairing doors and scraping paint from windows. A common laborer performing menial chores for a woman with a cloud of soft dark hair and eyes the color of the sea.

A woman whose beautiful face was matched only by the beauty of her soul.

Back in his own time he would have known how to woo such a woman. There had been a time when he'd held a position of respect in the world, when the good people of Boston had hailed him in friendship when he passed.

A time when he might have deserved a woman like Shannon.

But that time was no more and he wondered if it would ever come again.

Three more families had arrived during the night. Each woman had a story to tell of abuse and fear and the loss of self-respect. Their stories cut across all economic and social barriers, and each story reminded Shannon anew of how important these shelters were.

By nine in the morning, Shannon spent thirty minutes on the phone with a vocational school in Bridgewater, called for a repairman to fix the air-conditioning in both guest houses and refereed a loud fight between two of Pat Delaney's kids. Karen Naylor stopped by on her way to court to see if any of the women were interested in obtaining restraining orders against their husbands, but she met with resistance all around. The young lawyer did a great deal of *pro bono* work for the shelter and was often as frustrated as Shannon at the reluctance many battered women showed when it came to prosecuting the men who'd beaten them.

"I saw your friend Andrew," Karen said over a cup of coffee back at Shannon's house. "He was scraping paint off your windows."

"He enjoys working with his hands," Shannon said smoothly.

"An attorney who works with his hands? Not very likely."

Shannon offered up a bland smile. "What can I say? He's a Renaissance man."

"So, is it serious?"

Shannon arched a brow. "What's with all the questions?"

Karen pushed her coffee cup away from her and sighed. "It's been a while since I've come across something like this. I guess I'd forgotten how it felt."

"I don't think he meant to be rude."

"Maybe not," said Karen, "but he succeeded admirably."

"I wish there was something I could say to make you feel better."

Karen patted her on the forearm in an easy, affectionate gesture. "Not your responsibility, Shannon. Believe it or not, you can't change the entire world."

"I'm doing my damnedest," Shannon said with a smile.

"Speaking of which," Karen said, checking her Filofax, "I have an opening at one o'clock, if you'd like to come in and take care of the paperwork for the foundation." She looked back up at Shannon. "You did read everything, didn't you?"

"I'll get around to it."

"By one o'clock?"

"I promise."

"Ms. Wylie, we need to talk."

Dakota peered around the side of the huge stack of books she'd been hiding behind since lunchtime. "What's up, Dr. Forsythe?"

"You were fifteen minutes late. You know how we feel about lateness."

"My alarm clock didn't work."

"And you went home early yesterday."

She thought for a second. "I had a headache." *Didn't I?* She couldn't remember exactly what she'd said, only that she couldn't wait to get to Shannon's and grab a minute alone with Andrew McVie.

Dr. Forsythe tapped one loafered foot impatiently. "I can't talk to you with you hiding behind that stack of books."

She forced a bright, lighthearted laugh and rose to her feet, brushing decades of dust from her flowing paisley skirt. "Whatever gave you the idea I was hiding? I'm cataloging, for heaven's sake. That's all." *Right, Dakota. Just pray your nose doesn't start to grow....*

"Mrs. Payton will be in to make her bequest this afternoon. I'd like you to join us in my office to witness her signature."

Her brows knit in a frown. "What time is she coming?"

He frowned right back at her. Not a good sign. "Three o'clock. I hope that doesn't interfere with your schedule, Ms. Wylie."

It did, but she didn't think Dr. Forsythe would care to hear about it. "I have a luncheon appointment but I should be back by three o'clock."

His frown degenerated into a scowl. "Your work ethic is deplorable, Ms. Wylie. I would give great thought to my attitude, were I you. You're up for review in November. It would pain me to have to put you on probation."

What else could you expect from a man with an aura the color of a faded puce bedspread? He stormed off down the hallway and Dakota dived back behind the stack of books. Of course, none of this should have surprised her. Last night she'd dreamed Dr. Forsythe would try to throw a monkey wrench into the works and he had, just like clockwork.

Which also meant she was about to find what she'd been looking for. Closing her eyes, she visualized the book. It was a small, slender volume with a navy cover, no dust jacket and a chip in the bottom right corner. The frontispiece was missing and half of page eleven, but the name "Andrew McVie" was in the second sentence of the first paragraph on page 127.

She could see it all. She could almost smell it. But, damnation, where was the book hiding? It wasn't every day a psychic got her hands on proof that her best pal's new boyfriend was a time traveler. She flipped through the titles. *Apothecaries in Colonial New Jersey... Artists of the Revolution... Declaration of Independence: Call to Arms... Forgotten Heroes.*

"*Forgotten Heroes,*" she whispered, grabbing the book from the shelf. Her hand tingled as she cradled the volume to her chest. This was it. She didn't even need to turn to page 127 to make sure. She felt as if she'd been plugged in to a giant source of electricity and all of that electricity was zapping through her body right that very minute.

Though why Andrew McVie should have such an uncommon effect on her was beyond Dakota. He was an average man in every way. Average looks. Average height. Average coloring. Nobody she'd look twice at on a given day. And yet when she'd clasped his hand she'd felt the same sensation of pure electricity that she felt right now as she held the book.

She took a deep breath and flipped to page 127. First paragraph. Second sentence. *Pay dirt.*

In an act of courage unequaled at that time in the War for Independence, Boston lawyer-turned-spy Andrew McVie staged a daring raid on British troops near Jockey Hollow during the winter of 1779-1780 and single-handedly saved two of the most important members of the Spy Ring from certain death when—

"Darn," she muttered. The bottom of the page was torn but it didn't matter. She had seen enough to know the truth.

Shannon reached Karen's office at one o'clock on the nose, and by one-thirty the papers had been signed, sealed and notarized.

"Okay," she said as she placed the cap back on her pen, "now let me get this straight. If I decided to pack a sarong and move to Borneo and live on coconuts, the shelters would survive."

"Not just survive," said Karen, handing the documents to her secretary to photocopy, "but thrive. You've done an extraordinary thing, Shannon. I don't know if you realize how extraordinary."

"It's only money," Shannon said with a shrug. "There's a limit to how many diamonds one woman can wear."

Karen shook her head. "No, kiddo, trust me when I say there's no limit. You're exceptional."

Shannon brushed away the compliment with a wave of her hand. "So how are we doing with the overflow facilities? Last month's fund-raiser brought in plenty of promises, but how many followed through with satellite shelters?" She had new facilities under construction in Gloucester, Monmouth, Middlesex and Warren counties, but more were needed. It was exciting to see her brainchild grow, but the need for her brainchild was a constant source of sorrow.

Karen recited a list of names, only a few of which were regulars in the society pages. "See what I mean?" the attorney said, leaning back in her chair. "The ones with money and empty houses can't be bothered."

"We'll see about that at the gala this weekend."

Karen grinned. "You're going to hit them hard?"

"Like a sledgehammer," Shannon said, grinning back. "A sophisticated, well-dressed sledgehammer."

"You realize you don't have to do any of this, don't you? That's what the foundation is for."

"It's easy to say no to a foundation," Shannon said. "It's a lot harder to say no to me."

"The question, of course, is *why* do you do it? I was thinking about this the other day and I realized how little I actually know about you."

"I do it because it needs to be done."

"But there's more to it, isn't there?" Karen persisted. "Something personal."

Shannon just smiled. "You've been reading too many mysteries, Karen. Some things are exactly as you think they are."

"Not you," said Karen. "There's a lot more to you than meets the eye."

Shannon grinned and stood. "I'd better head home."

An odd expression flitted across Karen's face. "So how serious is it with you and Andrew McVie?"

"What makes you think there's anything between us, serious or otherwise?"

"He's living with you. That's a first to my knowledge."

"He needed a roof over his head."

"So now you're running a shelter for displaced Scotsmen?"

Shannon sighed. There was no avoiding this particular issue. "I know he has his problems, but Andrew is a decent man."

"I'm sure he is," Karen said, not sounding convinced.

"He just has a few things to learn about race relations."

"Don't we all?" Karen said in a dry tone of voice. "Every time I think we're making real progress, I run into someone like your friend and realize how far we still have to go."

Shannon gathered up her purse and portfolio. "I'll work on it."

Karen rose from her desk and showed Shannon to the door. "Take care of yourself," Karen said, giving her a warm hug. "You give me hope."

Andrew swung open the door to the white closet in the kitchen and stared at the array of foodstuff arranged within. Cold milk in a tall blue box, sticks of butter wrapped in shiny paper, chicken eggs nestled in a receptacle with depressions made to cup them like a nest. Two large beefsteaks rested on a glass shelf. Each was wrapped in pliable material that he could see right through. He bent and pulled out a bin marked Vegetables and saw an assortment that could have fed the Continental army.

Shannon had told him to help himself to anything he desired but he found that with such bounty to choose from he was unable to choose anything at all. In truth, he would gladly trade the contents of the white closet she called a refrigerator for a tankard of ale, a loaf of bread and a leg of mutton.

Surely there must be some bread in the house. In his world even the poorest families had bread in the cupboard. In the back of the refrigerator, behind a large metal cylinder marked V-8, he found a package.

The bread was mushy and sweet and not at all what he was accustomed to, but it filled his stomach. He ate five slices and took a few gulps of cold, thin milk and was about to return to his work outside when the telephone shrieked.

He tried to remember what it was Shannon had done to make it work, but before he had a chance to do so, it stopped shrieking and the sound of Shannon's voice filled the room.

"Sorry I can't come to the phone right now," she said, "but if you leave your name and number at the tone, I'll get back to you as soon as I can. Thanks."

He had started to say something when a peeping noise sounded, followed by a voice he didn't recognize. "This is Terri from the cottage. The kids went for a walk in the woods over an hour ago and th-they're not back yet. Do you think maybe you could drive over and help us? Sorry to bother you but we don't know what to do. Thanks a lot."

"I can find them," he said out loud to the empty room. He had walked those woods just the night before. It would not be a difficult task to find the children in the full light of day.

A few minutes later he crossed the yard behind the house, walked past the rectangular pond, then headed into the woods near the silver maple trees. He recalled a grove of pines a few hundred paces away, and a lightning-struck sassafras tree at a diagonal from the grove. The spot where the hot-air balloon had landed was some distance from there but Andrew found it without any difficulty, then stood perfectly still for a few moments, gaining his bearings.

He turned in the direction of the shelters, narrowed his eyes and slowly scanned each inch of leaf-strewn ground for signs of the children. It didn't take long. The leaves were disturbed near the shelter side of the woods, and he found a thumb-sized piece of bright orange paper with the strange words Peanut Butter Cups printed across it. It smelled sweet, like a candy, and Andrew reasoned one of the children had discarded it along the way.

In truth, it was a simple task to follow their path. It surprised him that the mothers were unable to do so.

Footsteps in the dirt, crushed blades of grass, a copper coin glinting in the filtered sunlight.

Up ahead he heard the high-pitched sound of young voices and he picked up his pace. Moments later he stepped into a clearing and found the four children sitting on a log, morose expressions upon their faces.

"Oh, great," said one, looking up at him with disgust. "They sent the guy who talks funny."

"'Twould seem to me you would welcome my appearance," Andrew said, maintaining his temper in the face of such disrespect.

"Are you a cop?" the only girl in the group asked.

"I am a lawyer," Andrew said.

The children looked at each other and burst into merry laughter. Andrew did not much care for the sound of that laughter, for it seemed to hold an unpleasant edge within it.

The oldest boy met his eyes. "So what do you call a lawyer at the bottom of the ocean?" he asked.

"A good start!" the Negro boy next to him called out as the two slapped hands together.

"You find the death of a lawyer a topic of amusement?" Andrew asked, wondering about the nature of children.

"Lighten up," said the girl. "It's only a joke."

"I thought humor was the object of joke telling."

The Negro boy frowned. "You didn't think that was funny?"

"No," said Andrew, "'twas nothing funny about it." He could feel his spine growing rigid in true Boston fashion.

"But I got it from a book," said the first joke-teller. "They got about a hundred lawyer jokes."

Andrew's brows knit together in a scowl. "What is it about lawyers that creates such mirth?"

The children looked at each other, then at Andrew.

"Lawyers are greedy," said the girl.

"They're bad people," one of the boys said.

"My uncle is a lawyer," said the oldest boy, who was then treated to a series of rude noises and much laughter from the others.

Andrew crouched down near where they sat on a fallen log. "The function of a good lawyer is to maintain order in a civilized world."

"Tom Cruise was a lawyer in *The Firm*," said the girl.

"Tom Cruise is a weenie," said the Negro boy, to cheers from the other boys.

"He is not," said the girl.

Andrew, thoroughly confused by this conversation, rose to his feet. "Your mothers are worried. 'Tis time you returned and put their minds at ease."

"It's boring back there," said the oldest boy. "There's only one TV."

"They don't even have Nintendo," said the Negro boy.

"I wanted to bring my Barbies," said the girl they called Angela, "but my mom was in too big a hurry to let me pack them."

They started walking back toward the shelters with Andrew in the lead. He did not know the nature of Barbie or Nintendo but he did know bone-deep fear when he saw it. The children hid that fear behind a cloak of rudeness and hilarity but it was still visible for those who looked beneath the surface.

He thought of his own David and wondered how the boy would have felt if violence between his parents had been part of his daily life. His imagination could not conceive of such a burden on so frail a pair of shoulders.

"How did you find us?" Angela asked, hurrying to keep up with him. "Derek and Charlie got us lost in the woods so deep we didn't think we'd ever get out."

"'Tis no great feat," Andrew said. "You need only know-how and where to look."

Derek, the Negro boy, fell into step. "Everything looks the same in here. It's just a bunch of trees."

Andrew chuckled. "Pine, fir, sassafras, silver maple, holly—"

"I see Christmas trees," Derek said, "but the others still look the same."

Christmas trees? Andrew wondered what a tree and Christ's birthday could have in common.

Charlie, the oldest of the four, lagged behind with Scott, the youngest. "Who cares about this, anyway?" he asked in a belligerent tone of voice. "Only Boy Scouts know that stuff."

Andrew looked back at him. "You would not have been fearful had you known your way about."

"I wasn't scared."

"You were," said Andrew in an easy tone of voice.

"They're babies," Charlie said. "They were scared, but I wasn't."

"You were, too," said Scott.

"Yeah," said Angela. "You wanted your mommy."

"'Tis normal to feel afraid in a strange place," Andrew said, "but the more you understand about the things around you, the less afraid you will be."

Angela looked up at him and smiled. "I'm afraid of the dark," she confided. "Daddy took out the belt last night 'cause he caught me sleeping with the light on."

Andrew caught sight of a deep purple bruise peering out from beneath the half sleeve of her bodice. In his mind's eye he saw the little girl, crouched in fear, as her father made to hit her. What kind of world was this that a child should bear the marks of violence upon her person? He could not help but wonder if the seeds for this violence had been sown in his own time.

And if there was something that could have been done to save little girls like Angie—or women like Shannon—from knowing a man's rage.

The little girl looked up at him, considering, then took his hand. They didn't speak, which was just as well, because the lump in Andrew's throat made words impossible.

CHAPTER FOURTEEN

SHANNON ARRIVED HOME from Karen's office feeling tired and vaguely depressed. Not that she regretted signing the papers that secured the future for the shelters. Knowing that her fortune would be put to good use was a deep and abiding source of happiness.

But it was something else, something more elemental, that had triggered the sense of time passing quickly. Too quickly for her taste. She felt as if she'd lived a lifetime in the past forty-eight hours, as if everything she said and did and felt had more meaning now than at any other time in her life.

From the start she'd felt connected to Andrew in a way that defied logic, almost as if their souls were linked together in some strange form of communication. Then, in the space of a heartbeat, she'd stopped hearing his voice within her heart. Was this how it would be then, she wondered, a gradual pulling away until he left her behind to start a new life on his own?

172

Sighing, she walked up the driveway and around the corner of the house toward the French doors in the back. She had her hand on the doorknob, about to go inside, when something caught her eye and she turned. Andrew was hard at work at the far corner of the yard beyond the pool, and at a distance behind him sat four of the kids from the shelter. Not that she saw the children. All she saw was Andrew.

He was magnificent.

She stood stock-still, car keys dangling from her fingers, unable to draw a breath.

Utterly magnificent.

There were no other words for the sight of him, stripped to the waist as he split firewood in the backyard. She stepped beneath the shade of the silver maple trees and watched as the muscles in his back and shoulders flexed with each powerful swing of his ax.

This was the real thing, she thought as hunger sprang to life deep in her belly. Bone-melting, heartstopping desire. She closed her eyes against a wave of pure heat radiating outward from the center of her being.

This was nothing she'd sought, nothing she'd expected to be part of her existence, but there it was in all of its elemental glory. The magical, life-affirming need to join with another human being and cast your lot with the future. She smiled to herself. Or with the past, as the case may be.

There has to be a way to make this work, she thought, watching him. She had wealth and position and influence. She could create for him a life that would surpass his wildest dreams if he would only let her.

The squeal of brakes brought her out of her reverie. *Please, not another emergency,* she thought as she hurried back toward the driveway to see who'd arrived. Sometimes they went weeks without seeing a soul, then all hell would break loose, the way it had last night.

She rounded the corner of the house in time to see Dakota leap from her battered '72 Mustang, holding a book aloft.

"Where is he?" Dakota called out as Shannon approached.

"In the backyard."

"Good," said Dakota. "This is important. I don't have time to faint right now."

"Very funny," Shannon said as prickles of apprehension nipped at the back of her neck.

Dakota glanced around. "Let's talk inside. This isn't the kind of thing you want anyone to overhear."

Shannon led the way into the kitchen, then leaned against the counter and looked at her friend. "So, what's with the book?"

"Page 127," Dakota said, handing the volume to Shannon. "First paragraph, second sentence."

Shannon checked the title. *"Forgotten Heroes."* Her hands began to tremble and she prayed Dakota wouldn't notice.

"Open it," Dakota urged, her voice high with excitement. "There's something I think you should know."

"This isn't another one of those New Age books about a man who saved the world with squash blossoms or something, is it?" *You know what it is, Shannon. This has something to do with Andrew....*

Dakota looked wounded. "I come to you with news that can change your life and you make a joke."

Shannon started to open the book, then handed it back to Dakota. "I don't think I want to look at this."

"He's from the past," Dakota said, pushing the book back to Shannon.

"That's ridiculous." She pushed the book back toward Dakota.

"Page 127," Dakota said, practically leaping around the room with excitement. "It's all right there."

"I don't know how to break this to you, Dakota, but people don't time travel. That only happens in the movies."

"It happens," Dakota said sagely. "We just don't hear about it."

"Uh-huh," said Shannon, striving for nonchalance. "And Martians are working at K mart."

"What you know about K mart could fit on the head of a pin." Dakota wagged a stern finger under Shannon's nose. "Just because you don't understand something is no reason to make fun of it."

"Sit down," Shannon said, gesturing toward a chair. When in doubt, fall back on hospitality. "It's hot as blazes outside. I'll pour us some iced tea."

"Nice try," said Dakota, "but no dice."

"You're not going to let up on me, are you?"

"Absolutely not."

"I know what this is going to be," Shannon said as she grabbed the book back from Dakota and thumbed through the first few pages. "Some kind of crazy allusion to a guy with a Scots accent who—" She stopped, looked up, drew a deep breath, then looked down again at the torn page.

In an act of courage unequaled at that time in the
War for Independence, Boston lawyer-turned-spy
Andrew McVie staged a daring raid on British
troops near Jockey Hollow during the winter of
1779-1780 and single-handedly saved—

"Shannon?" Dakota touched her arm. "Are you
okay?"

"No," said Shannon, sinking to the floor, "I don't
think I am." Knowing Andrew was from the past was
one thing. Seeing that fact right there in black and
white was something else altogether.

"Are you going to faint?" Dakota asked.

"I never faint. You're the one who faints."

Dakota crouched next to her. "Your aura's looking
a little pale."

"Leave my aura out of this."

"You knew, didn't you?"

"About my aura?"

"About McVie. He told you, didn't he?"

Shannon struggled to regain her wits. "Andrew
McVie is hardly an uncommon name. There must have
been hundreds of Andrew McVies alive back then."

"Check out the painting on the next page. If that's
not McVie I'll turn in my crystal ball."

With great trepidation Shannon turned the page and
found a reproduction of an eighteenth-century painting that depicted the Battle of Princeton. "I don't see
anything."

Dakota leaned over her shoulder. "Right there," she
said, pointing toward a figure in the lower left-hand
corner. "That's him."

Shannon looked. No doubt about it. That was Andrew right down to the stubborn jaw and muscular torso. "They say everybody has a twin."

"Did you see the caption?" Dakota asked. "It says his identity was kept secret until the end of the war so he could continue sneaking around, doing all sorts of heroic things."

Shannon was beyond coherent thought. Her brain felt as if it had suddenly turned to mush. *Dakota's got you dead to rights.*

"That's why I fainted, you know," Dakota went on. "The guy has a force field you wouldn't believe. It's like he's carrying two centuries of baggage along with him."

She grabbed Dakota's hand, all pretense abandoned. "You can't tell anyone about this," she begged.

"Of course not," Dakota said with indignation. "What kind of person do you think I am?"

"And you won't tell any of your psychic pals, or your mentor, or Dr. Forsythe."

"What about the *National Enquirer* while you're at it? I might be able to get a few thousand for the story." Dakota lifted her chin. "You insult me, Shannon. I'm not an opportunist."

Shannon rested her head in her hands. "I know you're not, but this is important. If it got out that Andrew's a time traveler, we'd be signing his death warrant. The media would eat him alive."

"I agree," said Dakota. She leaned closer to Shannon and lowered her voice. "So, how did he get here?"

"Remember that hot-air balloon you saw him dragging across the backyard yesterday morning?"

Dakota nodded.

"That's how."

"You're kidding."

"No, I'm not kidding. He landed in the woods during the balloon festival, just like I told you."

Dakota frowned. "But that's not possible. The first hot-air balloon flight wasn't until 1783...and it was in France or some place like that."

"I can't explain it. I can only tell you what happened." She hesitated, then decided to go for broke. "He—he said he made friends with a couple who time-traveled back last summer."

"What were his friends' names?"

"I don't know," Shannon said. "Radcliffe, Rutledge. I think her name was Emilie."

"This is so exciting!" Dakota grabbed Shannon's hand and tried to pull her to her feet. "Let's go tell him about the book. I'm dying to see his reaction. I mean, the man is living history—"

"No!"

"No? You *have* to tell him about it. Wouldn't you like to see your name in some history book and know you influenced the course of events?"

Shannon held firm.

"Oh," said Dakota, the light dawning. "He can't read, is that it? Don't worry, I'll teach him. What's one more student?"

"He was— I mean, he *is* a lawyer, Dakota. He can read."

"So what's the problem?"

"This." Shannon pointed to the date.

"The winter of 1779-1780," read Dakota. "So?"

She met Dakota's eyes. "Andrew left his world in August 1776."

"Time is fluid," said Dakota after a moment. "It might've happened."

"Time isn't *that* fluid," Shannon shot back. "Besides, wouldn't he remember doing something heroic in the middle of a blizzard in the middle of a war?"

"But it's here in black and white," Dakota said. "How do you explain it?"

"You're the psychic. I was hoping you could explain it."

"Maybe he goes back in time again."

Shannon felt a sharp stab of pain deep inside her chest. "Give me that book." She grabbed it from her friend and headed for the library.

"What are you doing?" Dakota ran after her. "That's museum property."

"Not anymore it isn't."

"Shannon! I'm in enough trouble with Dr. Forsythe. It's bad enough I took the book out of the building. He already thinks I'm a flake. If he finds out the book's missing, I'm out of a job."

"I'll pay for it." Shannon strode across the library and climbed the rolling ladder in the far corner of the room. "Plutarch's *Lives*. That's the ticket." She dropped *Forgotten Heroes* behind the tome. From the looks of the dust, Plutarch's *Lives* hadn't been touched in aeons. For once she was glad her cleaning service wasn't as thorough as they claimed they were.

She climbed back down the ladder, feeling quite pleased with herself until she saw the look on Dakota's face.

"I can't believe you did that," Dakota said.

"I'll write you a check," Shannon said defiantly. "I'll write you two checks. I'll buy you a house in Bermuda. Whatever it takes to keep you quiet."

"You don't look like yourself."

"I don't feel like myself."

Dakota narrowed her eyes and peered at Shannon. "Your aura's changing again. I swear it's Day-Glo orange now."

Because I'm doing something for me, Shannon thought. *Because I've waited all my life to find someone like Andrew and I can't let him go.* "You're not going to tell Andrew, are you?"

"I won't have to," Dakota said, placing a hand on Shannon's forearm. "This can't last, Shannon. This isn't his destiny. His future is somewhere else."

"You're wrong." Shannon backed away from her friend. "We make our own destinies, and this is where he wants to be. It was his choice, Dakota. Not mine."

"That ain't gonna work." Scott looked up at Andrew. "You need a power screwdriver."

"It will work," said Andrew, considering the eaves of Shannon's house. He had not the slightest notion as to what a power screwdriver was, nor would he ask any of the children who had been watching his every movement since he found them in the woods. There was something unseemly about a man of thirty-three years seeking counsel of a child.

His attempt to engage their interest in physical work had thus far been for naught. They seemed strangely content to sit and watch him move about as if he were performing for their amusement. He was reminded of the moving-picture cabinet in Shannon's house that thus far held little appeal for him.

"Where are your safety glasses?" asked Charlie, the oldest. "That guy on TV says you gotta wear them all the time."

"That guy don't know nothing," said blond-haired Angela. "My cousin's got a power saw in his basement and I never seen him wear glasses."

"That's 'cause he's stupid."

"Is not."

"Is."

"Is n—"

"Sweet Jesus!" Andrew roared. "Lend some assistance where it is needed and cease that infernal racket *now!*" Four young faces stared up at him, mouths agape, but nobody moved. Andrew pointed toward Charlie. "You will hold the ladder while I climb. And you—" he singled out Angela "—will fetch nails for me. And the rest of you will stack the wood."

"I don't know how to stack wood," said Derek.

"'Tis a simple enough task," he said.

The boy frowned. "D'ya think there are any spiders in the wood?"

"I cannot say with certainty but the wood is freshly cut. I do not believe spiders have found it yet."

"Okay," said Derek. "Then I'll do it."

"Good decision," said Andrew, biting back a smile. He did not hold a great deal of affection for spiders either.

He felt naught but affection for Derek. His black skin mattered not at all.

But Derek is still a boy, a voice inside him spoke. *How will you feel when he is a man and vying with you for a place in the world?*

He thought of his reaction to Shannon's friend Karen. Had he responded solely to her race and gender, or had there been something else at work, a sense that in this world he might not measure up to their standards of success? The idea was one he did not wish to pursue.

The children set to work with speed if not enthusiasm. The boys were dressed in a most peculiar fashion—baggy pants rolled up to midcalf, shoes the size of rowboats with the laces untied, strange caps with the bill worn in back. The girl wore short pants in a bright green color and a half-sleeved shirt that was many sizes too large for her small body.

They looked strange to his eyes, yet in many ways little had changed in two hundred years. Children still reacted to a strong leader and to discipline.

"Is this right?" Derek called out. He was lugging a good-sized log to the stack already begun near the back door.

"'Tis most right," Andrew said, climbing the ladder.

"You talk funny," said Charlie, holding the ladder. "Are you English?"

"I was born in Boston." He could not remember being as comfortable in the company of adults as these children seemed to be. To speak so freely to a man old enough to be your father—he could not imagine doing so as a child.

"They talk strange in Boston."

He reached down for a handful of nails. "They talk strange in New Jersey."

"Nah," said Charlie. "We talk normal."

"'Tis a matter of perspective."

Angela squinted up at him. "What's that?"

"Perspective is how you look at things." Across the yard Derek struggled to lift a second log.

"Take a smaller one," Andrew called out. "Better two trips than to overtax yourself."

Derek nodded then did as Andrew suggested, and Andrew found himself sharply reminded of his son. David had been much like that boy, eager for direction. Eager for guidance.

Eager for approval.

Aye, there is the rub. There had been so little time for them to spend together—six short years—and most of those six years Andrew had squandered in the pursuit of his career. Ofttimes weeks would pass when he did not see his son, weeks in which the boy changed in ways Andrew could but wonder at when he returned home.

His eyes swam with tears. He blinked rapidly and willed them to stop. He had done the impossible and traveled through time to a world two hundred years in the future, but he had never found the way to tell his son that he'd loved him and been proud of him.

"'Tis a fine job you're doing," he said to the children. "All of you."

"Thanks," said the one holding the ladder, "but now the gutter's crooked. You gotta do it over again."

Andrew looked, then looked again. "You are right."

"Yeah," said the boy, grinning. "I figured you'd wanna know."

"'Tis always better to know," he said, using the back of the hammer to remove the nails.

"Not everything," said the boy. "My mom says what you don't know can't hurt you."

"Your mother is wrong," Andrew said with conviction, thinking of a little boy who lived on only in his heart.

It was what a man didn't know that had the power to hurt most deeply.

CHAPTER FIFTEEN

DAKOTA ROUNDED UP the kids and took them back to the shelters a little before five o'clock. Shannon had always marveled at her friend's ability to relate to children without talking down to them, a particularly tricky proposition when you were dealing with children from families torn apart by abuse. Before the night was over Dakota would have not only determined their reading levels, but she would have won their hearts, as well.

Shannon wandered about the house for a while. She flipped on the news, watched a bit of it, then turned off the television. She couldn't concentrate on a magazine, didn't feel like listening to music. Actually she found it impossible to do anything but think about the book she had hidden in the library. How could she think of anything else with the battle raging between her heart and her conscience?

She sank onto the bottom step in the foyer and rested her head in her hands. The vision of him, shirtless in the fierce sunshine, burned against her eyelids. *Is this what you want for him, Shannon? Is he going to spend the rest of his days fixing loose gutters and splitting firewood?*

He'd been there only a handful of days, she reasoned with herself. You couldn't expect him to leap into a new life with career and future intact. Those things took time, even under more normal circumstances. Granted, he couldn't return to practicing law but there had to be something he could do, something important and fulfilling. Something that would keep him by her side forever.

There's nothing wrong with manual labor. Some people would say it's more honorable than practicing law.

But there was a limit to how many repairs he could do on her house. She had a brief, ridiculous vision of herself as Penelope, the wife of Odysseus, but instead of unraveling a tapestry each night, she broke windows and pulled down gutters—all so Andrew would have work to do the next morning.

You're a rich woman. You could start a business and make Andrew the CEO. He'd have a job and self-respect and—

"You idiot," she muttered, dragging her hands through her tangled hair. Who was she kidding? He was a proud man. A situation like that would be a sure recipe for disaster somewhere down the line.

He had no identification—good grief, the only driver's license he was likely to ever have belonged to Emilie Crosse, and she was alive and well and living in

1776. Any records pertaining to his existence were centuries old.

Think, Shannon. There has to be a solution. She'd created a new life for herself, albeit with a little help from the Feds. She'd overcome the horror of her marriage and found a way for other women to benefit from her experience. Surely she could find a place in her world for an extraordinary man like Andrew McVie.

But whatever she found, whether it was a position as a CEO or day work as a laborer, was there anything in her world that could compare to being a hero in the world he'd left behind?

"Dakota's wrong," she said, rising to her feet. Andrew had told her that according to Emilie and Zane there was no further mention of him in history books after the summer of 1776. What Dakota had found had to be a mistake . . . or maybe a coincidence.

For all Shannon knew someone had appropriated the name Andrew McVie and performed one lone act of heroism that managed to get itself reported in one lone history book. Big deal. It didn't prove anything.

The only thing she knew with certainty was that Andrew McVie was in her world and part of her life and she intended to do everything in her power to keep him there.

Shannon went outside around six o'clock.

"I'm going to fire up the barbecue and cook up juicy, politically incorrect steak," she called up to Andrew. "Do you like yours rare, medium or well?"

"'Tis still daylight," he said, wiping his arm across his forehead. "I will continue to work until dark."

"Those eaves can wait another day," she said lightly, watching him replace a board.

"They cannot," said Andrew. The pounding of the hammer provided a counterpoint to his words.

"Is something wrong, Andrew?"

"A strange question." He pounded in another nail. "'Tis nothing wrong."

"You don't seem like yourself." *Is that your guilty conscience speaking, Shannon?*

"Nightfall approaches," he said, "and I have much to do."

"If you change your mind, all I have to do is toss another steak on the grill."

But he didn't change his mind. Not that she really thought he would. The set of his jaw told her that more clearly than any words he could have spoken.

Something has changed, she thought later as she ate her steak on the patio and watched him work. For the past two days he had shadowed her movements, been part and parcel of her every waking moment. And now everything was different and she couldn't say why. It wasn't as if he knew about the book Dakota had found, for that was still safely hidden in the library, far away from curious eyes.

She speared a lettuce leaf from her salad plate and considered him. There was a barrier between them now, a sense of separateness that hadn't been there before.

She sat straight up in her chair, fork poised halfway to her mouth. She no longer heard his voice within her heart. That was the difference. The almost mystical connection between them that had swept away her sense of caution had been replaced by the sense that this interlude was only temporary.

Damn Dakota and her psychic nonsense. She pushed her plate away and sat staring out toward the pool. If Dakota's fortune-telling skills were half as good as she claimed, the woman would be picking lotto numbers, not working three jobs and wearing thrift-shop clothing.

Wonderful, Shannon. Now you're turning into a bitch as well as a liar.

She loved Dakota dearly and knew there was nothing phony or self-serving about her otherworldly talents. Shannon had seen too many of her friend's predictions come true to consign her to a nine hundred number on late-night TV.

But Dakota couldn't be right this time. Shannon was willing to fight the gods to keep this one chance at happiness from slipping through her fingers. Fate had brought Andrew to her and she wasn't about to let fate take him away.

Not in this lifetime or any other.

Andrew ceased work at dusk. He collected the hand tools scattered about the ground and was carrying them into the garage when Shannon appeared in the gathering darkness. She wore white pants that left her legs bare and a yellow bodice that revealed her midriff to his eyes. Her feet were bare, and even in the blue light of dusk he could see the pale pink color gleaming up at him.

He caught the scent of her perfumed skin on the soft night air, and a fierce hunger came to life deep inside his body.

"You must be hungry," she said, following him into the garage.

"Aye," he said. "The smell of beef on the fire has that effect."

"There's salad and corn ready now." She watched him as he placed the hand tools in the receptacle. "The steak'll be ready by the time you're finished."

He looked at her sharply. "You are a rich woman," he said. "How is it you do your own chores?"

"I don't always," she said. "Mildred usually cooks for me. Didn't I tell you about Mildred and Karl?"

"Aye," he said. "Still, I cannot imagine another woman of your wealth performing menial chores for a stranger."

Her sigh floated toward him and he wished he could reach out and capture it and hold it close to his heart. "I enjoy cooking, Andrew. Especially when there's somebody around to appreciate it."

They had turned to leave the garage when Shannon stopped abruptly.

"Sweet Jesus," Andrew said.

"The balloon." Her voice was little more than a whisper. "What on earth—?"

The covering he had placed over the balloon and basket had slipped off, revealing a most disturbing sight. The silk fabric of the balloon was faded almost white, while the basket appeared to be disintegrating before his very eyes. They looked as if they had traveled through the centuries and scarcely survived the journey.

The thought came to him that what had been done could not be undone, for without the balloon and its magic fire he was destined to live out the remainder of his days in Shannon's world.

"Poor Andrew." She placed a hand against his arm, and he felt her touch move through his body like a brushfire. "We'll find a way to make this work."

"Aye," he said. "I made my choice when I climbed into the basket, and I do not regret it."

"I hope you never will."

Will you still feel thusly in a month, lass, or will you wish me gone when I wish with all my heart to stay?

She met his eyes and he watched as a look of pure joy lit her lovely face from within. He did not know what had caused her to look at him with such wonder, but he knew that he would carry the memory with him to his grave.

Andrew ate as he did most things, with appetite and enthusiasm. After he finished, Shannon cleared the table then suggested they watch television in the den while they shared coffee and dessert.

"You still don't seem very enthusiastic about television," Shannon observed as they clicked past a "Cheers" rerun.

"'Tis like reading a book but without the challenge," he said. "There is no room for the imagination."

"Imagination is in short supply these days," Shannon said. "Most people want their entertainment as simple and easy to digest as possible." She channel-surfed until she landed on "I Love Lucy." "Now this is required viewing if you want to understand American culture."

It was a classic Lucy episode. Ricky was putting on a show at the Tropicana and Lucy wanted to be part of it.

"I do not understand his reluctance," Andrew said. "Why does he not grant her wish?"

Shannon grinned. "You've heard her sing. Lucy has no talent, that's why."

Andrew considered her statement for a moment. "I have seen no evidence of singing ability from Ricky Ricardo."

Her grin widened. "I think 'Babalu' is a masterpiece."

"Lucy is a comely lass," Andrew went on, a gleam of amusement in his hazel eyes. "She would be an asset to her husband."

"Another sexist statement! You must stop seeing women as adjuncts to men. We're free and independent and we don't need men to provide for us."

"I am a product of my time. I make no apologies for it."

"If you're going to make a life in the twentieth century, you have to adjust." She watched as he devoured a chocolate chip cookie in an exceedingly male fashion, and felt a delicious tingle of excitement. *You're in bad shape, Shannon. Getting turned on by a man eating cookies.*

"Turned on?" Andrew asked.

"Turned on?" she echoed.

"You do not know the meaning of the phrase, either?"

"I mean— It's just—" She stopped and took a deep breath. "We turn on lights and televisions and radios."

"That is not what you meant."

"How do you know what I meant? I don't recall saying anything like that."

"You did," he persisted. "I heard the words most clearly."

"I don't think so."

"Aye, Shannon." His voice grew lower, his tone caressing. "They were your words and I heard them inside my heart."

"I don't think we should talk about this." Talking might make it go away and that was the last thing she wanted to happen. Just a few hours ago she'd thought that magical connection was lost to her forever. But then, in the dim light of her garage, she had heard his thoughts as clearly as she heard her own and it seemed as if someone had handed her back her heart.

How could there be any doubt that she'd made the right decision when she hid the book Dakota had found?

He wanted to stay with her.

In her time. In her world.

When two people were so attuned that their thoughts were one, it had to mean their destinies were one, as well.

"You have experienced it also," Andrew said. "I know by the way you look at me, the things you say."

"It happened that very first night." She glanced away. "Yesterday your thoughts were closed to me until—"

"I know," he said. "It was thus for me, as well."

She met his eyes again, seeing beyond his physical self to some place deeper, more complex, more wonderful. "I have never felt this way before."

"Not with your husband?"

She shook her head. "I loved Bryant, but it was different." The love she'd had for her first husband had been built upon a foundation of family expectation and naiveté, and when harsh reality showed its face she'd accepted the blame the way other women accepted compliments. "Surely you loved Elspeth."

"With my entire heart," he said simply. "But when she left this world she no longer loved me."

"You can't know that," Shannon said, wishing she could ease his pain as he had eased hers.

"Aye," he said. "I can. On the last day I saw her, she said the love she'd held for me had died and only duty remained." His voice broke and he cleared his throat. "She was a good woman. She deserved more than I had been able to provide."

"The world hasn't changed very much in two hundred years," Shannon said after a moment. "We still make the same mistakes." Their gazes met. "And we still hope for a happy ending."

"As in a child's story?" he asked, a slight smile playing at the corners of his mouth.

"Is that so awful? Where is it written that the things we wish for can't come true? You wished to travel to the future and you did it, Andrew. And I—" She stopped abruptly as hot color flooded her cheeks.

He captured her hands in his. "What is it you wished for, Shannon?"

"You," she whispered. "I wished for you."

CHAPTER SIXTEEN

WORDS.

Plain words, simple in their meaning.

But with those words the world was his and everything in it.

Andrew's heart soared with joy as he drew Shannon into his arms. She was so small against him, her frame so delicate and womanly, that the need to protect her against the world battled his own fierce need to possess her right there on the floor as if she were a—

He pushed her away, struggling to douse the fires raging throughout his body.

"Andrew?" Her aqua eyes were wide, her lips soft and pink. Had she no knowledge what such a look could do to a man? "Is something wrong?"

"Aye," he managed with great difficulty. "You have an uncommon effect upon me."

"I'm glad."

Her words puzzled him. It was not the reaction he had expected. "That does not offend you?"

"It pleases me," she said in a voice that promised wonders beyond knowing, "for you have an uncommon effect upon me, as well."

"It is not my wish to cause you alarm."

"I know," she whispered, laying her hand against his cheek. "I think I've known that from the first moment."

"In my own time I would not hesitate, but here—" He shook his head. "I fear the rules of courtship are much changed."

"Court me, Andrew. Court me the way you would have if we'd met in your world."

He clasped her hand in his, marveling in the fragile bones that hid the strength of ten.

"'Twould be a slow and careful wooing." He bent his head forward and raised her hand to his lips. "There would be much time for walking together—" he pressed his lips against the palm of her hand "—and for social intercourse." He closed her fingers to hold the kiss. "And for watching the fire dance on a cold winter's night."

Her eyes seemed to grow darker as she watched him. "But it's summertime . . . what did you do in the summertime?"

"This."

She fit against him as if she'd been fashioned for his pleasure, and he knew that his pleasure had grown most apparent as she moved closer. His hands spanned her waist, that naked expanse of skin that had tantalized him the first time he saw her standing by the rectangular pond, and he feared his control would not withstand the temptation.

"A slow wooing," Shannon said in a dreamy voice. "Exactly how slow would that be?"

"Many months," he said as she linked her arms behind his neck. "A man might court his lady a year or better before—"

"Too long." She kissed the side of his neck. "We move a lot faster today."

"'Tis true," he said, blood rushing southward. "I have seen the speed at which you move."

"Life is short," she said. "That's one of the things we've learned."

"If my life ended at this moment, Shannon, I would die a happy man because I would be with you."

She pressed a kiss to the line of his jaw. "I'll bet you say that to all the girls you drop in on."

"I am not a flatterer. I speak what is on my mind and in my heart."

"I know," she said, placing her index finger against his lips. "I have heard all you have to say but now I want you to be quiet and kiss me."

Her words were powerful and they had a most amazing effect upon his person. He blazed to life, hungry for her yet painfully aware of his own strength.

"I am a...passionate man," he said bluntly. "I have no desire to cause you any discomfort." He would rather die celibate than hurt her in any way.

"I know you won't hurt me." She sounded surprised that he would say such a thing.

He thought of the pain she had suffered at her husband's hands, and persisted. "There are times when I do not know my own strength."

"I'll be the first one to remind you."

He cupped her face in his hands and met her eyes. "I have not been with a woman in a long while. I may be less than you expect."

"Never," she said, her voice fierce. "You are already more than I've ever dreamed."

He claimed her mouth with his, but in truth he knew that it was Shannon who was claiming him, heart and soul and body.

Somewhere in the background Lucy and Ethel were cooking up another harebrained scheme, but Shannon didn't hear a word.

Andrew swept her up into his powerful arms and, not breaking their kiss, carried her upstairs to her bedroom on the second floor. The door was ajar and he kicked it the rest of the way open with the tip of his boot and a thrill of recognition rocketed through her body. Without breaking stride he crossed the room toward the four-poster bed beneath the window and an instant later they were tangled together on the feather mattress.

He kissed her hungrily, as if he couldn't get his fill of the taste and smell of her. His naked hunger brought her to a fever pitch and she moved against him, running her hands along his back, down to his waistband, sliding her fingers beneath his shirt until she found his smooth, warm skin.

Was it possible to get drunk on the feel of a man's body beneath your palms? That powerful swell of muscle, the heat, the knowledge that you were playing with fire and looking to burn.

He spanned her waist with his hands, intoxicated by her smell, the satiny feel of her skin, the knowledge that all that separated him from paradise were a few thin layers of fabric and a supreme act of will.

They lay together on their sides, legs entwined, breaths mingling, hearts pounding wildly. She ran her hands up the length of his back and he feared he would lose all control.

"Nay," he muttered, moving away from her on the soft and welcoming mattress. "I am in danger of reaching the end before we have the chance to begin."

She reached for him, urging him closer by the look in her eyes, the soft smile on her beautiful mouth. With a groan he pushed her back against the mattress and straddled her hips. He found the closure of her short trousers but his fingers could not work it open.

"It's called a snap." Her voice was husky, different. He watched as she pulled the two pieces of fabric apart.

He fingered a tiny metal tab that waved just beneath the snap. "And this?"

"A zipper." She sounded unbearably alluring to his ears. "You pull down on it."

He did as she instructed, easing the tab over the gentle curve of her belly, lower, then lower still until he could feel her heat. "A zipper," he said as the garment fell open, exposing a small band of cream-colored lace to his gaze. "A new invention?"

"Not that new."

"'Tis amazing." He bent lower over her body, breathing deeply of her scent, then pressed his mouth against her belly.

She made a sound deep in her throat as he traced a design with his tongue. He tugged at the scrap of lace with his teeth. "A world of wondrous inventions."

She moved restlessly beneath him as he stripped her of her outer garment. His breath caught sharply in his throat as he gazed upon her shapely legs and hips, clad in naught save that wisp of lace so sheer he could see the thick, dark curls covering her mound. He cupped her with his hand, felt her wet heat against his palm, imagined burying his length deep inside her body and hearing her cry out as she found her release.

Shannon reached again for him, tugging at his shirt, fumbling with the buttons, baring his chest to her hands and mouth. She pressed her face against him at the point where his arm met his torso and drew in a deep, shuddering breath that he felt in all parts of his body. She seemed to find great pleasure in the sight and touch of him, and his own pleasure multiplied in response.

Her blouse was fastened with ordinary buttons and he quickly slipped them through the buttonholes, only to discover more cream-colored lace, this time hiding her breasts from view. But not entirely. He saw the dusky shadow of her nipples beneath the filmy barrier and with trembling hand he drew a finger across curve, then valley, then curve again.

"What is this called?" he asked, hooking a finger under a strap.

"A bra," she said. "Actually, a brassiere. The purpose is—"

"The purpose is plain," he said, "even to me."

Less plain, however, was how to remove the brassiere from her person.

"Having trouble?" she asked.

"'Tis a devilishly puzzling garment." He ran his hands beneath the stretchy fabric.

"Most boys can open a bra before they're fifteen," she said with an innocent smile.

"Are you implying I am less skilled than a child?" he asked, growing most annoyed with his lack of ability.

"You're a resourceful man," she said. "I have no doubt you'll figure this out."

And when he did she laughed, a soft, throaty, woman's laugh that pleased him beyond measure.

"See? I told you that you were a resourceful man," she said with obvious delight.

"Aye." His own delight was obvious, as well. The brassiere was still warm from her body. Indeed, it seemed to retain her shape with its own. He gazed down at her, his blood heating with a need that went beyond desire. She was small but beautifully made, as if an artist had created her from a dream of splendor. A dream he'd never dared dream before now.

He rose from the bed and removed shoes and stockings, then unfastened his trousers. The undergarments—briefs, she had called them—were an embarrassment and he felt more himself when he was naked on the bed with her.

"Come to me, mistress," he said, opening his arms.

She smiled, recognizing the endearment, and did as he bid her to do. There was nothing hesitant about her demeanor, nor anything coy. She seemed as eager for what was to come as he, without artifice or apology. He had never before known a woman with such a capacity for joy, and the sensation brought him close to the edge.

She lay at an angle across his body, her breasts flattened against the hard wall of his chest. He held her by

the hips, moving her slowly—wonderfully, deli-
ciously—against his arousal until she thought she
would faint with longing.

But it was more than longing. It was hunger, a hunger that went so deep, cut so close to the bone, that she
couldn't hide from it even if she wanted to. The hunger slashed through her defenses and exposed her
beating heart, the heart she'd thought locked away
forever.

I can take no more, Andrew. His cadence had
somehow become her own. *Now . . . please, now. . . .*

He slid his hand inside the leg band of her panties
and stroked her. "You are certain?" he asked.

She was beyond speech, beyond thought, beyond
everything but the moment—and the man.

He inched her panties down over her hips, her
thighs, then slid them off and tossed them to the floor.
"Nothing will happen that you do not wish to happen," he said as he poised himself over her body. "It
is for you to say."

"Yes," she whispered, opening her arms wide. "I
say yes."

With a groan he covered her body with his own. His
powerful erection pressed hard and fiery and magnificent against her belly. She cupped his face with her
hands and willed him to know that she belonged to him
alone, that traveling through time was nothing compared to the miracle of finding love when you'd given
up hope.

He fit himself between her legs. She felt him press
against her wet heat. She arched upward. He thrust
forward. She opened for him, surrounded him, met his
passion with more love and joy and wonder than she'd
ever believed one woman could hold inside her heart.

*   *   *

She gave him her body, but more than that she gave him back his soul. He knew the precise moment it happened. When he entered her, her aqua eyes opened wide and she looked at him, watched his face as he sank deeper into her willing softness, and she smiled. Smiled as if he'd somehow managed to gather up the moon and the stars and place them at her feet.

He had been with many women in his life. He knew that the moment of euphoria he found in a woman's arms never lasted the night. With the cold light of dawn came the realization that he was alone, had always been alone, would be alone until he drew his last breath.

But this time it was different. He pleasured her through the darkest hours of the night, and with the approach of dawn he took his own pleasure in the sight of Shannon, asleep in his arms.

Her thick tangle of lashes cast shadows across her cheeks. Her tousled hair lay soft against his shoulder. She stirred, turning onto her other side, and he felt a sharp pain in his heart as he saw the shiny white curve of the scar that her husband's knife had left behind.

He came from a rougher world than the one in which he found himself. Men ofttimes spoke with their fists, even within the four walls of their home. Somehow he had imagined better of the twentieth century. They had been blessed with riches beyond knowing and yet the same problems that had beset the men and women of his time still existed today.

Leaning forward he pressed his lips against the pale scar tissue, breathing in her scent. Not even those dark thoughts were enough to dim the joy she'd awakened inside his heart simply by virtue of her existence. The fact that she had lain with him, offered him the wonders of her body—was there a man in this world or any other who had ever been granted a greater honor?

She slept deeply, her bosoms rising and falling with the rhythm of her breathing. After a while he slept, as well. He did not dream, for nothing he could dream could compare to the wonder of lying there next to a woman such as Shannon.

In truth, he did not know what it was that awakened him, but he found himself drawn from the warmth of the bed he shared with Shannon. He crossed the room swiftly and went straight to the window, where he pulled the curtains and looked out on a landscape oddly dark for that hour of the morning.

The yard was shrouded in shadows. An unnamed dread filled him as he lifted his gaze to the tops of the trees and saw a most peculiar cloud cover towering up toward the heavens. He knew the striations of dark and light, the low whistle of the wind, the way it called to him like one of the sirens who lured sailors from the sea.

"The lighthouse," he murmured as the sense of dread grew stronger. That same cloud cover had enveloped the lighthouse on the day Andrew had left his old life behind.

He stood there as the cloud cover lingered then passed, feeling as if something had been asked of him and he had failed to answer.

"Andrew?" Shannon's soft murmur curled itself inside his ear. "Come back to bed."

"Aye," he said, turning away from the window. "'Tis the one place I wish to be."

CHAPTER SEVENTEEN

DAKOTA WAS HALFWAY OUT the door when the telephone rang.

"I can't talk to you now, Ma," she said, cradling the receiver against her shoulder. "If I'm late for the library one more time, Forsythe'll have my head."

"I had a dream," Ginny Wylie said in the tone of voice she reserved for major announcements.

"So what else is new?" Dakota mumbled, eyeing the clock over the refrigerator.

"Dakota? What did you say?"

"I really have to go, Ma. Why don't I call you at lunch—"

"This will only take a minute," Ginny said with the blithe confidence of a woman whose place in the world was secure. "You're going on a trip."

"To work," Dakota said, "if you'd let me hang up the blasted phone."

204

"I don't have to tell you any of this," Ginny said, sounding aggrieved. "I'm just trying to give you food for thought."

A car phone, Dakota thought eyeing her old Mustang in the driveway. *Give me a car phone so I can get to work on time.*

"You've met a man," Ginny continued, "and he's going to change your life forever."

The hairs on the back of Dakota's neck rose and she sank onto a kitchen chair. "A man?" She forced a laugh. "The only man in my life is Dr. Forsythe, and we both know how much he loves me."

"He's not handsome, but he's...compelling." Ginny drew in a long, noisy breath. "And he's not from around here—Dakota? Are you still there?"

"I'm here, Ma." *With my head between my knees.* She felt the blood rushing to her brain but didn't dare sit up straight for fear she'd pass right out on the floor. "Does this guy have a name?"

"Adam," said Ginny. "Andrew, maybe?"

The room swam in front of her eyes. "He's a friend of Shannon's," she whispered.

"There's more to it than that, isn't there?"

"I really can't talk about this now, Ma."

"Your future is tied up with his."

"I don't think so."

"Yes, it is," said Ginny, "and when he goes home, you're going to go with him."

She sat straight up and burst into laughter. "I don't know how to break it to you, Ma, but this time your dream radar is way, *way* off base."

"So where's he from?" Ginny asked. "Chicago? I know you hate Chicago."

"It's worse than Chicago."

"Denver?"

"Worse than Denver."

There was a long silence, then, "I'm not picking anything up on this, Dakota. Why is that?"

"Good grief," said Dakota, leaping to her feet, "will you look at the time! Gotta go, Ma. Talk to you later." She hung up the phone and raced for the door before Ginny had the chance to redial her number. Right on cue, it began to ring as she locked the door behind her.

Ginny was nothing if not persistent.

And accurate?

She closed her eyes and tried to imagine herself with Andrew McVie, but her mind was a blank screen. He and Shannon belonged together and nothing would change that.

But you know your future is linked with Shannon and Andrew's.

"Of course I do," she said out loud—never a good sign, even in the best of times. "That doesn't mean I'm going to be their shadow." As the only single Wylie sibling, she'd had more than her share of being the fifth wheel. She couldn't imagine spending her life in that position.

Andrew's stay here was only temporary. Of that Dakota was sure. And, God knew, she'd never seen two fates more intertwined than his and Shannon's.

So where does that leave you?

"I don't know," she said, starting toward her beat-up Mustang, which was parked at the end of her driveway. She supposed that left her where it always left her, playing the good friend, or the witty psychic sidekick.

Or maybe the catalyst.

She stopped dead in her tracks as she considered the notion. A catalyst? It didn't make sense. She hadn't brought Andrew and Shannon together, and she certainly would never do anything to keep them apart. Other than swoon every time she saw him, the only thing she'd done was dig up a dusty old history book that had turned Shannon into a crazy person.

Still, the feeling persisted that there was more to it than that. All her life she'd had the feeling she was meant for more than the mundane reality of everyday existence. Was it possible there was a grand adventure waiting for her, right around the corner?

Like maybe in the next hot-air balloon that floats by.

"Yeah," she said as she climbed into her car and started up the engine. "Right."

The only grand adventure in store for her was a trip to the unemployment office if she didn't get to the library before Dr. Forsythe.

"Three billion sold," Andrew read from the sign beneath McDonald's golden arches on Route 206 a few miles north of Princeton. He turned toward Shannon. "Three billion what?"

Shannon pulled into the parking lot. "Hamburgers."

Andrew looked at her with a blank expression on his face.

"Chopped beef that you form into patties and fry on a grill then serve on little round pieces of bread."

"To what purpose?"

"Your dining enjoyment. It's the same as the hamburgers we had at the restaurant before." She laughed and got in line behind a Chevy Blazer loaded with little kids. "Did I forget to tell you about the pickles, lettuce, onions, ketchup and special sauce?"

"Aye," he said. "You forgot."

A minute later she stopped in front of the menu board and a voice crackled through the speaker, "Welcome to McDonald's. Can I take your order, please?"

"Sweet Jesus!" Andrew leaned across Shannon to take a closer look. "Is there a machine to replace each one of us?"

"Just about," said Shannon.

"Your order, please," repeated the speaker voice.

"Big Mac, chef's salad, large fries and two iced teas."

"Drive up to window one."

"Real food will be found at window one?" Andrew asked.

Shannon grinned. "American classic cuisine at its best."

"'Tis a most amazing thing."

No, she thought a few minutes later as they sat together in the car and ate lunch. *The only amazing thing in this big wide world is that you're sitting here beside me.*

"So, what do you think?" she asked as he swallowed a bite of his first Big Mac.

He popped a fry into his mouth while he considered the question. "I think I should like another one."

"A junk food junkie," she said with a rueful grin. "Who would've thought it?"

He looked at the burger with suspicion. "Mayhap I will reconsider. 'Tis not a good thing to eat junk."

"You're so literal minded, Andrew. Junk food means quick food, fast food, anything that's not your regular sit-down dinner."

He attacked the burger again with gusto and she found herself shivering with delight. Last night he had brought that same exuberant appetite for pleasure to her bed. She had lived almost thirty years and had never known her body was capable of such transcendent delight until Andrew McVie took her in his arms.

She had gone to her ex-husband a virgin, both emotionally and physically, and Bryant had taken that naiveté and destroyed it. From the start she'd believed she wasn't good enough, pretty enough, sexy enough to satisfy him, and it had taken a very long time for her to understand that none of it was her fault.

She'd regained her self-respect but she'd never believed that sensuality would be part of her life. She told herself it was okay, that you couldn't miss what you'd never known, but there was a hollowness inside her heart that wouldn't go away.

Until last night.

She felt her cheeks redden and she looked away, a smile playing at the corners of her mouth. All it took was the thought of his strong hands stroking her inner thighs, the sound of his voice as he said her name over and over and over again to bring her once again to life.

So this was the secret, the force that made rational people into fools and fools into poets. She glanced toward Andrew and found him watching her. The sunlight brought out the golden flecks in his hazel eyes and she thought she'd never seen a man more magnificent—or glimpsed a heart so true.

* * *

Andrew remembered Princeton as a small town situated in the midst of heavy woods and lush farmland. For the most part, to his amazement, it still was.

In truth, the farmlands were diminished and the heavy woods were confined, but the character of the place was unchanged. Princeton was a small town blessed with intellectual and artistic energy, both of which were blended with a rural take on life that had survived the years.

When Shannon turned the car to the left and drove down Nassau Street, he found himself engulfed in memory of a time just a few weeks past—and many worlds away.

"A tavern once stood here." He pointed to the corner of Nassau and University Place. "'Twas a common meeting place for the spy ring."

"I hear your words," Shannon said, "but it's so hard to believe you're seeing Princeton from across two centuries."

"Emilie and Zane stood on that corner. It was there that she told me in her time women ruled countries and went to university and did all that men do, but I did not believe her." And now, with the truth in front of his eyes, he still ofttimes found it difficult to fathom. "She took great offense at my disbelief."

Shannon abruptly pulled the car off to the side and stopped.

"'Tis something wrong?"

"You loved her," she said flatly. "Didn't you?"

"Nay, Shannon, 'twas not love but infatuation."

"But you thought it was love at the time."

He would not deceive her, not even to make things between them go more easily. She deserved better from him than that. "Emilie was unlike any woman I had ever seen before. She spoke of wonders beyond knowing. 'Twas easy to mistake that for something more."

"And what about me? Would you have felt— Are you with me because I am the first woman you met or because you want to be?"

"I am with you because there is nowhere else in this world or any other that I wish to be."

An odd look drifted across her face, a look he had never before seen. "What if you could go back to your own time?" she asked.

"That question is not relevant, for the opportunity to do so does not exist."

"But what if?" she persisted, resting her hand on his wrist. "Now that you've seen this world, what would you do? Would you go back?"

"I would stay with you," he said, feeling the truth of his words deep inside his heart. "Whatever the time or place." He leaned across the small barrier she called an armrest and touched the soft skin of her cheek. He wished he could reach inside her head and banish all memory of the husband who had treated her so badly.

Mayhap then she could believe happiness was theirs for the taking.

Shannon parked the car in the U-Store lot, then she and Andrew walked over to Nassau Hall. Except for Dakota's involvement with the historical society, she'd never given much thought to the wealth of history that surrounded them in central New Jersey. But when you were walking with a man who'd been around when the history was being made, you couldn't help but gain a new perspective on things.

Some of the houses on Alexander and University boasted plaques that commemorated their dates of construction: 1752, 1768, 1772. Once Andrew placed his palm flat against the door knocker of a stately three-story house and said, ''William Strawbridge was a terrible merchant but a true patriot. He passed along many a message at great risk to his own family.''

Stockton and Witherspoon weren't streets to Andrew; they were people. Richard Stockton and his wife, Annis, who buried the family's silver—much as Andrew's friend Rebekah Blakelee had—to keep it safe from the marauding British soldiers. And John Witherspoon, who came from Scotland to be president of the College of New Jersey, only to become the lone man of God to sign the Declaration of Independence. People who had lived and breathed and fought in Andrew's own time. People who were remembered still.

As Andrew would be if he'd stayed in his own world.

No. She refused to think like that. She wasn't responsible for him climbing into a hot-air balloon and taking off for the twentieth century. He'd come here of his own free will and he was staying here for the same reason.

''We could drive over to Morven or Drumthwacket,'' she said as they started walking down University Place near the Princeton railroad station, where commuters caught the shuttle known as the ''dinky'' that connected them to the main line. ''I believe Morven was built before the war started.''

''Nay,'' he said, ''but there is one thing more I would like to see before we leave this place.''

''Anything,'' she said, summoning up a carefree smile that hid her guilty conscience.

"The Blakelee farm."

"I never heard of a Blakelee farm anywhere around here. Was it close by?"

"Aye," he said. "Naught but a short walk from the center of town."

"I doubt if it still exists, Andrew. You can see what's happened. Much of the farmland has been turned over to developers for housing."

"Your friend Dakota," he said. "Does she not work for an historical society?"

Dakota couldn't believe her eyes.

She'd just come back from a quick lunch at the pancake shop near the movie theater when she saw Andrew McVie and a grim-faced Shannon walking toward the reference desk. McVie was dressed in jeans and a plain white cotton shirt that strained against his powerful shoulders. He still didn't do much for her, but she had to admit he looked wonderful today. Especially with that ponytail. She'd always been a sucker for men with ponytails, and he looked exceptionally good with it.

Shannon, however, looked as if she was about to jump out of her skin.

I know you don't want to be here, Dakota thought, trying to send the vibes directly to her friend, *but can't you see what's happening?* Fate had the three of them all tied up together in one unwieldy package and there was nothing any of them could do to change that.

Wasn't this proof positive of that? Shannon would rather chew ground glass than visit the museum. And she certainly didn't want Dakota anywhere near Andrew.

But there they were, coming toward Dakota like a pair of intrepid bloodhounds in search of quarry. She looked from Shannon to Andrew, then back again. No, she was certain Shannon hadn't told him about the history text hidden behind Plutarch's *Lives,* which meant they wanted something else—something Shannon obviously wasn't too thrilled about. But what?

"Hi," she said, leaning across the reference desk. "Fancy meeting you guys here."

"Good day, mis—Dakota." Andrew favored her with a pleasant smile. "You are looking well."

"And you have wonderful taste." She glanced down at her Mexican peasant blouse and grinned. "Fifty cents at the thrift shop in Somerville." *I haven't swooned yet,* she thought. *It's a miracle!*

"This isn't a social call," Shannon said, a warning look apparent in her eyes. "We need some information about a revolutionary-war-era farm outside of town."

"Then you've come to the right place," Dakota said easily. "Whose farm?"

"The name was Blakelee," said Andrew. "Josiah and Rebekah."

"We have records in the archives," Dakota said, "but a master list on microfiche." She spun her chair around and turned on the machine. "Let's see what I can find out." She mechanically flipped through the pages. "There was a Blakelee farm between here and Griggstown but, according to the records, it passed into the creditor's hands in 1778." She spun back around to face Andrew and Shannon. "Much of the property was sold in the 1950s to a land developer but part of it was reserved under the Green Acres provision."

Andrew looked so distressed that her heart went out to him. "Are they—" He cleared his throat and began again. "What happened to the family?"

"It doesn't say here but, if you like, I can check some of our other records."

"I would be in your debt," said Andrew.

She shot a look in Shannon's direction. *You have to do something about his speech patterns,* that look said. This was 1993. Nobody was polite anymore, not unless they were displaced time travelers who hadn't learned the ropes yet.

"Give me a minute," she said. "Archived material is kept downstairs." She gestured toward the leather sofas lining the window. "Make yourselves comfortable." She glanced down and noted that they were holding hands. Apparently they were already more comfortable than she'd realized.

Oh, Shannon, she thought as she raced past the leaded windows that looked out on Dr. Forsythe's colonial-era knot garden. *Do you really think this is going to last?*

Hiding behind a pillar she looked back at the two of them, seated together on the sofa with the light spilling over them like a benediction. She closed her eyes for an instant, praying she'd been wrong, praying things would be different, but when she opened her eyes and looked—really looked—at Andrew, she found nothing had changed.

The man had no aura. The light around him was from the sun streaming through the windows and nothing else. He was as irrelevant and temporary in this world as a good hair day was to Lyle Lovett.

The wonder was that nobody else saw the things she saw when they looked at him. A chain of history followed him wherever he went. Thousands of lives were somehow tangled up with the fate of this one solitary man from another time.

Would those lives vanish into the mists if he remained here? Would it be as if they never existed, never had the chance to live and love and walk this earth? A wave of dizziness crashed over Dakota and she clung to the pillar for support. She rested her hands on her thighs and bent her head, struggling to regain her equilibrium for the second time that day.

Shannon loved him. You had only to see the two of them together to know that for a fact. And, God knew, she deserved the best life had to offer. But nothing good could come of flying in the face of history.

Unless that book was wrong.

The thought caught her attention and she straightened up, her head clearing. How many texts had she thumbed through that were filled with errors, both minor and major? Hundreds, that's how many. Scholars were not infallible, no matter what they might like the hoi polloi to believe. One book did not a destiny make.

Love was a powerful force, she thought as she continued on her way to the basement. She prayed it would prove to be more powerful than the sense of farewell that was growing stronger by the minute.

CHAPTER EIGHTEEN

"SHE IS GONE a considerable time," Andrew observed as he and Shannon sat on the couch and waited.

"I know," said Shannon, tapping her finger against the armrest. "Maybe she ran into Dr. Forsythe and he sent her to do something else."

"Dr. Forsythe?"

"Her boss. They have, shall we say, a confrontational relationship."

"She watches us as if she knows what we are about. 'Tis a most disconcerting notion."

"That's one of the problems with having a psychic for a friend. Keeping a secret is harder than it should be."

"She does not know how it was I came to be here, does she?"

"She knows about the balloon," said Shannon, shifting uncomfortably on the leather cushion. Hiding the history book was one thing; lying to Andrew was something else. "She—she seems to suspect there's more to it than that."

"Aye," said Andrew. "'Tis as I thought. It is in her eyes each time she looks at me."

But it wasn't anything like he thought. Dakota knew everything except for the fact that Shannon and Andrew were lovers, and considering Dakota's psychic antennae she probably knew that, too.

Shannon stood and smoothed the front of her walking shorts. "You know, it's beginning to look like Dakota's going to be stuck for a while. Why don't we just leave her a note and she can drop off whatever information she finds when she comes by to teach the kids?"

Great idea, but about thirty seconds too late.

Shannon and Andrew were halfway out the door when Dakota came racing across the room waving a sheaf of papers.

"Sorry I took so long," she called out, "but some idiot filed these with survey maps instead of death records."

Andrew recoiled noticeably, startling Shannon. *These are his friends,* she reminded herself. *A few days ago they were alive and well and celebrating their daughter's wedding.*

"It was a bit hard to find," Dakota went on, acting as if there was nothing unusual going on, "but apparently the Blakelees moved back to Princeton in 1785 and lived here until their deaths. Josiah died in 1799. Rebekah followed in 1801."

Andrew nodded, a muscle on the right side of his jaw jerking spasmodically.

"There is another couple," Shannon said, knowing he would not ask, "who once lived in Princeton with the Blakelees. I heard about them once—Zane and Emilie Rutledge.''

''Where did I hear those names before?'' Dakota wondered. She looked at Shannon, then her cheeks reddened. ''Give me five minutes and I'll see what I can do.''

Andrew reached for Shannon's hand as Dakota hurried away. '''Twas a generous thing you did.''

''I must be crazy,'' Shannon said with a quick laugh. ''Finding out about my own competition.''

''There is no other,'' Andrew said. ''No woman could compare to you.''

His words touched Shannon's heart and she pressed a quick kiss against his lips. ''I knew you wouldn't ask for yourself, so I figured I would.'' *Generosity, Shannon, or just your guilty conscience?*

Dakota was unable to find any information pertaining to Emilie and Zane Rutledge, but when Andrew mentioned that Emilie's maiden name was Crosse, the floodgates opened.

''Crosse Harbor,'' said Dakota as she handed Andrew a sheaf of papers. ''It looks like Emilie and Zane had a mansion near Philadelphia and a summer house on the Jersey shore. Since this is a New Jersey museum, that's how it was referenced.''

''How did Crosse Harbor come to be known by her maiden name?'' Shannon asked.

''Who knows?'' Dakota shrugged her shoulders. ''Maybe she was emancipated before her time. It's not that unusual for a woman of the era to wish to perpetuate her family's name in some way.''

'Tis Emilie as I knew her, Andrew thought. He looked toward Shannon and felt a wash of emotion

that warmed him, body and soul. *A woman unlike any other until you.* She met his eyes and he knew by the expression in their aqua depths that she'd somehow heard his thoughts and understood his meaning.

His eyes burned with unshed tears as he looked down at the top page. "The Rutledge family, one of the foremost families in the Commonwealth of Pennsylvania, was founded by Zane Rutledge and his wife, Emilie Crosse. Their five children, Sara Jane, Andrew—"

"I cannot read this," he said, folding the papers and stuffing them into the breast pocket of his shirt. *A child,* he thought. *A boy who carries my name . . .*

He could feel the eyes of the two women boring into him with iron-hot intensity but he could not find the words to explain his actions.

"We should go," Shannon said. "You know what rush hour on 287 is like."

Dakota seemed reluctant to let them leave. "If you wait a little bit longer, I might be able to find more information on the Rutledges of Pennsylvania."

"Nay," said Andrew a bit more gruffly than he intended. "'Tisn't necessary. I know all I need to about them."

Dakota walked with them to the door. "So I'll see you guys later. I'm bringing over a pile of 'Sesame Street' books my mother found at a yard sale."

"'Sesame Street'?" Shannon asked. "Aren't the kids a little old for that?"

"When you can't read it doesn't much matter if you begin with Ernie and Big Bird or Shakespeare. All that matters is that you learn to read."

It occurred to Andrew that Dakota was as extraordinary in her own way as his Shannon was. These women felt commitment to a cause beyond them-selves, as he once had, and he wondered if they knew how fortunate they were.

Dakota stood in the doorway and watched as Shan-non and Andrew walked hand in hand down the street.

"Coward," she whispered to herself. Maybe Shan-non didn't have the heart to tell him the truth about his destiny, but there was no excuse for Dakota. She wasn't in love with him. In fact, except for the way he looked at Shannon as if she was the best thing since sliced bread, she wasn't entirely certain she even liked him. What kind of man would leave a time where ev-eryone's effort counted, where one person could bring about changes that would affect a nation's destiny?

He had no business abandoning his true fate. So what if life was not what he had wished it to be? Maybe if he'd stayed put instead of leaping into the first hot-air balloon to come along, he might be carv-ing a place for himself in history, a place reserved for heroes.

Down in the archives she had uncovered two more documents with mention of Andrew McVie's heroism during the winter of 1779-1780 featured prominently in the text. *You don't understand,* Shannon had said. *He left in August 1776.*

And you don't understand, Dakota thought. *He's going back again.*

Shannon was quiet on the drive home. She blamed it on the rush-hour traffic, which was true enough, but that was far from being the entire reason.

You're getting good at this, Shannon. Bet you never thought you were such a skillful liar.

Lying? She hadn't lied to Andrew about anything. She'd sidestepped, underplayed and concealed, but she hadn't lied.

Can you look him in the eye and say that, Shannon?

"Oh, shut up," she muttered, exiting the highway.

He looked toward her. "Lass?"

"Nothing," she said. "I was just talking to myself."

"'Tis a bad sign," he said with a playful grin. "When I practiced law in Boston, that was cause for arrest."

"We're not in Boston," she replied.

"Aye," he said, rubbing his chin, "and this is not 1776."

She looked at him sharply. "You sound disappointed."

"That was not my intention. I am but stating a fact."

"I know what year it is, Andrew. I don't need you to point it out to me."

"You are unwell?"

"What makes you ask that?" Her tone of voice was cool enough to frost a margarita glass.

"'Twould seem the best explanation."

"I'm not entitled to a bad mood?"

"You do not wish an answer to that question."

She glared at him. "Wimp."

"I do not know that word."

"Good," she said. "It's an insult. Not particularly apt, but an insult."

"You are behaving in a most uncharacteristic fashion, lass. In truth, it appears each time you and your friend Dakota are in each other's company."

"You're imagining things."

"Nay," he said. "I know what I see and hear."

"Maybe time travel damages the gray cells."

"I do not understand the meaning but I believe it to be another insult."

What in hell are you doing, Shannon? This is the man you've waited your entire life to find and now you're pushing him away with cheap wisecracks a cut-rate comic in Las Vegas wouldn't touch.

She turned onto the long, winding driveway that led up to the house. She wanted to tell him she was sorry, but the words wouldn't come. She felt brittle as glass, as if the slightest movement would shatter her heart into a thousand pieces.

She suspected Dakota had found something more about Andrew, probably more proof that he had saved the world or something equally grand and heroic...and impossible if he didn't go back where he came from. Shannon could feel the truth of her suspicions deep inside, in the place where her guilt was growing bigger by the minute. She'd thought her heart would stop beating when Dakota handed over those pages about Emilie and Zane.

She glanced over at Andrew and saw the bulge of photocopied papers in his breast pocket. God only knew what information they contained.

The question, of course, was why reading about people who were two hundred years dead should bother her as much as it did. Those people were no more real to her than Julius Caesar or Napoleon or Genghis Khan. How was it Andrew's friends exerted an influence over her across the centuries?

Maybe it's because you don't believe it's over.

She glanced over at Andrew, who was looking straight ahead, his jaw set in granite.

Maybe it's because I love you.

He turned to meet her eyes.

Neither said a word as she pulled the car into the garage.

The moment lengthened, shimmered, wrapped itself around their hearts and drew them closer together.

"I'm sorry," she whispered. "I've been hateful."

"And I have been a fool." From his pocket he pulled the sheaf of papers Dakota had given to him and ripped them in half. "The past is done."

Shannon watched as the pieces of paper drifted to the ground near the hot-air balloon and prayed Andrew would never regret his decision.

They lay together that night in a spill of moonlight. Their lovemaking had been sacramental, a joyous celebration of the miracle that had brought them to this time and place. If there was anything more to ask of life, any blessing she'd been denied, Shannon couldn't imagine what it was. Lying there in Andrew's arms she felt a sense of wonder that filled her with delight and made her feelings of guilt seem insignificant.

"Are you happy?" she murmured, her lips brushing against his chest. "Is this everything you thought it would be?"

"A strange question, lass, considering the events of the past two hours."

She laughed softly and circled his nipple with her tongue. "I want you to be happy," she said fiercely. "I don't ever want you to wish you'd stayed in your own time. We can make this work, Andrew. I know we can.''

Her words caught him by surprise. He'd never understood a woman's need for constant reassurance. Apparently it was one trait that had survived throughout the centuries.

He grabbed her by the waist and pulled her up the length of his body until her mouth was but a kiss away from his. ''Have I expressed dissatisfaction?''

''No, but—''

''Am I here with you, in your bed?''

''Yes, but—''

''Then say no more, for we have other business to conduct between us.''

''You couldn't possibly... I mean, we just—'' A low, throaty laugh. ''How positively amazing!''

''Aye,'' he said, reaching between them until he cupped the hot wetness between her legs. ''Amazing.''

She was slick with their spent passion. He slipped one finger into her willing body and felt his shaft grow hard as her muscles tightened around him. With his thumb he toyed with the lush curls that covered her mound, then gently rubbed the source of her greatest pleasure. She arched against him and her soft moan of delight brought him close again to madness.

He wanted more. He wanted to worship her, glory in her, brand himself with the smell and taste and heat of her.

''I will not hurt you,'' he said as he moved her to the edge of the bed. ''You believe that, do you not?''

''Yes,'' she whispered. ''I believe that.''

He knelt on the floor next to her and spread her thighs, burying his face at her most secret, woman spot. He found her with his mouth. She smelled of sex and of life...hot...sweet...as ripe and juicy as a fresh peach on a summer's day.

She arched against him, presenting herself for his lips and mouth and tongue, and he took all that was offered and demanded more. She spent herself again, her cry of ecstasy ringing out in the quiet room, and he found himself close to ecstasy at the sight and sound of her passion.

He lay with her on the mattress and held her close as her heartbeat slowed.

"No one," she whispered, kissing his mouth... tasting herself upon him. "No one but you. Not ever."

He understood the meaning of her words and they filled him with a sense of triumph. "Only me, Shannon," he said, his voice fierce with pride. "From this day forward, there is only me."

She leaned up on one elbow and even in the darkness he could see the shimmer of emotion in her beautiful eyes. "Lie back down," she said in a tone that brooked no argument. "Now it is your turn."

He had never before known a woman who so firmly took control of the act of love. Even the whores with whom he'd taken his ease were paid to do a man's bidding. Such enthusiasm and invention were beyond his ken. He did not know whether to protest or go willingly.

In truth, he had not time to make that decision, for his beautiful Shannon made it for him. She trailed kisses down his torso, his belly, until she reached his manhood. He ached for her touch but she was coy, fingering him lightly with teasing strokes along the inner muscles of his thigh, cupping him, then withdrawing her touch until he felt he would explode with need.

"You play a dangerous game, lass," he said as she drew her tongue upward from the base of his shaft. "A man can be contained for only so—"

His moan was wrenched from the depths of his being as she took him in her mouth. Her movements were tentative at first, as if such an act was alien to her, but her eagerness and desire to pleasure him were so intense that she quickly discovered how to bring him to a fever pitch. She suckled him, she teased him with her lips and tongue and teeth, she fondled him as if the weight in her palm brought her pleasure.

Indeed, she seemed by her demeanor as if the act of bringing him pleasure brought her such, as well. He would not have thought it possible that a woman could derive physical satisfaction from pleasuring her man, but the proof was undeniable.

"No more, lass," he said, grabbing her by the shoulders and drawing her up the length of his body. "'Tis a release we will find together."

She smiled at him, a smile of dark pleasure and understanding, then straddled him in much the same way she had straddled him the night they met. But this time it was different. She was naked, in both body and soul, hungry for the act of completion that could only come with the joining of a man and a woman in sexual congress.

He lowered her onto his hard shaft, slowly, gently, until with a sigh of pleasure she took his full length. She moved to an inner rhythm, one he swiftly made his own, and moments later they found paradise together.

I love you, lass, he thought as he fell back to earth.

He heard her voice in the darkness. "Aye," she said.

CHAPTER NINETEEN

"REMEMBER," SAID SHANNON the next morning as she moved her hip closer to his, "this was your idea."

"I know that, lass."

"It might hurt."

"Aye."

She shifted her weight and set herself. "On the count of three. One...two...three!" Andrew went flying over her right shoulder and landed with a thud on the grass at her feet.

"See?" she asked, crouching next to him. "A woman *can* best a man."

Andrew lay there on his back and stared at her without moving.

She bent over him. "Andrew?" She placed a hand on his chest. "Are you okay?" There was no response. Her heart beat faster. "Andrew! Don't do this to me.... Say something, please."

With a roar he gathered her to him and rolled her onto her back, covering her with his body. "'Tis a parlor trick you play, lass," he said while she laughed. "Naught but a strange sleight of hand."

"It's called karate. Anyone can do it." She grinned. "After many years of practice, of course."

He kissed her soundly. "A most unusual skill for a woman to possess."

"A necessary skill for a woman to possess if she's smart. I wish I'd known how to do this when I was married. Things might have been very different." At the very least, she would have left Bryant at the first sign of violence.

"And this is what you teach the women who come through your shelters?"

"Among other things, yes." She took his hand and he helped her to her feet. "Mostly we teach women self-respect. Learning to defend yourself is a great way to start."

He was quiet for a moment. "The girl Angela has need of such knowledge, as well."

"Damn," Shannon whispered. Children were so vulnerable. To suffer at the hands of a parent was unthinkable. "It starts so early."

"Is there something you can teach the children that would give them this self-respect you talk about?"

"There are all sorts of role-playing games that the social workers—" She stopped. "That sounds ridiculous, doesn't it? Those kids need something more than role-playing to give them confidence. They need someone to teach them how to find their place in the world."

"Aye," said Andrew, "and they need someone to teach them how to find their way through the woods."

He shook his head. "Within shouting distance of the house and they could not find the path back again. 'Twas a sorry thing to see."

"That's it!" Shannon grabbed his arm. "We could do a kind of mini Outward Bound program."

"I have no knowledge of Outward Bound."

Enthusiasm bubbled through her. "One of the things we've lost in my world is the ability to live without modern conveniences. Outward Bound takes people into the wilderness and forces them to develop survival skills."

"'Tis something those children would be well served by."

"Would you?" she asked, excitement building.

"I do not follow, lass."

"You could take them camping for a night, Andrew! I know they'd have a wonderful time and, best of all, you could pass on what you know about living with nature."

"My knowledge is of another time."

"Some things don't change. Basic survival skills, for example. Technology can't help you when you're alone in the woods with only your wits."

"'Tis something to consider."

"It could be great fun, Andrew," she said. She smiled at him. "Besides, I could use a refresher course myself."

"You should have been a lawyer, lass, for you plead your case with great skill."

She wound her arms around his neck. "We need to do it soon. It's Thursday already and I doubt if any of them will still be here this time next week."

"Then we will do it tonight."

She kissed him hard. "Not tonight. I'm not ready to share you with anyone tonight."

His beautiful hazel eyes twinkled with delight. "When will you share me, lass?"

"I've been meaning to talk to you about that, Andrew. How would you feel about escorting me to a charity ball on Saturday night?"

"What is the alternative?"

"I attend alone."

He bristled and she loved him for it. "Then I will escort you."

She grinned up at him. "You'll need a tuxedo."

"Tell me what it is, lass, and I will decide if I do."

"It's a type of formal apparel."

His sandy brows slanted downward. "Would it require another visit to the tailor?"

"Of course."

"Then I will not go. That man measures more than the length of a seam."

Shannon started to laugh. "They have your measurements on file. I'll go to the mall and you can stay here."

"'Tis fine with me. I noted that the garage needs repair," he said. "I will tend to it while you are away."

She glanced up at the sky. "Looks like a storm is brewing. I'd better get out and back before those black clouds open up."

She kissed him, then ran back to the house to change her clothes. Andrew's smile vanished when she disappeared inside.

Those are not storm clouds, lass, he thought, looking up at the sky. Once again it was the same cloud cover he'd seen the day he climbed into the hot-air balloon...and the same cloud cover he'd seen at dawn yesterday.

Mayhap there was nothing so peculiar about those clouds after all, he reasoned as he crossed the wide expanse of lawn and headed toward the garage. They seemed to occur in this world with some frequency, if the past few days were any indication.

The garage was open and he stepped inside. His intention was solely to gather up the hand tools and set to work, but he found himself drawn to the corner of the structure where he'd stored the basket and balloon.

"'Tis a mistake to look," he said aloud as he approached. What did it matter if the silk of the balloon had faded even more or if the basket looked as if it had traveled through a nor'easter? He did not seek a way back to his own time.

Still, his curiosity could not be denied. He pulled the cover from the odd contraption and stared in disbelief. This time it was not the fading of the fabric that gave him pause; it was the nature of the fabric itself. The color had remained constant since last he viewed it but the silk was thinner, almost transparent in nature, so sheer it looked as if it could not sustain a puff of smoke, much less the magic fire that had transported him there. The torn pages Dakota had given to him were scattered about and he pushed down the stirrings of curiosity.

"No matter," he said, turning away. Emilie and Zane...Josiah and Rebekah...they were gone, all of them. Their lives had been played out long ago. It was his turn now. His turn to choose the life he deserved.

He was not looking to leave this place. Not so long as Shannon loved him.

*   *   *

"You look awful, honey."

Dakota looked up from the stack of papers she was cataloging. "Mom! What are you doing here?"

Ginny Wylie was the mirror image of her daughter, except twenty years older. They shared the same short-cropped black curls, dark eyes, funky clothes sense and psychic abilities. Over the years the latter had made the mother-daughter relationship rocky at times and sublime at others. The one thing it never was, was boring.

"I had another dream," Ginny announced. "I had to come see for myself."

Dakota removed her glasses and rubbed her eyes. "Well, now you've seen, Mom. I'm still here, still single. I haven't run off with some mystery man. Satisfied?"

Of course, Ginny wasn't. She sat on the edge of the desk and considered Dakota. "You've gained weight."

"Thanks, Mom. Have you noticed the bags under my eyes, too?"

"I'm not being critical, honey. I'm worried about you."

"There's nothing to worry about," Dakota said, wondering where this was leading. "I'm fine."

"No, you're not."

"Is this a psychic assessment or a maternal judgment?"

"A little of both." Ginny leaned forward and grabbed Dakota's hands in hers. "You've been having dizzy spells, haven't you?"

"I'm not pregnant, if that's what you're asking."

Ginny made a face. "Of course you're not pregnant. You need a man to get pregnant."

"Thanks again, Mom," Dakota said dryly. "I'm fat, light-headed and manless. And people wonder why I'm considering therapy."

"They've been here, haven't they?" Ginny lifted her head and practically sniffed the air like a bloodhound.

Why waste time denying it? This was as bad as when Dakota was sixteen and praying Ginny's ESP wouldn't come up with the fact that she was dating the town bad boy. Unfortunately that sounded more exciting than it actually was. In her day, the Princeton High School bad boy was a rich kid with an overbite and five overdue library books.

"Yes," Dakota said at last. "They were here yesterday."

"You can feel it in your bones," Ginny said. "The man has quite a force field around him."

"Tell me about it," Dakota muttered.

"That's why you've been fainting, isn't it?"

"I haven't been fainting. I've been swooning. There's a difference."

"Is it only when he's around?"

You're good, Mom. I have to grant you that. "He doesn't have an aura, Mom. Standing next to him is like standing at the edge of a black hole in space." *Great going, Dakota. As if she doesn't know enough already.*

"So when's he going back?" Ginny asked with the same matter-of-fact tone she used to ask if you wanted more mashed potatoes.

"Back where?"

"Wherever he came from." Ginny waved her hand in the air. "To 1588, 1776, 1812. It's somewhere around there."

"What makes you think he's from another time?"

"I have no idea," said Ginny. "I just know it's true."

Dakota tried to sidestep the issue. "He's living with Shannon."

"Not for long," said Ginny. "He has an opportunity to go back right now but he isn't paying attention to the signs."

Dakota swallowed. "You feel that, too?"

"Who wouldn't?" countered Ginny. "It's clear as the nose on your face."

"What if he doesn't go right now? Will he get another chance?"

"The window is shrinking," Ginny said with conviction. "Sooner or later he'll lose his opportunity."

"And then what? He won't die or anything, will he?"

"I don't know," said Ginny. "But there will be far-reaching repercussions. His future is tied in with the futures of many others. That's one thing I'm sure of."

Dakota thought of the papers she'd given to Andrew. She wondered how he felt reading about the struggles his friends had endured during the war, the dangers they'd faced. "I wish I could make Shannon see that."

"She's in love with him, isn't she?"

Dakota nodded, wishing she had some Oreos. "I'm afraid so."

"Tell her not to worry," Ginny said with breezy assurance. "She can go with him."

Dakota had to laugh out loud. "You make it sound so easy."

"It is easy," Ginny said. "Just follow your heart."

"Most people don't have to follow their hearts across the centuries."

"Life's an adventure, honey. Most people are scared to death of living out their dreams."

Dakota was reminded of the time fifteen or sixteen years ago when her parents had taken the family to see *Close Encounters of the Third Kind.* They'd all been mesmerized by the story of ordinary people hand-picked by extraterrestrials to experience life on an-other planet. After the movie Ginny had asked the kids what they thought about the movie, and Dakota's sib-lings had all agreed they'd like to see the inside of a spaceship but they wouldn't like to live there.

"I would," Dakota had piped up. "I'd go to outer space in a minute."

Her brothers and sister had laughed and teased her mercilessly but Ginny had met her eyes, and in her mother's look Dakota had seen understanding and admiration.

"I really should get back to work, Mom," Dakota said. "Dr. Forsythe's been on my case lately."

Ginny made a face. "Oh, who cares about him. You're not going to be here forever, honey."

"You're a regular ray of sunshine," Dakota said. "First you tell me I'm fat, then you tell me I'm head-ing toward unemployment. What's next, Mom? Gonna tell me there's no Santa Claus?"

"Very funny." Ginny leaned across the desk and kissed her daughter's cheek. "Don't forget what I said, honey—life's an adventure."

"What exactly does that mean?"

"You'll know when the time comes." Her mother's aura was a sunny lemon yellow, probably just like Mother Teresa's.

Dakota let out a sigh of exasperation. "This is how psychics get a bad name," she said, feeling irritable and out of sorts. "If just one of us could answer a question in plain English, we'd all be a lot better off."

"I'll ignore that," said Ginny. "Your aura's looking a little off today." She patted Dakota's hand and stood. "The Fountain of Vitality has a sale on ginseng. You might want to stock up."

With that her mother swept out of the library in a cloud of patchouli, leaving Dakota staring after her.

Of course, Dr. Forsythe chose that moment to pop out of his office.

"You know how I feel about visiting with friends on work time, Miss Wylie."

Dakota looked up at him blandly. "You've mentioned it a time or two."

"Friends visited you yesterday." He made it sound like a crime against humanity.

"With a legitimate question of an historical nature." *Don't look at me like I graduated from Romper Room. I went to college, too, Forsythe.*

"And what about that oddly dressed lady who was sitting on your desk?"

Dakota grinned. "That was no 'oddly dressed lady' sitting on my desk, Dr. Forsythe. That was my mother."

His cheeks reddened. "Well, keep her off your desk."

"I'll do my best," said Dakota.

"See that you do."

"Puce," said Dakota.

He looked at her. "What was that?"

"I said puce. Your aura's puce. You really should do something about that, Dr. Forsythe."

Dr. Forsythe stormed off, muttering something about insubordination, but Dakota just smiled. *You're right, Mom,* she thought. *I won't be here forever.*

She wondered how she would like unemployment.

CHAPTER TWENTY

THE SALESCLERK at the men's store at Bridgewater Commons had turned fawning into an art form. Shannon, never a fan of groveling adults, found it difficult to mask her distaste.

"You're certain you can deliver the tuxedo by tomorrow afternoon?"

"You have our word, Ms. Whitney," he said with a slight bow of his head. "The End of Summer Masked Gala is a most important event here in Somerset county. We would never let any of our illustrious patrons down." He bared his teeth in an approximation of a smile. "Your friend is a lucky man to be so well taken care of."

Of all the nerve, Shannon fumed as she headed across the sunny corridor toward Lord & Taylor. The salesman made it sound as if Andrew was a gigolo or something. A kept man, if there really was such a thing. Women picked out suits and shirts and all sorts of things for their husbands. Entire sitcoms had been created around that premise. For all that cretin knew, Shannon was Andrew's wife, out to do some more clothes shopping for her husband.

Feeling a little touchy, are you? an annoying voice asked.

She marched through the cosmetics department, scarcely noticing the squirt girls with their loaded perfume bottles, ready to assault unsuspecting customers. Of course she wasn't feeling touchy. The only thing she was feeling was annoyed that she'd let an obsequious salesman get away with that untoward remark.

Right, that annoying voice continued. *And this has nothing to do with what you saw in the garage, does it?*

She wheeled past the DKNY display of lush autumn knits and headed for the down escalator. She'd been doing her best to push it from her mind but apparently her best wasn't good enough. The image of Andrew, standing before the hot-air balloon and basket, was as vivid in memory as it had been in reality. She'd noted the faded silk, the crumbling basket, but more than that she'd noted the look in Andrew's eyes.

He hadn't seen her standing in the shadows as he ran his hand along the rim of the gondola, an odd expression on his face. You didn't have to be clairvoyant to know that he had been thinking about the life he'd left behind. There must be something he missed about his old life, something he longed for.

I'll make you forget all of it, she thought as she headed for the men's department. *Whatever it is, I'll find a way to make it all up to you.*

She was flipping through a display of white dress shirts when she had the uncomfortable sensation that someone was watching her. She glanced over her right shoulder and noted a well-dressed man in a business suit peering at her from behind a rack of silk ties.

She went back to looking at the shirts. If he was looking to strike up a conversation with her, certainly he'd get the message that she wasn't interested.

"Excuse me," he called out.

She turned with studied reluctance. "Yes?"

"Don't I know you?"

"I don't think so."

"I'm sure we've met before," he said, walking toward her.

"I don't believe so."

He extended his hand in greeting. "Linc," he said. "Linc Stewart."

"I'm sorry, Mr. Stewart," she said, moving away, "but you must have me mistaken with somebody else." The man was nothing if not persistent.

"Now, wait," said Linc Stewart. "Don't tell me. I'll remember your name in a second."

"Really, Mr. Stewart," she said, starting for the up escalator, "I'm in a hurry. I'm sure I'd remember if we'd met."

"Kitty...Katie...Katharine! That's it. Katharine Morgan."

The shock of hearing her old name on his lips sent the blood rushing from her head and she feared she would pass out at his feet.

"You okay?" he asked, his voice deep with concern. "Let me get you some water."

"I'm fine. It's just—" She searched frantically for a workable lie. "I'm pregnant and I tend to get dizzy at the drop of a hat. John—my husband—told me to slow down but you know how it is...." She favored him with the most dazzling smile at her command. "I'm afraid I'm not your friend Katharine Morgan," she said easily. "Sorry."

He considered her for a moment while her life passed before her eyes. "No," he said, "I guess you're not, but let me tell you, you could be her twin."

"I must go," she said, stepping onto the escalator. "It's been lovely talking with you."

She didn't draw a deep breath again until she was safely behind the wheel of her car and back on the highway headed for home. The odds against bumping into someone who knew her from her old life must be a million to one. Whoever this Linc Stewart was, he couldn't have been an important part of either her or Bryant's daily existence. And she hadn't been an important part of his. It was one of those random meetings that made for three minutes of conversation over dinner and then were forgotten.

"That's what you should do," she told herself as she turned up the road that led to her estate. "Forget about him." It was a fluke, one of those bizarre occurrences that happen every now and again and amount to nothing. Bryant had been on parole for over six months now and there hadn't been so much as a whisper of trouble. He was somewhere in California and, please God and the judicial system, destined to stay there.

She longed to see Andrew, to feel his arms around her, to push the whole strange incident from her mind. She left the car at the top of the driveway, then ran into the garage. Andrew wasn't there. She turned to leave, but that damn balloon stared at her from the corner.

Then the flutter of torn papers on the ground caught her eye.

It was obvious Andrew hadn't looked at them. Shannon, however, found herself compelled to gather them up and see what was important enough for Dakota to photocopy and press into Andrew's hands when she knew how Shannon felt. She brushed off some dirt and flipped through the half pages. Much of the information was boring detail about the Blakelee farm, the crops they'd grown, the dimensions of the original house. But buried in that minutiae was a paragraph that made her blood run cold.

She stuffed the torn pages into her purse, then ran outside. She didn't see Andrew anywhere. She tore around the side of the garage toward the backyard. He wasn't there, either.

"Andrew!" Her voice sounded shaky, not at all like herself. "Andrew, where are you?"

"Here, lass."

She spun around.

"Look up."

He was perched on the top rung of the ladder, working on the roof of the sun room.

"Oh, Andrew...." With that she burst into tears.

He had never seen her cry before. The sight tore at his gut, and he jumped the ten feet to the ground, landing hard, then raced to her side.

"Shannon, lass..." he murmured, gathering her into his arms. "There, now...don't cry...."

"I never cry," she said, sniffling as she struggled to regain her control. "I can't believe I'm doing this."

"'Tis nothing unnatural. Crying soothes the soul."

"M-my soul doesn't need soothing."

"Something caused this, lass. Tell me what it is."

"I don't know." She buried her face against his shoulder. "Nothing...everything." She looked up at him, face streaked with tears. "I'm not making any sense, am I?"

"None at all," he said, holding her close. He pulled away slightly so that he could look deep into her eyes.

"I couldn't find you, Andrew," she said after a moment. "You weren't in the garage, then I didn't see you in the yard. I don't know what came over me. I thought you'd gone away."

"Where would I go, lass, when I have all I could ask for here in my arms."

She reached up and took his face in her hands. "We don't have to stay here, Andrew. There's a whole big world out there for you to learn about, and we can go and see it all."

"You have a life here," he said, uncertain where this was leading. There was an edge to her voice, a touch of something akin to desperation. "People who rely upon you."

"The foundation runs itself. I signed the papers the other day. I could run off to Borneo and live on coconuts and the foundation would be just fine." Her eyes flashed with a fire unlike any he had seen before. "Anything I do for them is extra, more for me than for anyone else. By this time next week there will be a twenty-four-hour-a-day staff to keep things running."

"You sound unhappy."

"I'm not unhappy. I'm glad things are going well. Don't you see? I'm rich, Andrew! I have enough money to take us anywhere we want to go. We won't live long enough to spend all the money. I'll take you on a jet plane, in a helicopter, on the Concorde, buy you a car—''

''Enough!'' His tone was harsh but that could not be helped. ''What in bloody hell has brought this about, Shannon? I am not a man who takes from a woman. I make my own way in this world.''

''Oh, don't be ridiculous,'' she said, brushing away his words. ''First you have to experience this world before you can make your way in it. And trust me, Andrew, there's more to the world than New Jersey.''

''We will see the world when I can afford that privilege.''

''I can afford it now, Andrew. Why should we wait?''

''I am an educated man. I will find a way to secure a living in your world.''

''Oh, God, Andrew . . . you just don't understand. You have no identification, no birth certificate, no résumé, no driver's license. For all practical purposes, you don't even exist.''

''In my time a man's presence was enough to prove his existence.''

''Life is more complicated now.''

''There are records of my birth and marriage in Boston.''

''I'm sure there are,'' said Shannon with a sigh, ''but they're from the eighteenth century. We're going to have to get you some fake identification, and soon.''

''That can be done?''

''Yes,'' she said, ''but it will take me some time to ask around and find out where we can do it.''

''It was done for you,'' he observed, ''when you created this new life for yourself.''

"I had some help," she reminded him. "I had the government behind me."

"We will ask the government to help me."

"It doesn't work that way, Andrew."

"The government is in contact with you, to see that you are safe."

"Actually, nobody is in contact with me. The government created my new identity and then they bowed out."

"Did the government provide your wealth?"

She shook her head. "The wealth was mine. My trust fund came through when I turned twenty-one."

"So what you are saying is that although I exist, I do not really exist until I have papers to prove that existence."

"Well, yes," Shannon said. "I suppose I am. But don't you see? None of that really matters. I'll buy you some papers some place, you'll get a passport, then we're off to see the world."

"When I am able to pay for the experience."

"We'll talk about that," Shannon said, her jaw set in a stubborn line.

"Aye," said Andrew. "We will talk about that."

Shannon brightened. "The masked ball on Saturday night! Why didn't I think of it before? You'll meet every important person in the state. We're bound to connect with someone who can help us."

"You put great store in an evening of entertainment."

"Oh, the ball is a lot of things, Andrew, but entertainment isn't one of them. Charity events are work, same as going to the office."

"And you believe some profit might be gained from attending?"

"I can almost guarantee it."

And because she was so beautiful and so kind—and because he was so much in love with her—Andrew almost believed it.

Four women from the shelter sat on the grass Friday morning and looked up at Andrew as he painted the front door of the cottage. Shannon was sitting on the step next to him, just out of reach of his paintbrush. They had brought the women together to outline their plans for the mini Outward Bound camping trip, and so far the response had been less than overwhelming.

"I don't know about any of you," said Pat, "but I'm not letting my kids spend the night in the woods unless I'm with them."

"Wouldn't catch me in the woods in the middle of the night," said her mother, Terri, shuddering. "Too many creepy-crawly things all over the place."

Derek's mother, Rita, laughed. "That's the point, isn't it? Getting used to bugs and strange animals and no bathrooms." She looked at Shannon. "I've heard about this kind of thing. It's a confidence builder, right?"

"Exactly. It's been used by breast cancer patients, business executives—" Shannon gestured toward the women "—people like you and me."

"You?" said Pat with a short laugh. "I know you said you went through it, too, but—" She gestured toward the house and the estate grounds. "Kinda hard to figure what your problem was. If I had your money, I'd have left a long time ago."

"It's not always a question of money," Shannon said, not wanting to minimize the importance of being financially secure. "Yes, I had money but I didn't have something else that was a lot more important."

"Keys to the safety deposit box?" Pat asked.

"Guts," said Shannon. "And self-respect. If you don't have those two things, you don't have anything at all."

"And you think a night in the woods will give us guts and self-respect?" Pat asked with obvious skepticism.

"I think it's a damn good place to start."

There was a long silence. Shannon wondered if she'd gone too far and alienated the lot of them, but they needed to hear the truth.

"I don't know about the rest of you," said Rita, breaking the silence, "but I could use a night out. Count my kids and me in, Shannon."

"Not me," said Terri. "I'm going to stay in and watch a movie."

Pat looked at her mother, then at Shannon. "I'll go, but if I see one spider I'm out of there."

"And your kids?" Shannon asked.

"They love spiders." Pat smiled for the first time in days and Shannon felt a burst of elation.

"My kids are older than yours," said Sara, "but if we're still here Sunday, I'll try to convince them to tag along."

The women joked among themselves about the problems inherent in trying to convince teenagers to do anything at all.

Shannon looked up at Andrew. "Looks like we'll have our work cut out for us."

"Aye," he said, "we will, at that."

Their eyes met and held, and for a moment she remembered another man, other promises, and she thanked God for bringing Andrew McVie into her life.

CHAPTER TWENTY-ONE

"YOU LOOK MAGNIFICENT," said Shannon on Saturday night as she gave a final adjustment to the cloth about his neck.

"I look the fool." Andrew grimaced at his reflection in the mirror. "No man, save a Virginia plantation owner, should wear so many ornaments upon his person."

She considered him, her eyes twinkling with delight. "A bow tie, a cummerbund, cuff links, your basic tuxedo... that's not very much, Andrew."

"'Tis more than I like."

"You're a hunk," she said.

"I take offense, mistress."

"Don't," she said, starting to laugh. "That's the highest compliment for a man these days."

"Has the sound of an insult about it."

"Well, it isn't. The women are going to be falling all over themselves, Andrew. I hope they won't turn your head."

"Would you be feeling proprietary, lass?"

"Aye," she said, kissing his mouth. "Very proprietary."

"'Tis a higher compliment to me than any other."

In truth, the highest compliment of all was that a woman of such beauty and splendor should desire his company. The sight of Shannon in her floor-length white silk gown shot through with shimmering threads of gold put him in mind of celestial beings. Diamonds glittered at her throat and dangled from her ears. A narrow gold bracelet, also studded with diamonds, graced her right wrist.

"'Tis a king's ransom, Shannon." It struck him most forcefully that in his entire lifetime he would not be able to provide even one of the gemstones she wore with such ease, and that realization was not a happy one. "A man could live forever in my world with the money from one of your earbobs."

"I'll remember that next time I buy a plane ticket to 1776," she said with a saucy toss of her head.

He smiled at her jest, but for an instant found himself wondering how it would be to return to his own world with such a woman by his side.

"The limousine will be here any moment," she said, fetching a small beaded bag from the table near the door.

"I do not understand the need for another person to drive when you are most capable."

She gestured toward her slim-fitting dress. "You can't work a clutch in a Versace gown."

"This limousine, how does it differ from a car?"

"It's bigger," she said, adjusting her earbobs. "And it's terribly impressive."

"You wish to impress others?" That did not sound like the Shannon he had come to know.

"At events like this I do. The more impressive you are to others, the more likely they are to support your charity. It's a game, Andrew. Like playing chess but with real, live pieces." She met his eyes. "Karen Naylor and her date will be sharing the limo with us."

"The Negress lawyer?"

"Must you label her that way?" Shannon countered.

"I am not here long, lass. How else am I to remember the various players?"

Her dark brows drew together in a frown. "I have the feeling you remember Karen quite well."

"Because she is a Negress?"

"Because she's African-American."

"A cumbersome phrase."

"But accurate," she shot back. "A problem that might not have had such tragic consequences had the men of your time seen fit to prohibit slavery."

"You speak as if I had the power to change the course of events. I was not privy to the discussions at Carpenters' Hall, mistress. My opinion on the keeping of slaves mattered little in the scheme of things."

"You're wrong," said his beautiful warrior woman. "How can you, of all people, say that the opinion of the common man doesn't matter? The revolution was based upon the opinion of the common man."

"And that rebellion had not enjoyed much success when I took my leave."

"Maybe if—" Shannon stopped abruptly, horrified by what she had been about to say. *Maybe if you hadn't left . . .*

"Finish your sentence, Shannon. I am eager to hear your words."

"Forget it," she said. "There's no point to this discussion." Certainly not if she was going to say something as idiotic as that. She'd been on edge since Thursday morning and that odd encounter in Lord & Taylor. It had been so long since she'd heard her old name, much less met anyone who associated her with it, that she'd found herself looking over her shoulder more than once, almost as if Bryant somehow was going to find her again.

Ridiculous, she thought. She had a new home and a new identity. The odds of Bryant ever finding her were a million to one.

About like the odds of meeting Andrew McVie?

Fortunately the doorbell sounded, signaling the arrival of the limousine and putting an end to further conjecture.

"The masks," she said, looking around.

Andrew moved next to her, blocking her way. "They are in my keeping."

She nodded, then waited, but he didn't move. "We should go, Andrew. We don't want to keep Karen waiting."

"Aye," he said. "We would not wish to do that."

"Make an effort," she said in a soft voice. "Please don't make this difficult for everyone." If they were going to share their lives, it would have to begin now.

"I am not the ogre you paint me to be, lass. I am in new circumstances and doing my utmost to bend my will to the greater will of the times in which I find myself."

Unexpected tears filled her eyes. "I know you're not an ogre. It's just—"

"You wish me to see your friends in a favorable light."

"And I wish my friends to see you in a favorable light, as well."

"I had not thought of it in such terms."

"I know," she said, reaching for his hand. He was so strong within himself, so sure that his way was the right way, that the opinions of others were of little consequence. *This isn't the world you knew, Andrew. This is my world and you must learn to live by its rules.* Why was it that thought suddenly filled her with great sadness?

"I will make an effort," he said, "although those rules are ofttimes difficult to understand."

She smiled, feeling once again connected to him in the deepest way possible between two people, deeper even than the act of love. "I can't ask for more than that, can I?"

"Nay," he said, "you cannot." He shot her a bemused glance. "But I am of the opinion you will try."

Shannon had told him to avoid the topics of politics, religion and sex, but it appeared to Andrew as if he alone refrained from discourse on those subjects. He heard odd bits of talk about such things as test tube babies, gay rights and born-again Christians, and found he could understand little.

"You're very quiet, Mr. McVie," said one of the women at their table. "Surely you must have an opinion on abortion."

"Aye," he said, "and that opinion is as personal as the topic itself."

"Right to life," said the woman with a knowing nod of her head. "Typical evasive answer."

He felt Shannon's concerned gaze from across the table but this stranger's barb made him wish to deal with the matter directly.

"I stated no preference in the matter," he told the woman, "only that my opinion is of a personal nature."

"You're among friends, Mr. McVie," she continued. "Why not share your views with us?"

"Because my views are of no consequence in what is a private matter between a man and his wife."

Her painted blond eyebrows lifted above her mask and she laughed. "'Man and his wife.' What a quaint notion." She turned toward her companion, dismissing Andrew in a most obvious fashion.

He felt a hand on his arm. "Great job," said a familiar voice.

He looked to his right and saw Karen standing next to him. She wore the same bejeweled mask everyone but Andrew sported. "There was much left unsaid."

"She'd never hear you, Andrew. The woman's head is filled with cement."

"You heard the conversation?"

"Every last phrase. Not many people hold their own with Lydia. You deserve the croix de guerre."

He glanced toward Shannon, who was engaged in conversation with the silver-haired man who had accompanied Karen. He sensed, however, that she was fully aware that Karen was at his side.

"There is much intolerance of opinion at this party," he said.

"You noticed." Her tone was dry, but he heard the leavening note of humor.

They watched as Shannon rose from her chair to dance with the silver-haired man.

Karen smiled at him. "If you ask me to dance, I won't say no."

"If I ask you to dance, you will be most regretful, for I was cursed with lack of ability."

"So was I," Karen said. "That's why John is dancing with Shannon. Why don't we show them we're not lost causes?"

She was a woman of wit and charm and he was not unaware of the olive branch she extended toward him. They both shared a Harvard education, a dislike of fools and a strong affection and respect for Shannon. In truth, he could not think what else was required as a point from which to start.

He rose and inclined his head in her direction. "Lack of ability does not mean lack of the ability to *learn*. May I have the honor, Miss Naylor?"

She laughed and gave him her hand. "You may, Mr. McVie."

Together they took the floor.

"I thought you couldn't dance," Shannon said when they exchanged partners for the next song.

"And that is true," Andrew said, sweeping her into his arms.

They took a few steps and Shannon started to laugh. "You're right," she said. "You can't dance."

"And neither can Miss Naylor. We were a most agreeable combination."

"So I noticed." She forced them to a stop. "I'll lead, you follow." They began to move again on the beat. "See? You have potential."

"Aye," he said. "'Tis a miracle."

"Thank you, Andrew," she said softly. The sight of him dancing with Karen had given her hope.

"There is no reason for thanks, lass."

"I know it was hard for you."

"No harder than it was for Miss Naylor. She is a most intelligent woman and a true friend to you."

"I know," said Shannon. "I'm glad you realize that."

"It occurred to me that she is living my life, had I been born in your time."

"What an odd way to look at it, but I suppose that's true." They were about the same age, had the same educational background, the same drive.

"Now I am a lawyer without a practice and a farmer without land. It would seem my only claim upon this world is a result of your generosity. Every man in this room has a trade save for the man with whom you have cast your lot."

"Do you think I care about that, Andrew? You can't choose a profession before you learn all there is to learn about the world you're in. We'll travel. You'll get to learn all about the country... all about the world. Then you'll know what it is you were meant to do."

He fell silent and her heart went out to him. *You'll find your way, Andrew,* she thought. *Just give it time.*

The masks came off at midnight with great fanfare.

"As if we didn't know exactly who everybody was," Karen said with wry amusement. "The rich are *definitely* different." She grinned at Shannon. "Present company excepted, of course."

"Of course," said Shannon, grinning back.

Andrew and Karen's companion, John, were engrossed in conversation. Shannon couldn't imagine what they had in common but they seemed to be getting on well and for that she was grateful.

"Photos, everyone!" Madolyn Bancroft, coordi-nator of the gala, popped up at their table. "We have the *Star-Ledger, Philadelphia Inquirer, New York Times* and *Town and Country* waiting for you. Smile pretty!"

"Smile pretty." Karen groaned. "That woman is so perky there are times I want to strangle her."

"I know what you mean," said Shannon. "But that's probably why she's so good at what she does."

They rose from the table and moved toward the fountain, where the photographers were gathered snapping pictures.

Shannon drew Andrew aside. "They're going to photograph us," she said sotto voce. "They'll aim the camera in our direction and you'll see a bright light flash."

"And that captures our image, does it not?"

She smiled. "Depends how good the photographer is."

They took their places.

"Great," said one of the photographers. "Good contrast. Now you, mister, put your hand at the lady's waist. Big smile . . . big smile . . . great! You'll see the results in the morning paper, folks."

"'Tis an amazing thing," Andrew said as they made room for Karen and John to be photographed. "Our image on paper for the world to see."

She thought of the man who'd recognized her at the mall, and a shiver of apprehension moved through her. All evening she'd found herself looking at the masked faces and wondering if Linc Stewart might be here, as well. Foolish thoughts. Ridiculous, idiotic nonsense. If only she could put it from her mind.

"Lass? Are you unwell?"

"I'm fine," she said, summoning up a smile. "Just tired."

"Aye," he said, his hazel eyes twinkling. "The thought of bed holds definite appeal."

You've had your photo in the paper before, she told herself as they left for home. *There's nothing to worry about.* It might be the best thing that could possibly happen. Linc Stewart would see the picture and discover that her name was Shannon Whitney, not Katharine Morgan, and the whole thing would be forgotten.

Karen suggested they stop at the Bridgewater Diner for coffee and conversation, but neither Shannon nor Andrew was much in the mood.

They rode home in silence, a silence that seemed different from any that had come before.

"We shouldn't have gone to the gala," Shannon said later as they lay in bed together. "You had a terrible time."

He didn't deny it. "They talk and talk and nothing comes of it. You say they were the best the state has to offer and I did not see a man or woman of true accomplishment among the lot of them."

She leaned up on one elbow. "Andrew, how can you say that? Philip Stallings is president of the biggest computer company short of Microsoft. Francesca Duval is CEO of Le Visage Cosmetics, a Fortune 500 company. Lee Prescott is—"

"Yet among them I did not see a happy face."

"Dinner was an hour late," she said with an uneasy laugh. "Nobody was very happy about that."

"There is more to it than that, Shannon. Those men and women have all that I came here to find, and still—"

"I know," she whispered. "I know."

They didn't make love. Instead they held each other close and waited for the dawn.

CHAPTER TWENTY-TWO

"'Tis not right to leave you alone," Andrew said the next afternoon. "This trip into the woods can be done another day."

"No, it can't," Shannon said firmly. "Most of these kids will be gone in a day or two." She smoothed the collar of his work shirt. He looked much the way he had the first day they met, and less like the man she had created. It was not a thought she wished to pursue. "Besides, I'm exhausted after last night. I don't think I have the energy to rough it with the rest of you explorers." She had dozed for a little while just before sunrise, only to awaken to find Andrew standing by the window, staring up at the towering cloud cover.

"Your fatigue does not worry me, lass. 'Tis the fact that you will be unprotected that causes me concern."

"I was unprotected, as you put it, for quite a few years before you dropped into my life, Andrew." She

260

softened her words with a kiss. "I think I can manage one more night."

"The doors and windows have been repaired and you will use the mechanical alarms."

She saluted. "Yes, sir."

Apparently he didn't see the humor in the salute, for his expression remained serious. "I understand more now than on that first night. Your world is a place of violence and cunning. If the alarm can guarantee a measure of safety, you will use it."

She wrapped her arms around him, glorying in his strength and solidity. "Poor Andrew. I should never have told you to watch the news on television."

"'Twas more than that, lass. I left in the midst of a rebellion, only to find a war raging right here."

"I'll admit we have problems, but it isn't as bad as all that."

"Social anarchy," he said, warming to the topic. "Good men—" He paused, a sheepish smile spreading across his face. "Good men *and* women without a way in which to make a living, while the devil's own thrive."

She couldn't argue the point. "We have wonders that didn't exist in your time, modern medicine for one. People no longer die from smallpox and influenza. Certainly that makes up for at least some of our shortcomings."

"This world has you," he said. "That is wonder enough for me."

She walked outside with him and found Dakota waiting in the driveway, perched atop her beat-up Mustang.

"Need an ex-Girl Scout and former librarian on the camping trip?" Dakota asked.

"Former librarian?" Shannon countered while Andrew headed for the garage. "Forsythe fired you?"

"Fired. Sacked. Got the pink slip. I'm finished."

"We shouldn't have dropped by that day."

"It wasn't you, it was my mother. She sat on my desk and told me about her dreams."

"He fired you for that? The man's a beast."

"Yeah," said Dakota. "And cheap, too. So far, no severance pay."

"Isn't that against the law?"

"Try telling that to an academic despot. You won't get very far."

Shannon lowered her voice. "You're not serious about the camping trip, are you?"

"Actually, I am. Two of the kids, Derek and Angela, told me about it and asked me to tag along." She grinned ruefully. "And since I don't have anything else to do, I said I would."

"I don't think it's a very good idea."

"If you're afraid I'm going to swoon every time I brush elbows with Balloon Boy, I promise you I won't."

Shannon laughed despite herself. "Don't call him Balloon Boy, please! That's our secret. Besides, how do you know you won't swoon?"

"Because I've had a long talk with myself, that's why. If I'm ever going to figure out why he doesn't have an aura, I'd better stay conscious."

"That's the second time you've brought up that aura. What do you mean, he doesn't have one? I thought even inanimate objects have auras." She'd seen Kirlian photography in some magazine once, where scientists claimed to have caught the aura of both a carrot and a garden rock.

Dakota's eyes darted toward the garage, the swimming pool, everywhere but Shannon. "Well, yeah," she said, finally meeting her eyes. "Most objects have an aura, but he doesn't."

"Of course he does."

Dakota brightened. "You've seen it?"

"Well, of course I haven't seen it. You're the one who sees things like that. I'm just saying, he's here, he's real, he must have an aura."

"You'd think so, wouldn't you?"

"Maybe I'd better go on this camping trip with you, after all."

"I didn't know you'd decided against it."

Shannon shrugged. "I'm tired, headachy and PMS-ing up a storm. I figured I'd stay home and give the rest of you a break. You won't—"

"Tell him I know he's from the past?" Dakota broke in. "Not if you don't want me to."

"I don't want you to," Shannon said.

"Thank you for making that clear."

She took Dakota's hands, desperate to make her friend understand her position. "It's not you," she said. "It's me. It's Andrew. It's the two of us together. The best thing for both of us is for him to cut ties with the past and make a life for himself here. You can't live in two worlds forever."

Dakota was silent, but the expression in her dark brown eyes spoke volumes.

"You're not going to start that 'this is only temporary' routine again, are you?"

"I guess not."

"I can give him a life like he never dreamed, Dakota. He'll never want for anything. How can his world offer him anything to compare?"

Dakota didn't say anything.

She didn't have to.

That passage in *Forgotten Heroes* had said it all.

Andrew and Dakota left an hour later to meet the others at the shelter and begin the great camping expedition.

Shannon waved goodbye, then opened the French doors and stepped into the sun room. It was a beautiful house but it had never seemed like a home until Andrew. Of course, it wasn't the house. She'd lived in enough different places to know that. It was being with him that made her feel connected to the world, safe and cherished and filled with hope for the future. *Their* future.

Don't say anything, Dakota, she prayed silently. *Let us make our own decisions.*

She'd been tempted to join them, but she was so bone-deep weary that the thought of trekking through the woods—even if they were *her* woods—was more than she could contemplate. At least she knew why she was tired. Typical PMS exhaustion.

And maybe a touch of regret?

She leaned back on the chaise and closed her eyes.

"Yes," she said to the empty room. "Regret."

Regret that there wouldn't be a child of her union with Andrew McVie. The emotion was so primal, it cut so deep that it stole her breath. She hadn't thought about children in years. It was as if that part of her heart had been sealed away and forgotten. But loving Andrew had thrown open the doors and windows and made her want things she'd thought beyond her reach.

Husband. Home. Children. The entire American dream, no matter the century.

She settled down on the sofa and tried to imagine herself back in Andrew's world. There would be no central air-conditioning, no big-screen TV or VCR. A war raged as the nation struggled to be born, while men and women of character sought to carve a place for themselves and their families.

She closed her eyes, letting the images come to life. So much could be done, she thought. So many mistakes could be avoided. *You're a born crusader,* Dakota always said, looking to save the world from its own excesses. What would it be like to go back to the beginning and have a chance to do it right?

Their children and their children's children would go forward with knowledge that would make them leaders, and all of it would happen simply because Shannon Whitney and Andrew McVie met and fell in love one warm summer's night in central New Jersey.

Central air was a small price to pay for such riches.

But, of course, it was ridiculous to even think about it. It wasn't as if she could drive over to the hardware store, buy a propane tank and fire up the hot-air balloon. There was no explanation for what had brought Andrew into her life, and she could only pray that same mysterious force would not see fit to take him from her.

She tried to read but couldn't concentrate. She scanned the latest copy of *People,* then tossed it aside. *Newsweek* and *Time* quickly followed suit. Television held no appeal. She'd already leafed through the Sunday papers and had been relieved to note that the picture of her and Andrew was a grainy shot, buried on page three of the Living section. She couldn't resist, however, and clipped the photo and article and set it aside.

The good thing about PMS was the fact that it explained more than her sudden exhaustion. It put a lot of other things into perspective. The way she'd overreacted to that man in Lord & Taylor the other day. And the jolt of apprehension she'd experienced last night at the ball when faced with the photographers.

Life was good, she thought, closing her eyes as fatigue washed over her. Each day Andrew adapted to another quirk of twentieth-century life . . . and the shadow of his old life grew fainter. Less threatening. He no longer tried to wind quartz timepieces or talk back to the answering machine, although last night when he'd pounded the table while the others applauded the singer, they'd locked eyes and burst into delighted laughter.

"Yes, life is good," she murmured, drifting toward sleep. And, as long as they were together, it would only get better.

"Straight to the matter," Andrew said, plunging deeper into the woods.

"I thought you were gonna show us how to find our way around," Charlie said.

"That is what we're about."

"I don't see us doin' nothing special," said Angela. "We're just walking."

"We're doing more than walking," Dakota said. "Right, Andrew?"

"In truth, there was much to be learned if you had looked with open eyes."

"A bunch of trees and plants," said Derek. "Big deal."

"Aye," Andrew said, "'tis a big deal, indeed. Skunk, raccoon and deer are nearby."

"No way," said Charlie. "I didn't see anything."

Andrew squatted near a fallen tree and pushed aside a handful of dead leaves. He gestured toward a series of depressions in the soft earth. "See the shape of the hooves clearly rendered, the way they overlap? The sign of a deer walking at a normal pace." He then gestured toward scrapes on the bark of the fallen tree. "'Twas a fine supper for a doe or buck."

They crowded around him, disbelief turning slowly to wonder as he showed them the five-toed mark of a skunk and the distinctive impression of rabbit. "A young rabbit can be taken by hand," he said in a most ordinary tone, "but many a man has starved on a diet of rabbit alone. 'Tis not enough fat to—"

With that little Angela burst into loud sobs. "Mommy! He says we have to eat bunnies."

Angela's mother stepped forward to hug her daughter while the other mothers gathered around.

"I have no wish to make the child unhappy," he said, patting the girl on the head, "but 'tis a fact of life that to survive we must ofttimes perform unpleasant tasks."

A look passed between the women and then Angela's mother met his eyes.

"Go ahead, Mr. McVie," she said. "I think it's time we all learned how to survive."

Jules, the shelter's driver, called a little after five o'clock.

"I didn't wake you, did I, Ms. Whitney?"

"No, of course not," Shannon lied, stifling a yawn. "New arrivals?"

"Looks like," said Jules. "We're taking this one to the house you rented in Morristown, but I don't have the key."

"I don't think I—" Shannon thought for a second. "Karen has it." Now that the papers had been signed, sealed and delivered, Karen and the foundation would be handling the day-to-day running of the shelters. "Wait a minute," she said. "I forgot to give her the key. It's right here."

Jules was silent for a moment. "I gotta be at the police station in Flemington in twenty minutes to pick 'em up, but I could swing by and get the key after."

"Whenever you can, Jules. I'm not going anywhere."

"Don't want to be a bother, Ms. Whitney. Just leave the key in your mailbox and I won't have to disturb you."

"You're good at this," Dakota said to Andrew as he struck a spark from a rock with the blade of his knife. "You don't meet too many lawyers who can start a fire without a match."

"You were to gather tinder," he said, meeting her eyes. "I see no contribution from you."

"I gave at the office," she said, then stopped. Of course he wouldn't understand the reference.

"You are a good friend to Shannon," he said, watching her.

"I like to think I am."

"You are," he said. "I know that for a fact, but what I do not understand is why you dislike me as you do."

"I don't dislike you," Dakota said carefully.

"Aye," he said. "You do."

Dakota took a deep breath. "I'm worried, that's all."

"I will not hurt Shannon. You have my oath."

"I know you won't hurt her intentionally." She touched his forearm. "But—"

She felt as if she was falling end over end through space, tumbling toward the earth, faster and faster and—

Her eyes opened and she found Andrew kneeling over her, extending his cupped hands.

"Drink this," he said.

She looked at the brackish water.

"Where did you get that?" she asked.

"From the stream."

She shuddered. "Not on your life. I'm not a fan of toxic waste."

"Each time we meet, mistress, you swoon." He crouched closer to her. "What would be the reason?"

"It's— I . . ." Her words faded.

"You know." Andrew's voice was low so that the others could not hear. "You have known from the start."

She looked away. "I promised Shannon I wouldn't talk about this."

"You have second sight. My mother did, as well."

Her eyes widened. "You believe in such things?"

"I believe there are things beyond understanding."

He smiled and she started to laugh. "All things considered, I suppose you would." After all, the man got there from an eighteenth-century hot-air balloon.

"But there is something else you see, isn't there?"

"Look, Andrew, I really can't talk about this. Shannon's my friend and I told her I wouldn't."

"God's oath, mistress, there are two things I
swear—I will not hurt Shannon and I will never leave
her."

Dakota's eyes welled with tears. "You will leave,"
she said. "That's one thing I'm sure of."

She could feel it in her bones.

Shannon awoke with a start. She'd dozed back to sleep
after Jules called. The key, she thought, stretching la-
zily. The key to the Morristown house was still in her
purse instead of in the mailbox where she'd promised
Jules it would be.

Stifling a yawn, she stood, tightened the belt on her
silk robe, then padded barefoot to the sun room. She
switched off the alarm to the French doors, stepped
outside, then hurried around the side of the house and
down the driveway to the mailbox.

Clouds slid across the moon, obscuring it, while she
walked back up the driveway. *Too dark for me,* she
thought, wrapping her arms around her chest. Strange
how eerie your own driveway could look at night when
the house was empty...when you'd gotten used to it
being not empty.

She would have laughed if anyone had told her it
was possible to miss someone as much as she missed
Andrew. The man had been gone only a few hours and
it felt like days. *He's in the woods, not Wyoming. He'll
be back tomorrow morning.* She was almost tempted
to venture into the woods herself, flashlight and com-
pass in hand, and look for him.

Almost, but not quite.

She heard a rustling sound from across the yard and
shivered. It gave the old phrase "the night has a thousand eyes" a brand-new twist.

She reached for the handle on the French doors, then paused. Too many strange noises. This time it was a snapping twig to the left. Some enterprising bureaucrat should outlaw strange noises on dark nights when a woman was home alone.

The wind rustled the trees and she caught the scent of something unfamiliar mingled with the smell of pine and hot summer air. A fragment of memory danced just beyond reach but she couldn't bring it forward into the light.

She swung the door open and was about to step inside when something hit her hard from behind and sent her sprawling, face first, to the floor of the sun room. Her right knee struck the tiles first. She waited for the pain to start but it didn't.

Maybe you had to breathe to feel pain... but she couldn't breathe... or think... or feel anything. There was only terror and the deep certainty that her worst fears were about to come true. *Andrew.* His dear face flashed through her mind. *Dear God! Will I ever see you again?*

She closed her eyes, face pressed to the cool tile floor. She tried to make herself small, insignificant, invisible, but the world was narrowing down, growing smaller and smaller, until she was the center and there was no place left to hide.

"This is scary," Derek said. "Are we lost?"

Andrew smiled. "Far from it." He pointed up toward the sky. "See that band of stars arcing upward?"

Derek nodded. "You mean the Milky Way?"

"Aye," he said, although the term was unfamiliar to him. "Follow a straight line with your eye from the handle of the Plough to the brightly shining star. The polestar will always guide you.''

''I don't get it,'' said Derek. ''It's just a dumb star. Why don't we use a map?''

''Rambo's got night-vision goggles,'' said Charlie. ''That's what I'd use.''

''Sometimes you have naught save your God-given wits to guide you,'' said Andrew. ''What would you do if—'' He stopped abruptly. ''Did you hear someone call my name?''

Derek shook his head. ''Uh-uh.''

''Not me,'' said Charlie.

Inexplicably the hairs on the back of Andrew's neck began to rise and he stood.

''Something is wrong,'' he said, turning to Dakota. ''Do you feel it, too?''

Dakota tilted her head. ''What do you mean? A storm or something?''

'''Tis Shannon,'' he said, the dread inside his chest growing. ''You do not sense a darkness settling over her?''

Dakota shook her head. ''But that doesn't mean anything. Trust your gut. We'll be fine.''

He gestured toward the others. ''I do not wish to add to the women's distress.''

''I was a Girl Scout,'' Dakota said. ''Not that you know what a Girl Scout is. This is survival training. We'll manage.''

His brow furrowed. ''I will not leave you unprotected.'' He handed her his knife. ''Use this well.''

''I hope I don't use it at all.'' A small smile tilted Dakota's mouth as she accepted the weapon. ''Go to Shannon. I promise everything else will fall into place.''

CHAPTER TWENTY-THREE

"GOOD TO SEE YOU AGAIN, Katharine," her ex-husband said, yanking Shannon to her feet by her hair. It was the voice she'd heard every day of her marriage and in every nightmare since the divorce. "So where've you been hiding yourself?"

Bright waves of pain blurred her vision. She caught the image of a tall, handsome man in a hand-tailored suit. The kind of man you'd see in a corporate board-room or a five-star restaurant. She tried to get into position to knock him off balance but her knee gave way and she staggered against him. His fingers were still threaded through her hair and he pulled again. She wondered how it was her scalp didn't separate from the rest of her.

Think, Shannon! You know how to deal with this. Just don't be afraid... think! His height gave him an advantage but she knew she could best him if she could just regain her footing.

"Surprised to see me?"

She wouldn't answer him. He could go to hell before she'd answer him.

He reared back and swung at her, holding her head still so she absorbed all of the blow and more. The iron taste of blood filled her mouth and she tried not to gag.

"Not talking, Katharine?" His fingers dug into her scalp. "You never used to be this quiet."

With his other hand he grabbed her face, forcing her to look into his eyes. Once, a long time ago, she'd thought those gray eyes were beautiful. How wrong she'd been . . . how pathetically, tragically wrong.

She thought of Andrew. His infinite tenderness, the strength that was as much a part of him as his hazel eyes. A rough man, from a rougher time, and yet he knew more about love—in all of its aspects—than Bryant could ever understand.

"You had a lot to say to the police, didn't you? And you didn't shut up when you talked to the lawyers and the judge. What's wrong, Katharine?" His laugh made her tremble. "Will you talk to me if I call you Shannon? That's your new name, isn't it? Shannon." He looked at her, long and slow, his gaze traveling up her legs, over her belly, lingering on her breasts. "You don't look much like a Shannon." His fingers pressed harder against her temples until she felt as if her head would explode. "Shannon puts out, doesn't she? The way I remember it, Katharine didn't much like it."

For a moment she was that other woman again, the girl who'd come to him in hope and joy, eager to build a life with him, a life they could share someday with children. She could feel her strength ebbing away, her hard-won self-esteem crumbling beneath her. *No,* she told herself. *Don't let him win. You've come so far....*

She wasn't that woman any longer. She was some-body new, somebody strong. She'd left Katharine Morgan behind and created a woman who would fight for the right to live life without fear.

You're not going to win, Bryant. Never again....

He pulled at her hair hard, snapping her head back with the force, making her bones rattle.

Let yourself go, she told herself. *Make him think he's winning, and you can take him by surprise....*

Her gun was useless, locked away in the coat closet in the foyer. Bryant would kill her before she made it into the hall. Her adrenaline was flowing fast, scream-ing for her to fight Bryant *now* and with every weapon at her disposal. But she couldn't. She had to control her need for revenge because the element of surprise was the best weapon of all.

Letting go was the toughest thing she'd ever done. She felt physically sick at the thought of the pleasure Bryant would take from her weakness.

It's the only way, Shannon. You can't get to the gun. Andrew isn't around. There's no one to hear you scream. The mailbox was at the far end of the drive-way. Unless Jules walked up the path and rang the doorbell, he'd never know anything was wrong. And even if she could hit the alarm, she knew it would be over before the police arrived. Bryant had violated his parole, flying across the country for this confronta-tion, and Shannon wasn't naive enough to believe he'd risked his freedom for anything less than seeing her dead.

She had only herself and her wits to save her.

She sagged against Bryant, forcing her arms to hang loosely at her sides, her legs to go limp. He caught her roughly by the shoulders, his strong fingers digging into her flesh. She knew that the pain would come later, but it didn't matter.

Survival was all.

The house was ablaze with light. Andrew breathed a sigh of relief when he noted that Shannon's car was parked in the garage as it should be.

Still, apprehension tugged at him and he moved quickly around to the back of the house. Ofttimes in the evening they sat together by the swimming pool. He had no wish to cause her alarm, appearing like an apparition from the shadows, but he would not rest easy until he saw her lovely face and could reassure himself of her well-being.

The French doors were closed. His brows knit together as he stepped closer. The red light above was blinking. Was it not supposed to glow steadily to indicate the alarm system was guarding the door as it should? That she was alone inside the house and unprotected made his very blood run cold.

He climbed the steps and reached for the handle. Had the woman no sense? She would not like it, but he intended to speak harshly to her. This was a dangerous world. He would see her safe or know the reason why.

"I've been watching you, Katharine," Bryant said as he dragged her into the kitchen. "That guy you're shacking up with is gone for the night."

She nodded, trying to look submissive rather than terrified. Bryant's rage fed off terror.

"This isn't going to take long." He flung her aside and she fell against the kitchen table. The table skidded on the shiny tiles, sending two of the chairs crashing to the floor and taking Shannon with them. The pain in her right knee was intense. Balance and control were everything when it came to using karate. What if she couldn't stand up when the time came?

I don't feel the pain, she told herself. *There* is *no pain.*

He ran his hand along the countertop and grimaced. "Still not much of a housekeeper, are you, Katharine?"

"I'm sorry," she whispered, the dutiful ex-wife, while bile rose into her mouth. "Mildred and Karl are on vacation."

"You never did understand how to run a household. You held me back, Katharine. Another woman would have understood what I needed." He fingered a glass left in the sink. "That's why I had to explore other avenues."

"I understand." She cast her eyes down, praying he didn't realize she was calculating the distance between them and planning her move. "I'm sorry."

"I'm sorry," he mimicked, moving toward her.

Come on, Bryant... keep walking....

He was about twelve feet away from her. His Italian loafers barely made a sound against the tiles. "Is that all you can say... I'm sorry?"

Ten feet away. *Okay... okay... this is it.*

She shifted her weight to her right hip, leaned back on her arms. Her muscles contracted in preparation. It was all a question of leverage and angles. Balance on the right hip, lash out with the left leg. Simple, clean, powerfully effective.

Just a little closer, Bryant, just get in range.... She'd done it a hundred times in class. A kick to the groin would stop even a bastard like Bryant in his tracks, but she had to do it right the first time, because if she didn't, she would be dead.

The sun room looked much as it had hours ago. Andrew, his senses alert, moved carefully through the room and took its measure. The chaise longue was pushed slightly out of position and as he moved to right it, he noticed the belt to Shannon's robe under the glass-topped table.

He bent to retrieve it and as he did he heard the crash of furniture from the kitchen. *Sweet Jesus,* he thought. His premonition of danger had come to pass. Pressing himself flat against the wall, he moved slowly toward the hallway that led to the kitchen. Shannon's voice floated toward him. He could not distinguish her words but he recognized that her tone was both timid and uncertain, unlike any he had heard from her before.

The man's voice held the cultured tones of education and privilege but there was no mistaking the menace behind the words.

Her husband, Andrew thought with certainty. In his mind's eye he saw the pale curve of the scar on her shoulder blade and his gut twisted. The man who had committed that crime against her person was on the other side of the door. A red mist of rage clouded his vision and the need to spill the man's blood burned within his breast, yet he knew that to burst into the room without first knowing the situation could cost Shannon her life. Still, the taste for blood grew stronger with each second that passed and he wished he still had his knife.

*   *   *

"Come on, Shannon," Bryant said. "Let's go for a little walk upstairs."

He stepped into range.

Now! Do it now! Shannon centered herself, met his eyes, then lashed out with a vicious kick meant to tear straight through the bastard's groin and come out the other side. She caught him in the thigh but fell short of her goal.

"You bitch!" He lurched to the left then turned back toward her.

Panting, she tried to crawl away from him, struggling to ignore the stabbing pain in her right knee and the smell of fear that suddenly filled the air. He grabbed her by the hair and pulled her back across the floor.

"You feel like playing rough?" he asked. "I can play rough."

She watched as he pulled a small revolver from the waistband of his trousers where it had been concealed by his jacket. Grinning, he aimed it at her.

"How rough do you want to play, Shannon Whitney?" He pressed the gun against her temple. "We can do this fast or we can do this slow. Your choice."

She spat on the floor at his feet.

He jammed the gun deeper into her temple.

A buzzing sound started inside her head. It wasn't supposed to end this way. Not here. Not like this. She'd come so far, learned so much, found the one man on earth who was everything she'd dreamed a man could be. But none of it mattered any longer.

Her strength, her dreams, her future—everything was gone in the space of a heartbeat.

Bryant had won.

And she had lost.

Andrew, she thought. *If only...*

She called to him. No words were spoken aloud but still they reached Andrew's mind and heart as clearly and truly as if they had been.

The connection between them defied space and time and he somehow knew not even death could break the bond that drew them together.

But she would not die. Not that gallant, beautiful woman who had captured his heart. He would lay down his life if it meant that she would live.

He propelled himself across the room with power born of love. The other man was tall and broad but Andrew held the element of surprise. He used his entire body as a battering ram, knocking the bastard to the floor. They crashed into the tumbled kitchen chairs, then slammed into the stove.

"Andrew!" Shannon screamed. "He's got a gun!"

Her warning came an instant too late. Andrew found himself pinned on his back with a pistol jammed into his mouth and the face of evil looking down upon him. He leveled his gaze upon his enemy. *Kill me if you must, but spare her. She has suffered enough by your hand.*

He knew the truth of what would happen. The man would not leave before he had sent them both to their Maker.

From the corner of his eye he saw Shannon crawling toward them.

Run, damn you, lass! I am of no consequence in this world. You must survive!

Run? She wouldn't run. There was nothing on the face of the earth that would make her leave Andrew.

"This is it, pal," Bryant said, setting himself. "Say your prayers."

In that instant Shannon didn't feel the pain. She didn't feel the fear. All she knew was that the man she loved was in danger and she was the only one on earth who could save him.

Few people were given a second chance. She wasn't about to waste it.

Grabbing hold of the legs of a kitchen chair, she leapt to her feet and swung that damn chair at Bryant with every ounce of power, every day of helpless anger. She swung that chair for herself and for every woman who'd ever passed through a shelter—and for every woman for whom it was too late. The chair caught him between the shoulder blades and it caught him hard.

He dropped to the floor, body held at an odd angle, then, with a cry of pain, went unconscious. The gun fell from his hand and skittered across the floor.

Andrew scrambled to his feet and reached for the weapon.

"Don't!" Shannon said. She grabbed the pistol from the floor and aimed it at her ex-husband. It would be so easy to pull that trigger.... "Get rope from the pantry and tie his arms and legs before he comes to."

Andrew looked sharply at her—and at the gun in her hand—then did as she asked.

"He probably has a broken shoulder," Shannon said dispassionately. "I should put him out of his misery."

"Nay, lass," said Andrew, covering her hand with his own. "He is not worth the price you'd pay." The bloody bastard deserved to die, but Shannon would carry the mark on her soul forever. He knew he could do the deed and suffer not a moment of remorse. "Give me the weapon. I will do it for you."

"Don't touch the gun!" She took a step back. He feared she would shoot her husband then and there, but she did not. "We can't let anyone know you were involved, Andrew. How could we explain your existence to the police?"

"The police will understand once I explain the facts to them clearly."

"You have no identification, no way to prove who you are. They'd take you away. Please," she said urgently, "go back into the woods and don't come back until the police are gone. Protect yourself, Andrew."

"I care not about my own well-being. 'Tis you I care for, lass. You alone."

"Then do as I say," she pleaded. "It's our only hope."

"I will not leave you again."

A look of sadness shadowed her face. It was unlike any look he had seen thus far and he knew a different taste of fear. "Yes, you will," she said softly and then she said no more.

He left the house through the French doors and lingered in the backyard long enough to see her set the alarm then trigger it with the muzzle of the gun to alert the authorities. Swiftly he headed into the woods to make certain all was well with Dakota and the others.

Their trail was easy to follow, even in the darkness. He counted the sleeping forms, reassuring himself that each was accounted for, then looked toward Dakota, who was awake and sitting by the dying fire. She brushed at her cheeks as he approached.

"It was Bryant, wasn't it?" Her voice was low.

"Aye," said Andrew, squatting by the fire.

"Is he dead?"

"I regret to say he is not. I wished to accomplish that with my own hands but failed."

"Is Shannon all right?"

"To the eye, yes. Beneath the surface, I cannot tell. Something troubles her."

"Bryant's return, probably."

"Nay," said Andrew, "'tis not that. She wishes to speak of it later and I—" He stopped and shook his head. He would not give voice to his fears. He had failed Shannon as he had failed Elspeth, as he had failed everything and everyone in his life. Regret lay bitter on his tongue.

Emilie had come to his time believing him a hero who saved General Washington, only to discover it was her own husband who did so.

And now, with Shannon, when he had wished to save her with his courage and gallantry, he had instead found himself with the barrel of a pistol shoved into his mouth—as trapped and useless a figure of a man as ever he had been.

He had believed this world of the future was where he would find riches and success beyond his wildest imaginings. In truth, he was but a babe in the woods, destined to rely upon Shannon's generosity for his daily bread.

You deserve better, lass, he thought, staring into the dying fire.

She deserved the hero he could never be.

CHAPTER TWENTY-FOUR

SHANNON WATCHED as the blinking lights of the last police car disappeared down the road that led to her house. The sound of the vehicle crunching along the gravel seemed very loud in the predawn stillness.

It felt strange to be alone in the house again. She stepped in through the French doors and stood in the middle of the sun room. She'd always loved the sun room, with its polished oak floor and the pale yellow chaise. Now she could never look at it again without seeing Bryant.

She wrapped her arms across her chest and took a deep, calming breath.

The fact that Bryant had found her surprised her less than the way it had happened. He'd known her whereabouts for weeks now and it had nothing to do with the man she'd met in Lord & Taylor.

Bryant was a lot more clever than that. He'd put people on her trail while he was still in prison, and this

midnight visit had been the climax of a carefully con-
structed plan. He'd checked in with his parole officer
that morning, then boarded a friend's private jet for
the flight east. If his plan had gone as he'd believed it
would, Bryant would have been asleep in his west-coast
bed when the authorities came looking for him.

And she and Andrew would be dead.

Prison didn't seem half good enough for him.

She walked slowly into the kitchen, then bent to
right the chairs, feeling the sharp edges of pain in her
knee and rib cage. But that pain was nothing compared to the deep longing she felt for the life she'd been
denied. They couldn't stay here any longer. Bryant had
seen to that. She had to move on, find a new home,
build a new life, same as she had done before. Had any
place ever felt like home? She couldn't remember. Not
with her parents. Not with Bryant. This house had
come close to being home, but that special sense of
belonging hadn't happened until the moment Andrew
McVie had walked into her life.

How ironic that the one man on earth who had
made her believe in the future was the one man she
could never have.

She sat at the table and rested her head on the cool
surface. She was tired of fighting the inevitable. He
didn't belong here. This world didn't deserve a man
like Andrew McVie.

And maybe neither did she.

Tears sprang to her eyes and she didn't try to wipe
them away. She had the right to cry. Damn it, she'd
earned that right. And it wasn't because her entire life
had been turned inside out tonight or because her head
ached or her knee throbbed. It was because there was

a sorrow inside her heart, in a place so deep she hadn't known it existed until Andrew.

She'd believed it could work, that somehow she could offer him something so wonderful, so lasting, so overwhelmingly *right* that he would never again want for the things his old life could provide. She couldn't pinpoint the change, couldn't put a name to the forces that were at work, but when he risked all to save her from Bryant's rage, she knew beyond doubt that he deserved so much more than a life in the shadows.

"You are more than I deserve, lass."

Her entire body was galvanized by the sound of his voice. She lifted her head and saw him standing in the doorway.

He opened his arms wide.

The distance between them vanished and she went into his arms, glorying in the touch and smell and sight of him. He was everything good and strong and decent the world had to offer and in that instant she knew she loved him enough to let him go.

He sensed the change in her immediately. Her body stiffened and he felt as if a wall of glass had been placed between their souls.

"I am not the woman you think I am, Andrew."

He considered her carefully, his own soul aching at the sight of the bruises blossoming along the side of her delicate jaw. "Aye, lass. I know that your identity is not that with which you were born."

"That is not what I mean."

Despair hovered in the shadows but he refused to acknowledge it. "Then say it plainly, Shannon, for I have no wish to guess at the meaning of your words."

She pulled away from his embrace. "Come with me," she said. "There is something you need to know."

He followed her through the hallway and into the library. She pointed to the top shelf of the middle bookcase. "Behind Plutarch's *Lives,*" she said, her voice taut. "There's a book that I want you to have."

He reached up, pushed Plutarch aside, then removed a slim volume from the shelf. *"Forgotten Heroes,"* he said, reading the title on the spine. The irony was not lost on him.

"Page 127," said Shannon quietly.

"There is nothing for me in this book." He pushed it toward her.

"Page 127," she repeated.

He found the page in question. "'Tis half torn," he observed, scanning the paragraphs. "What value can this—" He stopped abruptly. Blood pounded in his ears like the roar of the ocean as the words seemed to leap up at him from the printed page.

In an act of courage unequaled at that time in the War for Independence, Boston lawyer-turned-spy Andrew McVie staged a daring raid on British troops near Jockey Hollow during the winter of 1779-1780 and single-handedly saved two of the most important members of the Spy Ring from certain death—

"I lived," he said, dumbstruck. "I do not know how it is possible, but my life was lived out in my own time."

"I know," she whispered. "It's your destiny."

High color darkened his craggy face and he began to pace the room. "This cannot be. This is not what Emilie told me of my fate."

"Emilie was wrong."

"You cannot say that with certainty. That page was torn."

"Yes," she said sadly. "I can say it with certainty."

He ignored her. "Where did this bloody book come from?"

"The library."

"Dakota's library?"

"Yes."

"The woman does not hold me in esteem." He glared at the book as if it were a viper, coiled and ready to strike. "'Tis a joke of some kind, made to tear us apart. You should have burned it in the hearth."

"And what if I had? That wouldn't change anything, Andrew. Your fate is there in black and white."

"How did it come to be hidden on your library shelf?"

"I put it there."

"You kept it from me?"

"I didn't want to lose you." She met his eyes. "You gave me back my heart, Andrew. I'll never forget you—" Her voice broke and she could say no more.

"Do you think so little of me, lass, that you believe words in a book could make me turn from you? Magic brought me here and I see no magic awaiting to take me back." He reached for her hand and headed for the sun room and the French doors. "I will prove it to you."

The sky was growing light as she followed him across the backyard and into the garage where the balloon rested.

"See this," he said, pulling the cover from the balloon and gondola. "The fabric turns to dust, while the basket could no longer carry a child." He grabbed the lip of the gondola and began to drag it from the garage, not stopping until it rested in the middle of her curving driveway. "No magic fire, Shannon. No strange clouds come to carry me back. 'Tis a lie, that book, and nothing more."

"There is something more," she said.

"I do not wish to see it."

"You must."

He gripped her hands tightly in his. "Why is it you push me away, lass, when I have no wish to leave?"

"It is not up to either of us, Andrew. It was decided a long time ago."

"Aye, and this country is the proof of that. My existence played no part in her growth."

"What about the men you saved?"

He looked away. She saw a muscle in his jaw twitch. "They have no meaning to me when compared to all that I have found with you."

"Oh, Andrew," she whispered. "There is so much you don't know." She reached into the pocket of her robe and withdrew a wrinkled sheaf of papers.

"Dakota again," he said with an impatient shake of his head. "I grow tired of the woman's nonsense."

She pushed the papers toward him. "I did my best to piece them together."

"There is no purpose to this, lass. It changes naught."

"The spies you saved—"

"I do not want to hear this."

"Andrew, listen to me! You saved Zane Rutledge and Josiah Blakelee."

"That cannot be."

She fanned the patched pages out and waved them beneath his nose. "Three separate sources and each says the same thing. You saved their lives, Andrew. The children we read about, the farms, the families they founded—none of it will happen unless you return."

"You are my destiny," he said to Shannon. "You are all that I want."

"You must go."

"There is nothing else in life beyond you."

"You would never be happy. You need so much more than that. You *deserve* so much more."

"No," he said, his voice fierce. "You are all that I need."

He kissed her with a hunger that left her breathless.

"Andrew, look!" She pointed toward the sky. "Those clouds! I've seen them before."

He said nothing, but made to kiss her again.

"Last week," she said in a voice of wonder. "When you landed in the woods."

"Aye," he said, "and twice since." He turned away from the balloon and he had no need to see the clouds.

"That's it, isn't it? That's how it happened."

"Still, it cannot be," Andrew said forcefully. "There was a magic fire propelling the balloon and that fire does not exist any longer."

"What if the fire appeared," she pressed, her aqua eyes alight with a dangerous glow. "What would you do?"

"I would turn away," he said, "for I have no wish to leave you—not in this life or any other."

She rose on tiptoe and peered over his shoulder. "Oh, God! Andrew, look!"

"Nay," he said. "I will not."

"It's happening.... My God, Andrew!"

Slowly he turned and saw a sight that was beyond reason. The basket appeared to his eyes as perfect as it had on the day he climbed aboard. And the balloon—Sweet Jesus! The balloon was a vivid crimson red and it was growing larger with each second. Had the clouds somehow rejuvenated the balloon?

"The magic fire," he whispered, staring in wonder at the flames rising up from the basket to inflate the balloon. "This cannot be."

"Maybe not," said Shannon, grabbing the lip of the gondola, "but it's happening right here in front of us, Andrew, and we both know why."

He thought of Zane and Emilie and their hopes for the future...of Rebekah and Josiah and their children. Did their futures rest on his shoulders alone? Was he meant to be a hero, after all, the kind of man Shannon deserved?

But what did any of it matter if they were separated by time, destined to live out their lives in loneliness?

"I love you, Shannon Whitney," he said. "I would mark myself a liar if I said the past does not call to me but, in truth, I cannot envision a world without you."

"Then ask me, you fool! Ask me to come with you."

"I cannot," he said, his heart at war with his head. His gesture encompassed the house, the land, the rectangular pond. "How can I ask you to abandon all that you have for love of me when I can offer you naught save a life of hardship and uncertainty?"

"Wealth doesn't guarantee happiness, Andrew," she said quietly. "I know that firsthand."

"You do not know what you are saying, lass."

"I know exactly what I'm saying. I know what it's like to be rich, but I don't know how it feels to be happy. You can show me, Andrew. Only you can do that."

"I have no home, no prospects, not even the guarantee that we will end up in the same world I left behind."

"I don't care," she said as joy filled her heart. "I have enough faith for both of us. Don't you see? *This* is why you came, Andrew. You came to find me."

He looked at her hard and then his hazel eyes crinkled and his mouth curved upward and laughter—joyous laughter—rose up from the depths of his lonely soul. "Aye," he said, gathering her into his arms. "And I will never let you go."

"There are things I expect from you," she said sternly. "I want to love and be loved in return. I want us to be partners. I want us to be kind and tolerant of each other's faults. And I want your children." A smile played at the corners of her mouth. "Did you hear me, Andrew? I want to bear your children."

"Aye," he said, his voice gruff with emotion. "'Tis great good fortune that we wish the same things from life, mistress."

"And about that 'mistress' business, Andrew." She poked him in the chest with her forefinger. "I think we'd better make it legal."

"You are proposing marriage?"

She looked up at him, then started to laugh. "Will you marry me, Andrew McVie? Will you carry me off into the sunrise in your hot-air balloon and make an honest woman of me? Will you love me forever and ever?"

"I would gladly take you as my wife, lass, but know that I do not believe in divorce. When we say our vows before God, we will be wed into eternity."

"Eternity," she said, her voice a whisper. "I can't imagine anything that could please me more than sharing eternity with you."

They turned to look at the balloon, which bobbed high above the gondola now.

"'Tis almost ready," Andrew said. "Soon it will begin to rise."

"We can't go yet," she said, reality sinking in. "I have to pack my belongings."

"There is no time, lass. It will leave with us or without."

"One minute, Andrew! I'll be back in time. I promise."

She was as good as her word. She returned moments later, carrying a large satchel.

"You will turn my hair gray, lass," he said, swinging her into the basket as the balloon shuddered, eager to rise. He tossed in her bag then leapt in after her. "What was of such importance that you risked our future?"

"Patience, Mr. McVie." Her smile was one of mystery and promise. "You'll find out in good time."

He reached for the satchel and she pushed him away, laughing, but not before he saw a most familiar item tucked among the assortment. "'Tis the picture of us from the newspaper."

"For our children, Andrew." The look she gave him was one of such love that it filled his heart with joy. "It will help us explain a miracle."

He thought of a girl with her beauty and generosity of spirit, of a boy with her courage and wit. Once he had thought himself destined to walk this world alone, but then he found Shannon and suddenly the future glittered before him, more precious than gold.

"'Twas an adventure," he said, holding her close as the balloon shuddered again then began to rise.

"I know," Shannon whispered, resting her head against his shoulder. "But now it's time for us to go home."

"Aye," he said, as the sun pierced the clouds. "'Tis time we did, at that."

EPILOGUE

"YOU DON'T LOOK SO GOOD," the little girl said as she peered up at Dakota.

"Thanks a lot," said Dakota, ruffling the child's hair. "I'm getting too old for these late nights." She glanced around the front yard of the shelter. "Everyone accounted for?"

One of the mothers flashed her the thumbs-up sign.

They had arrived back at the shelter as the sun rose over the tops of the trees. If it hadn't been for the strange clouds towering overhead, it would have been a beautiful morning. As it was, the kids were ready for breakfast. Their mothers looked pleased to have made it through the night.

And Dakota felt as if she'd been run over by an eighteen wheeler.

"I make great scrambled eggs," said one of the mothers. "You're welcome to stay."

295

"I'd probably fall asleep with my face in the toast." She grabbed her purse and car keys. "I'm going to head for home."

"Take some doughnuts with you," the woman said. "You're too thin."

"God bless you and your children and your children's children," said Dakota while the woman filled a bag with jelly doughnuts. "I don't know who decided double-digit dress sizes were against the law but the man should be shot."

Her car was covered with a light mist and she ran the wipers for a few seconds to clear the windshield. She wondered how Shannon and Andrew were getting on but decided against stopping by. God knew, they'd been through enough for one night. Besides, she wasn't feeling all that well. She was not only tired but weak, as if she'd been sick in bed for weeks and this was her first day on her feet.

Bed, she thought, backing down the driveway and turning right on the road. Bed and a good twelve or eighteen hours' sleep should do it.

A flash of something red caught her eye and she braked slightly. It wasn't anything much, just the tiniest hint of something barely peeking over the trees by Shannon's house. An odd fluttering began deep inside her chest. It reminded her of the way she'd felt each time she'd swooned over Andrew McVie. Strange that she'd be feeling that way now when he was nowhere in sight.

She looked toward the red spot over the treetops and the fluttering intensified.

"The balloon!" The words tore from her throat. It was happening right this very minute and she suddenly knew this was Andrew's last chance to go back where he belonged.

Minutes later the Mustang skidded to a stop in Shannon's driveway, and Dakota found herself staring at the balloon and gondola as they drifted a few inches above the driveway.

Her heart did a little leap as she saw Shannon and Andrew waving to her from the basket. *They're together,* she thought with elation. *And they're going home.* Her eyes swam with tears as she noticed the shimmer of gold all around them, bathing the two travelers in its benevolent glow. And they even had matching auras....

The balloon began to rise higher. Already the gondola was a foot off the ground.

"Wait!" she yelled. "I have something for you."

"Hurry!" Shannon called out. "We haven't much time."

She tried to race, but her legs felt leaden and she had scarcely enough energy to put one foot in front of the other.

The gondola rose another foot.

"It's jelly doughnuts!" Dakota yelled, tossing the bag to them. "Don't squish them, whatever you do." They might need a snack. After all, their next meal was a century or two away.

The bottom of the basket was at waist level. The crimson silk was growing more vivid in color; the gondola, even more substantial. She looked down at her hands...her arms. Her aura was gone. She touched the basket. Her aura returned. She released the basket, then watched in horror as her physical self seemed to grow transparent, almost as if she were about to disappear.

Fatigue made her head swim, and she struggled to hang on to her equilibrium. She felt so weak, so temporary, as if her soul and her body were parting company. Dear God in heaven, she was dying! The only thing anchoring her to the mortal world was that hot-air balloon, and in another second it would be gone and she—

Shannon stared at her in obvious horror. "Andrew, my God! We have to do something."

"What's the matter?" Dakota managed to say. "I finally found a diet that worked...." *Always leave 'em laughing, Wylie. Can't you even be serious when you're about to kick the bucket?*

Andrew leaned forward until he was half out of the gondola. "Give me your hand."

"Absolutely not. If I swoon again, I'm a goner."

"As I see it, mistress, you have but one choice."

He leaned over the basket and grabbed Dakota by the arms, swinging her into the gondola with them as the balloon rose toward the clouds.

"A fifth wheel in two centuries," Dakota said as her heartbeat slowly returned to normal. "It's not too late if you want to back out. Tell me to leave, why don't you? I could jump. I'd probably only break a leg or two but what's a fractured limb between friends?" She waited. "Guys, I was just kidding. If you want me to leave, I'll—"

But Andrew and Shannon hadn't heard a word. Wrapped in each other's arms they were already in a world of their own.

A big fat lump formed in Dakota's throat and she blinked back tears. There was something about destiny being served that brought out the romantic in her.

"A fifth wheel," Dakota said, turning away. But somehow the words no longer stung.

They sailed up into the clouds and her fears vanished like the morning mist. It was a beautiful late-summer day. The sun was shining. The air was sweet. There was an adventure waiting for her out there and she was glad she was her mother's daughter, eager to take that first step into the unknown.

She heard the sound of soft laughter and turned toward Shannon and Andrew. The golden glow still surrounded them, but there was something more, something that had nothing to do with auras, and everything to do with the power of love. Her eyes grew misty as she shamelessly watched them. Andrew looked at Shannon as if he held the secret to life in his arms. And Shannon! Shannon looked up at Andrew with such pure joy that Dakota found herself struck once again by the miracle of love.

You never knew when it would happen to you. You never knew where. He could be a doctor, lawyer, Indian chief, or a renegade patriot spy. The only thing that mattered was that you'd found the other half of your heart.

She smiled and turned away once again as Shannon rose up on tiptoe for Andrew's kiss. Sometimes you even had to travel across the centuries to find it.

Her stomach growled and she plucked a jelly doughnut from the bag. *Raspberry,* she thought as she took a bite.

It was a good omen.

She could feel it in her bones.